THE WISHING TREE IN IRISH FALLS

JEN GILROY

SOUL MATE PUBLISHING

New York

THE WISHING TREE IN IRISH FALLS

Copyright©2019

JEN GILROY

Cover Design by Anna Lena Spies

Published in the United States of America by
Soul Mate Publishing
P.O. Box 24
Macedon, New York, 14502

ISBN: 978-1-64716-041-8

ebook ISBN: 978-1-68291-936-1

www.SoulMatePublishing.com

For Papa, with love and happy memories.

A good man and father whom I miss so much.

Since this book is about music, it's in remembrance of you.

Acknowledgments

Thank you to my editor, Janine Phillips, for loving *The Wishing Tree in Irish Falls*, providing valuable feedback, and helping me polish this manuscript to share it with readers. I'm also grateful to Deborah Gilbert and the team at Soul Mate Publishing for support and guidance in bringing this book to publication.

Much appreciation to Anne Barr and her daughter Leia of Nana B's Bakery in Merrickville, Ontario, Canada. In sharing helpful insights about running a small-town family bakery, they helped shape the fictional Quinn's Bakery.

Ian Angus and Diana Fisher answered my questions about radio stations large and small, and I'm grateful for their help in clarifying technical details. I hope my fictional radio station does justice to the real-life radio station experiences they shared with me.

Additional thanks to Ian Angus who answered questions about recording studios and that aspect of my fictional world.

Gratitude to all the teachers, musicians, choir directors, and choir members who have brought music into my life. My own 'life in music' also influenced this book.

One of my wonderful readers, Liz Deshayes, named the kitten, Olivia, in a contest on my Facebook author page. Liz chose the perfect name, and I'm happy a reader has a part in this story.

I'm also very grateful to the readers who buy my books, borrow them from libraries, reach out to me on social media, send me messages, and write reviews. It's because of you I can do what I do.

Special thanks to reader Lynn Folliott for supporting me on social media and being a dear friend across the miles.

I appreciate the many book bloggers and reviewers who share my writing with their readers. A particular shout-out to Linda Levack Zagon of Linda's Book Obsession, and Susan Peterson of Sue's Booking Agency, for everything they do to support authors and readers, including me.

As always, I'm grateful to my agent, Dawn Dowdle, for her guidance, encouragement, and help in making my writing better.

I particularly thank author friends Susanna Bavin and Kate Field for wise counsel and support in writing, as well as life.

And at an especially difficult time, Susanna's encouragement, virtual tea and cake, and then hosting me at her home by the sea in Wales made all the difference.

Not least, my husband, teen daughter, and Floppy Ears, our rescue hound, bless my life in ways large and small. Thank you for the love, support, and being the family that is both my center and rock through life's ups and downs.

Chapter 1

"No." Annie Quinn balanced a tray of blueberry muffins against one hip and eyed her sister across the bakery counter.

"You only had one date with him." Tara's hazel eyes held a teasing glint that Annie hadn't glimpsed in over a year.

"One too many." Annie slid the plump muffins into the glass-fronted case. Her sister meant well, but she was done with being set up. She could find her own dates—*if* she wanted to.

"Blake seemed perfect." Tara's voice had a wheedling note. "There aren't a lot of new, single guys around here, and he's sure easy on the eyes." She rearranged a tiered display of scones near the cash register and avoided Annie's gaze.

"He spent most of the date talking about Siamese cats. He has two and takes them to cat shows most weekends." Annie counted the muffins, each juicy blueberry a succulent reminder of a perfect Adirondack summer day. "Besides, Hannah took one look at him and did that eye roll of hers. She calls him Blake the Flake."

"Your daughter's sixteen. We invented that eye roll when we were her age." Tara's mouth lifted into a lopsided smile. "You like cats. Maybe Blake was nervous and didn't know what to talk to you about."

"I was nervous at first too. Your daughter checking out your date is enough to make anybody nervous, and Hannah was pretty obvious. But when we got to the restaurant, whenever I tried to change the subject, Blake went right back to cats."

"So maybe he didn't work out, but you need to stay in the game." Tara joined Annie behind the counter and flicked a dust cloth along the display cabinets. "You're only thirty-five. That's way too young to sit at home every Saturday night, eat Nanaimo Bar Cheesecake, and watch movies with me." The sadness in her sister's voice tore at Annie's heart.

"I like watching movies with you." But even if she didn't, Tara needed her and she'd do whatever it took, however long it took, to be there for her. Tara wasn't only Annie's sister; she was also her best friend. "As for Nanaimo Bar Cheesecake, it's better than sex any day."

The brass bell over the door of Quinn's Bakery jingled, and Annie's head jerked toward it. She opened her mouth and closed it again. A man stood on the threshold, backlit by the bright April morning. He wore cowboy boots, faded jeans, and a white T-shirt under an untucked gray shirt. Amusement glinted in his eyes as he glanced between her and Tara.

"I'm looking for Annie Quinn." His voice had a mellow Southern drawl.

"That's me." Her face heated, and she set the empty muffin tray on the counter with a thud. At her age, she should have learned to keep her big mouth shut, at least when she was at work. Quinn's was a family business, but it was still a business.

"Seth Taggart." The door slid shut behind him, and he reached the counter in three long strides. His boots hit the retro-inspired blue-and-white tiled floor in a syncopated rhythm that echoed the beat of a hundred chart-topping songs. "Jake Kerrigan's nephew."

"We didn't expect you to get here until Friday." Annie's pulse skittered and she darted a glance at Tara by her side.

Her sister stared at Seth, then her eyes narrowed and she gave Annie a knowing look. The kind of look that, back when they were teenagers, meant "hot guy alert."

Ignoring Tara, Annie turned back to the man who faced them. "It's Wednesday," Annie continued. But any day of the week, Seth Taggart was so not who and what she'd expected.

"Didn't you get the message I left on your cell? I texted and e-mailed you too." When he smiled, the lines around his nose and mouth deepened, and his expression was warm, yet sexy.

"Uh . . . I've been on kind of a technology detox over the past few days." Her face heated. Thanks to a careless teenager and kitten as mischievous as she was cute, Annie also had bills it would take her until summer to pay off.

"I hope me turning up a few days early isn't a problem." Seth's smile changed and became easy and polished. The kind of smile Annie had learned not to trust.

"Of course not." She made herself smile back, even as Tara's gaze drilled into her. "Jake's apartment is upstairs, along with the radio station. You'll want the keys and . . ."

She stopped. She'd done it again. Always happy-to-help Annie. She needed to learn to think before she spoke. How could she be sure this guy was who he said he was? As the executor of Jake's will, she had a responsibility to be duly diligent. It was her legal responsibility, as the attorney from the law office three doors down had reminded her only yesterday over a plate of lemon squares. "You need to show me some identification first."

"Sure." He pulled a wallet from the back pocket of his jeans and slid out a driver's license. His fingers brushed hers as he passed the laminated card over the counter.

"Jake was a good man." Tara folded the dust cloth into a tidy square and stuck it in a drawer.

"So I hear." Seth's voice was a low monotone.

Her fingers still tingling from his brief touch, Annie held the license between her thumb and forefinger and scanned the details. California. The name Seth Taggart beside a picture of a man with the same short brown hair and strong jaw as the one standing across from her. A Los Angeles address and date of birth, July 2. He was thirty-seven, soon to be thirty-eight. Two years and a few months older than her.

Seth took the license back from Annie and tapped one booted foot on the floor with a rhythmic beat that made her think about things she didn't want to think about. Like hot summer nights, the melancholy twang of a guitar, and the sharp fragments of a broken dream.

"I'll get Jake's keys from the kitchen. Do you want a coffee while you wait?" Her words tumbled over each other. "Or a muffin?"

"You haven't lived until you've had one of Annie's blueberry muffins. They're our muffin of the day today." Tara grinned and leaned both elbows on the counter. "Big blues is what folks here call them."

Annie felt her face grow warm again. "They're ordinary blueberry muffins."

A lot like her. Her palms went clammy. Once, she'd been a starry-eyed girl with a golden voice who'd imagined she could make it in the music industry. But nowadays, she was an ordinary person, and she'd worked hard to convince herself that all she wanted was to raise Hannah and live her everyday life. And if it was sometimes boring, like her date with Blake, she only had to remember the alternative. Then boring looked just fine.

"A muffin sounds good. Coffee too, black." Seth's lips tilted into another smile, a lot less polished and way too likeable.

Her stomach fluttered and she pressed a hand to her throat.

"Unless you have any of that, what did you call it, Nanaimo Bar Cheesecake?"

"Not today." Annie's breath quickened and she bit her bottom lip hard. That cheesecake wasn't ordinary. Or boring. And whenever she made it, she felt like someone else—a woman who was fearless and who didn't let anything—or anyone—stop her from going after her dreams.

"We sold out of that cheesecake over Easter, and Annie hasn't had time to make more yet. It's her secret recipe and, along with the muffins, she's famous for it here in Irish Falls."

Annie winced. How had she let herself be defined by cheesecake and muffins?

Tara touched a finger to her lips. "I'm Tara, her younger sister." She stuck out her hand, and Seth took it.

"Only by eleven months." Annie didn't know why she felt compelled to point that out, but she did.

"So not quite twins?" Seth quirked a dark eyebrow, and his expression was amused.

"Irish twins born less than a year apart." Tara grinned. "We have another sister too, a year younger than me, but she doesn't work here. Annie and I run this place with our older brother and—"

"The keys." Annie backed through the swing door into the bakery kitchen.

Tara's throaty laugh rang out, joined by Seth's deeper one, and then the coffee pot rattled.

Annie pressed her hands to her blazing cheeks. The kitchen was empty in the brief lull between the buzz of their early morning baking schedule and the lunchtime rush for sandwiches and Quinn's hearty soups. Her purse hung on the hook it always did in the sunny alcove next to a window overlooking the waterfall from which Irish Falls took its name. Peace, roots, and brimming with beauty everywhere she looked, Irish Falls was what she'd needed when she'd come back home all those years ago.

But despite that sense of comfort and belonging, something important was missing and Annie couldn't deny it any longer. Hannah was almost grown up and soon, she'd go off to college. When that happened, who would Annie be and what would she do? Her stomach clenched. She had to become the heroine of her own life. She didn't want to be a sad and lonely mom who Hannah didn't want to visit. She wanted to be a mom who found new interests—and new dreams.

She grabbed her purse and dug in it until she found Jake's key ring. As she curled her fingers around the shiny brass music note, her throat tightened. "Why did you have to go and die?" she whispered. "What will I do without you? You'd have helped me become the person I really am— the person I need to be. You valued me for more than my baking."

Jake's laugh, full of warmth and love, echoed in her head and she pictured his deep-set blue eyes with the wrinkles fanned out around them, still sharp and wise until the end. *"The big guy upstairs didn't give me much choice, Annie girl. But you'll be fine. That person you need to be has been inside you all along. She's just been quiet for a while. And don't forget, you're the daughter of my heart. The daughter I wished for."*

Annie's eyes smarted and she gazed out the window again. On the other side of the waterfall stood the wishing tree with bits of paper and charms tied to its branches with ribbon and string. They held the hopes and dreams of people near and far—except her. Once, she'd wished on that tree too. But, along with being set up with guys like Blake, tying foolish wishes to trees was another thing she was done with.

Seth laughed again, and Annie yanked off the hairnet she wore for work. Taking charge of her life meant figuring out who she was now and what she wanted. It didn't mean wishing for things she couldn't have or dreaming a dream that would end in heartache.

~ ~ ~

From across the bakery counter, Tara's high-pitched voice kept up a running commentary, but Seth barely registered her words. He should have tried harder to reach Annie in person before turning up here, but he'd wanted to get out of LA and hadn't thought a few days would make a difference. He drained the cup of coffee, and the taste of regret overlaid the dark Columbian roast.

The swing door behind the counter creaked open, and Annie reappeared. Her cheeks were flushed and tendrils of red-gold hair curled around her face. "I've got the keys. I'll take you upstairs and show you around. Until after Jake passed, none of us knew he had a nephew. Well, I guess the lawyer did, but you've had a loss and all of us, we're sorry and . . ." She stopped and jangled the keys.

"Jake and I weren't close." He shifted from one foot to the other and stared at the immaculate floor.

"The lawyer said you work in the music business. That you're a songwriter." Tara slid a glance at Annie. "Jake sure loved music. That must be why he left you his radio station."

Seth picked up the paper bag from the counter that held the muffin he'd asked for to go. He was still a songwriter—a good one. He'd written hits for movies, TV, and Broadway shows, as well as for some of the biggest recording artists in the country. He was in a creative dry spell, that was all. And once he got out of it, he'd find another contract—and maybe even another collaborator. Things would work out because he wasn't the kind of guy to let life happen to him without fighting back.

"About the station . . ." He hesitated at the sadness in Annie and Tara's eyes. He was here to settle Jake's estate as fast as he could. Then he'd go home to LA and get his life—and career—back on track.

"That station's real popular." Annie walked around the end of the counter to his side. Like her sister, her petite figure was covered in a frilled white apron with "Quinn's, Est.1920" in green script across the chest. "We never miss the morning show, and at lunch there's a golden oldies slot. My mom loves that one because those songs are the ones she and my dad danced to back in high school. Before he got sick, Jake did requests and Mom . . . he knew that was important to her." She stopped, her bottom lip wobbled, and she swallowed. "You okay to look after things here for a bit, Tara?"

Her sister nodded and, over the counter, made frantic hand gestures in the direction of Annie's apron.

"Oops." Annie pulled at the apron ties behind her back, dropped the keys, and reached forward at the same time Seth did. The top of her head bumped his chest. "Sorry." She jumped back so fast she hit the bakery case, and he held out a hand to steady her.

"Easy."

Her slender hand was small and soft, and her nails were unpainted. Her hair smelled of cinnamon, lemon, and fresh bread. Good, honest smells, together with something else; a sweetness that caught him and held.

She yanked her hand away like she'd been scalded. "I'm not usually so . . ." She fumbled with the apron and wrestled it over her head then bent to pick up the keys. The green T-shirt she wore underneath rode up to expose a curve of creamy skin above black jeans that shaped her body in all the right places.

Seth blinked and swallowed. He must be more tired from the cross-country drive than he thought. Or else there'd been something in that coffee he'd inhaled in the hope it would yank him out of the stupor he'd lived in for the past few weeks. After a lot of years in LA, much of his traditional Southern upbringing hadn't stuck, but some of his grandmother's teachings still held strong. And one of the things she'd drilled into him, along with please, thank you, and never making a scene in public, was that a man kept his eyes on a woman's face, no matter how enticing the rest of her was.

Annie handed the apron to Tara and gave him an assessing look. Her blue eyes darkened like she could see into his soul and the core of the man he was. Then her gaze drifted beyond him, out the sparkling bakery window with its mouthwatering display of sweet treats, to his truck with the California license plate, angle parked in the space out front. She turned and grabbed a chunky knit sweater from a hook by the door. "We'll take the outside stairs." She pulled open the door and led the way onto the bustling street, waving at a group of women coming out of a quaint storefront several doors down.

As he followed Annie around the corner of the two-story, red brick building along a narrow gravel path bordered by several trees still bare of leaves, Seth breathed in the crisp April air mixed with an earthy scent. Amidst the foreignness of this small upstate New York town, a dot on the map miles from any interstate that, until a week ago, he'd never heard of, it was a familiar and comforting smell that took him back to his Georgia childhood.

Annie clattered up a set of gleaming white stairs, and her bulky sweater hid those sweet curves he shouldn't let himself notice. "Are you coming?"

The morning sun turned her shoulder-length hair a rich copper.

"What's that noise?" He raised his voice above a roaring sound.

"Irish Falls." She gave him a half-smile, and a pair of dimples dented her cheeks. "The main waterfall is behind us. That's why Jake rented the second floor. He wanted to live and work beside water. After a while, you don't notice it."

Annie pulled open a glass door with KXIF and "Sound of the Adirondacks" printed on it in black letters. Behind the empty reception desk, a dog barked.

"Hey, Dolly." Annie dug in her sweater pocket and pulled out a treat.

A white dog with brown spots bounded over, wagged its tail, and took the snack from Annie's open palm.

"Dolly?" Seth took a step back and bumped into one of the two gray-upholstered chairs that flanked a small table stacked with magazines. He'd never had a dog. His grandparents hadn't let him have one when he was a kid, and his adult life had been too busy for pets.

"Jake was a huge Dolly Parton fan. He had every album she made. The radio booth is over there." Annie gestured across a short expanse of beige carpet toward the corner of a glass-enclosed studio. "The morning show ends at ten, and then it's the farm report before the Lunchtime Jukebox. That's the oldies show I told you about. The staff can't wait to meet you. They all have other jobs so they come in and out."

"What about the receptionist?" Seth glanced at the empty desk. A fluffy pink sweater was draped over the back of the desk chair and a pair of fluorescent green-framed glasses sat beside the computer.

"Oh, Sherri will be back in an hour or so. Her dad has Alzheimer's and she takes him to a special singing group every Wednesday morning."

"But what about phone calls? Like from a listener or someone who wants to buy an advertising slot?" Seth tried to keep his voice level. How could you run a business if your receptionist wasn't there during working hours? "And what if someone comes in? She left the door unlocked."

"Everybody around here knows about Sherri's dad, so they wouldn't call right now. But even if someone did, Sherri forwards the phone to the bakery while she's out. She works part-time reception and does cleaning for the station and a couple of other local businesses too. She's the most honest person ever, so she makes up the time and more. Anyway, most people leave their doors unlocked here, at least during the day." Annie's voice was laced with what sounded like laughter. "Small-town life."

He wasn't a small-town guy, but even the most sophisticated security system money could buy hadn't protected him from the kind of theft and betrayal that was more insidious—an inside job. Seth's stomach twisted and he looked at Dolly, who nosed his boots. "Dolly was Jake's dog?"

The dog whined, and the mournful sound reverberated in Seth's chest.

"She sure was, and she's grieving for Jake. I've been looking after her, but I can't keep her in the bakery, and I have cats who don't like dogs at home." Annie shook the key ring and extracted a silver key. "Besides, Dolly's happier here. I think she feels closer to Jake."

"What kind of dog is she?" Seth studied the animal at his feet, who looked back at him with woebegone brown eyes.

"A mutt with a whole lot of hound is what Jake called her." Annie bent and rubbed Dolly's floppy ears. "He found her by the falls two summers ago. He advertised, but nobody claimed her. Maybe Jake needed her as much as she needed him."

"And now?" Seth flinched as the dog's brown gaze turned hopeful.

"She's yours." Annie moved away from the reception desk, and he followed her down a carpeted hall that ended at a wood-paneled door. "Jake wanted you to give her a home." She turned the key in the lock and the door swung open.

Seth rubbed a hand across the back of his neck as Dolly bounced up to him and nosed his boots again. He wasn't going to take on Jake's radio station. And he wasn't going to take on a dog, either. Along with selling the station, he'd find Dolly a nice family. A few kids to play with would perk her up in no time.

"Jake didn't have a lot of things. My mom and some other folks in town gave him most of the furniture after he rented the apartment. His home was a place to sleep, eat, and do whatever woodworking project he had on the go. He was a good carpenter and most people around here have something he made for them or their kids." Annie flipped a switch on the wall, and a ceiling light went on. "Except from coming in to empty the fridge of perishables and water the plants, I haven't touched anything."

Seth glanced around the compact living area. A red plaid sofa sat along one wall, with a coffee table in front. A vintage dinette set was in front of a window flanked by two spider plants with a simple wooden chest of drawers to one side. Yet, the simplicity was deceptive. Even from ten feet away, the piece bore the imprint of a master craftsman. In fact, it was similar to a cabinet Seth had admired a few months before in a high-end furniture store in LA.

"The last time I saw Jake I was seven. I don't know why he left me his radio station or his dog. I didn't even know where he was until that attorney tracked me down." And he'd tried to not think about Jake, either. Or those sultry Southern evenings when, as his mom had gotten sicker and sicker, he and Jake had built a clubhouse in the shelter of a giant oak draped with Spanish moss—an oasis of safety in a big and scary world.

Annie's blue eyes softened. "You must have meant a lot to him. He also left you his guitar." She opened a closet and took out a battered case. "This guitar was Jake's most prized possession."

Seth swallowed the unexpected lump of emotion as more memories surfaced. "Jake visited my mom and me a couple of times a year. I remember he had a guitar. He'd play it for us." That ramshackle carriage house in the old part of Savannah his mom had rented from a friend of a friend was where Seth had spent the happiest years of his childhood.

A gentle smile spread across Annie's face. "Jake was a wonderful musician. He could play anything. He asked me to bring his guitar to the hospital. It's a Gibson. He said it gave him comfort. He played right up to the day before he died." Her voice was reverent.

Seth made himself reach out and take the guitar case from her. Then he knelt to open it and take the guitar out. He cleared his throat. "It's the same guitar he had all those years ago." He ran his hand across the gleaming soundboard and then caught up a rosewood pick and held it tight.

An image flashed into his mind as clear as if it had been yesterday. He'd sat on Jake's lap in the carriage house kitchen, the Christmas he was six, the year before his mom passed. Jake had shown him how to hold this same guitar and where to put his fingers on the strings. Together, they'd made sounds that weren't like any Seth had ever heard before. In the circle of Jake's strong arms, something in Seth's soul had shifted and changed.

Then his mom had smiled, and Jake smiled back and launched into a song like the ones Seth heard on the radio that sat on the scarred kitchen counter. His mom's high voice blended with Jake's lower one, and Seth had clapped along in time to the music. And happiness—along with a new and unexpected sense of completeness—had swelled inside Seth.

"You need some time. I'll leave you alone." Annie's voice pulled him back to the present.

"Wait." He set the pick back in the case and got to his feet. "How did Jake die? The lawyer didn't say." And he hadn't asked, too caught up in his own life to wonder about the end of someone else's.

"Lung cancer." Annie's voice cracked. "He was never a smoker, at least not when I knew him, but he played a lot of clubs before he came here. Maybe secondhand smoke from years ago, that's what the doctor said. It was quick." Her bottom lip trembled. "At first, he didn't tell us he was sick. He was a private guy."

Seth exhaled, and Dolly edged closer to his legs and whined again, a cross between a cry and a groan. He couldn't let himself think about Jake. Or about all the other losses that had led him here, to this woman with the kind eyes tinged with unexpected wariness. He had to move forward. "I plan to sell the station. I should have a buyer lined up in the next few weeks. I've already put out feelers to a couple of media companies."

And once he talked to the lawyer and dealt with the paperwork, he'd be out of here. Then he could reconnect with his son and he'd get back in the game with his career, too.

Songwriting had been good to him before and it could be good to him again. Not only did it more than pay the bills, it had enabled him to care for his son and make a home for the two of them, things he couldn't have done if he'd stuck with his teenage dream of being on the road with a band.

"Media companies. You mean chains?

He nodded.

"But this is a small, locally-owned station. Jake . . . that was important to him. He wanted to have a trusting, personal relationship with his listeners. Local content for local people and local advertisers too." Annie's tone was cool, and she crossed her arms in front of her chest.

Seth took a deep breath. "I understand, but I talked to some of my contacts in New York City and LA and, these days, small local stations are an anomaly. Most aren't commercially viable, either. Any chain would still serve the local market with news and weather, but you'd get more programs and more support too. There's what? A few thousand people in this town? In Buffalo and—"

"Irish Falls isn't Buffalo and bigger isn't always better." Her voice had a sharp edge he hadn't expected. "I take it you haven't seen Jake's will yet?"

"No, all the attorney said was Jake left me the station and I had to come here to go through the paperwork and instructions." And his uncle's unexpected generosity meant he'd have more than enough money to tide him over until he found his muse again. He'd had dry spells before. He'd dealt with sharks before too. And each time, he'd bounced back stronger than ever.

Dolly sat on Seth's feet and draped her tail across the guitar case like a furry white scarf.

"Jake left instructions all right." Annie's voice was low and had a telling quaver. "You can't sell the station and claim the proceeds unless you run it for six months. He also wanted you to give Dolly a home for life."

"What?" Seth took a step back, and Dolly yelped. "What kind of will is that?" He bent to give the dog an awkward pat. He had nothing against this dog or any other, but a pet was a big commitment and he wasn't good at commitment. Besides, did his condo even allow pets?

"Jake's will." Annie's mouth got tight. "You have to run—"

"I heard you, but there has to be some way out." Seth rubbed the back of his neck and moved to the window that overlooked the falls. The roaring sound was even louder there. "The lawyer will have to find a loophole. What was Jake thinking? I can't stay here for six months. My life's in LA. Apart from high school and when I first moved to California, I haven't worked in radio broadcasting for years. Besides, what am I supposed to do in a place like this? It's pretty, sure, but . . . ." He stopped and stared out the window.

Tall trees with thick trunks lined a street that ran downhill from the falls toward a river bisected by a swing bridge. A small stone church nestled into trees on the other side of the falls beyond a park with a baseball diamond and war memorial. Multi-colored clapboard houses encircled by white picket fences had kids' bikes and skateboards propped out front. Laundry danced in the breeze on clotheslines framed by a bright blue sky. The whole vista was as picture perfect, small-town America as the scenes on the decorative plates his grandmother had collected and displayed in the shadowy dining room of her big house in Savannah.

He turned back to Annie. She'd picked up Dolly and held the dog in front of her like a shield. Although her mouth still trembled, her expression was carefully blank. "Jake updated his will a week before he died. I didn't know what he wanted. I didn't know about you then." Her voice was low. "And I don't know what he was thinking. Maybe he wasn't thinking. I mean, it would be strange for a guy like you to stay here . . ." She stopped. "If you don't want the station, the attorney and I will sell it and the proceeds will go to charity. It's your choice."

It was. And in Seth's suddenly way-too-complicated life, the radio station, the dog, and even the woman standing in front of him, with a haunted expression in her eyes that hit him like a punch in the gut, were all complications he didn't need.

Chapter 2

"Hannah Geraldine Quinn. If I have to ask you one more time . . ." Annie raised her voice above the Carrie Underwood song that blared from Hannah's bedroom.

"What?" Her sixteen-year-old daughter's strawberry-blonde head appeared over the railing at the top of the stairs. "I already told you I'm busy."

"I'm busy too, and I need your help." Annie gripped the newel post as she mentally counted to five. "There are two of us in this family, and dinner won't cook itself."

Hannah's head disappeared, followed an instant later by silence, and then the clump of her feet across the upstairs hall and down the stairs. "I have a ton of homework. I shouldn't have to help make dinner."

"You've been at school all day. I've hardly seen you." As Hannah reached her, Annie smoothed the curls that tumbled over her daughter's shoulders.

Hannah let out a sigh before she gave Annie a one-armed hug. "Sorry."

"It's okay." Together they moved through the front hall to the kitchen at the back of the house. Annie had painted the room a warm gray and lined pots of red and white geraniums on the broad windowsill to catch the afternoon sun.

"I hate it when you call me Geraldine. It's an old lady's name." Hannah reached for the head of lettuce and several tomatoes Annie had set out on the countertop.

"It's because of your Nana Geraldine we have this house to live in."

And not a day went by that Annie didn't miss her grandmother. Although nobody in the big-hearted Quinn family had judged when she'd come back from her freshman year of college pregnant with Hannah and no husband or boyfriend in tow, it was widowed Nana Gerry who'd suggested she move in with her under the guise she needed company. And with gentle love and understanding, it was Nana Gerry who'd helped Annie put the broken pieces of her life back together.

"You've told me that like a gazillion times." Hannah pulled a paring knife out of a drawer. "It's great Nana left us her house, but couldn't you have given me a different name? I don't even remember her."

Annie reached into the fridge for the lasagna she'd taken out of the freezer to thaw that morning. "After me, Nana Gerry was the first person to hold you on the day you were born."

And she'd shared in the all-consuming, unconditional love for her baby daughter that had rolled over Annie like a tidal wave. A love that had washed away the past, blotted out regrets, and helped her look to the future with hope.

"When I make it big in the Nashville music scene, what if somebody finds out my middle name's Geraldine?" Hannah sliced tomatoes into chunks.

"*If* you make it big in Nashville or anywhere else, nobody will care what your middle name is." Annie slid the lasagna into the preheated oven. "But you have to make it through high school and college first."

"You know I don't want to go to college." Hannah's tone was sullen, and her mouth was set in a stubborn line. "You have to start young in music."

Annie wiped her hands on a colorful kitchen towel to stop the trembling. "You're a smart girl, and I want you to have something to fall back on. A college degree gives you options. You could study music education at college so you could teach alongside singing and writing your songs." And she didn't want her daughter's life to turn out like hers had. Annie's vision blurred as tears pricked behind her eyes. "What if music doesn't work out? What will you do then?"

"It *will* work out." Hannah dumped the lettuce and tomatoes into a glass salad bowl. "Lots of successful people didn't go to college or else they dropped out. Besides, I've got the money I've saved up and Nana Gerry left me, and everybody says I've got talent."

"You do, honey, but sometimes . . ." Annie hesitated. "There are lots of teens with talent. To make it in a place like Nashville or any big city, you also need hard work, resilience, and a lot of luck."

Most of all, you needed to trust the right people and not give away parts of yourself you couldn't get back.

"I have all those things." Hannah opened a drawer in the oak sideboard and pulled out two red quilted placemats.

"If I'd had something to fall back on beyond a high school diploma, maybe I wouldn't have had to work in the bakery." Annie held up a hand to stop whatever Hannah was about to say. "Quinn's is a good business, sure, and I like my job and working with my family, but I want more for you."

"I could work in Jake's radio station for a while. I worked there last summer. He said I have natural talent, remember?" Hannah dropped cutlery on the table with a clatter. In the cat basket below the window, Hazel, Annie's elderly tabby, opened a sleepy eye and nudged Olivia, Hannah's white and gray kitten.

Annie moved away from the oven and toward the cats. "You *are* talented, but it's no longer Jake's station, sweetie. We don't know what the new owner plans to do with it." Except, she'd seen the expression on Seth's face when he'd talked about lining up a buyer. He didn't understand that local radio was the lifeblood of a town like Irish Falls, and he didn't realize how many people depended on it, far beyond those who worked there. Jake hadn't only run a local business, the station helped support other local businesses too.

Her jaw got tight and she picked up a felt toy mouse from the floor beside the cat basket and tossed it for Olivia to chase. "There are other radio stations in bigger towns you could work for, but first, and if you don't want to teach, you could study broadcasting or music production at college. Or musical theater, or music therapy even. You've always liked helping people. There are colleges right here in New York state that offer all those programs. And I'm sure Nana Gerry would have wanted you to use the money she left you to help with your education."

"All Nana Gerry said in her will was that money would be mine when I turned eighteen." Hannah's voice was earnest. "I don't want to spend another four years in school. I want to learn by doing. When I sing or write music, it's like I'm who I was meant to be." The setting sun that streamed through the kitchen window made a fiery halo around Hannah's head as she grabbed paper napkins out of the holder. "I don't expect you to understand."

Annie leaned against the kitchen island. The wall clock that had been in her family for several generations ticked in a steady rhythm with her thoughts. "You might not think so, but I do understand. I had a dream of making it as a singer once." Except, sometimes, no matter how badly you want it to, your dream doesn't come true. There were people who'd take your dream and make it their own. The same ones who'd use you and toss you aside like stale baking.

"But—"

"I'm not saying don't go after your dream, but you also have to be practical. Don't get so caught up in the dream that you forget about the rest of your life." Annie made herself put one foot in front of the other and cross the kitchen to reach her daughter. "I love you more than you can ever know, at least not until you're a mom yourself. It's my job to worry about you and help you make good choices."

Hannah's expression softened, and the dark eyes with dark lashes that were one of the few physical legacies of her father turned pleading. "I have to make it in music. I just have to."

"I know, but you're only sixteen. Why don't you at least get some information about colleges? You could talk to the guidance counselor at school. I'm sure she'd have good ideas. If there's any campus you want to visit, we could go together." Annie smoothed Hannah's silky curls. Maybe an outsider would have a better chance of reaching her headstrong daughter and could help her see she could choose more than one path.

"I'll be seventeen in August, but I guess it wouldn't hurt to get information, even though I'm not going to change my mind."

"I don't expect you to change your mind." Like Annie wouldn't have changed hers at Hannah's age. "All I ask is you take time to consider all the options."

Hannah gave her a sunny smile. "From the bus on my way home from school, I saw some guy carrying stuff up to Jake's apartment. What was that about?"

Annie blinked at the sudden change of subject. Hannah had also inherited her father's ability to filter out anything she didn't want to hear. "That would have been Jake's nephew, Seth Taggart. He turned up this morning a few days early."

"He's hot. He sure rocked that dark, brooding look."

He did, and that was why Annie had to be on her guard around him. She'd been burned by that type once and learned lessons to last a lifetime. "Seth Taggart is way too old for you."

"Mom." In addition to the eye roll, the word was full of teenage sarcasm. "I meant for you." Hannah grinned. "He's gotta be better than Blake the Flake."

"Blake's a perfectly nice man." *If you like safe and predictable*, whispered a little voice inside Annie.

"He looks like he's been washed and ironed." Hannah's smile widened. "Seth Taggart worked a rumpled and sexy groove. He was wearing a great pair of boots, too. Can you see Blake the Flake in cowboy boots?"

Annie could, and the comparison wasn't in Blake's favor. "Hannah—"

"Geraldine Quinn." Her daughter stuck out her tongue. "You need to get out and have some fun."

"I do get out." Annie's mouth went dry. "Who took you to New York City for that concert last month and to Smuggler's Notch for spring break? I also go to the gym with Auntie Tara, and there's Auntie Rowan's book club. I ski in the winter and rollerblade in the summer. I sing in the church choir and do yoga." She pressed a hand to her stomach. All those things *were* fun, but she did them either solo or with her daughter and sisters.

"I meant fun with guys." Hannah made a disgusted face. "The book club is all women and ditto the yoga studio. The youngest man in the choir is Mr. Flaherty and he's retired, and you only go to the gym when Auntie Tara makes you. As for skiing and rollerblading, they're not exactly team sports." She pulled a chair away from the kitchen table and sat. "Sure, we do lots of great stuff together, but it's not like you're going to meet men with me in tow. And you won't do online dating, either."

Annie let out a breath. "You're still at home and I have a busy schedule. It's not the right time for me to have a relationship." She dated when she wanted to, but right now she didn't want to. She had a lot of other things to figure out first. "You've been talking to Auntie Tara."

"Nope." Hannah propped her chin in her hands and her expression turned serious. "But if you want me to change my way of looking at things, then you need to change your way of looking at some things too. What will you do when I leave home?"

Annie's chest hurt. Although she didn't want to think about what her life would be like without Hannah under the same roof, she had to. And if she didn't take charge of her life now, maybe she never would. "Okay." She exhaled. Perhaps she'd gotten a bit set in her ways and she could change that. But Seth was off limits for all sorts of reasons, none of which she could share with her daughter.

Hannah clapped her hands. "How long is that Seth guy going to be in town?"

"I don't know." If what Annie had glimpsed in his face was right, he'd bail on his inheritance and the station would be sold before the leaves came out on the wishing tree.

She shut her eyes and breathed a silent prayer to God, the saints, and Nana Gerry, too. Her demons were her demons. They had nothing to do with Seth Taggart.

~ ~ ~

Seth rolled over in bed. The buzzing noise wasn't in his head. It came from the alarm on the ancient clock radio on the nightstand beside him. He fumbled for the switch on the bedside lamp.

The buzzing was joined by a bark, and then a cold wet nose bumped his cheek.

He hit the light and then the alarm and lurched to sit upright as the bed springs creaked in protest.

"Dolly?"

The dog stared back at him before she propped her paws on Seth's bare shoulders. Her big brown eyes were level with his nose.

"What do you think you're doing here?"

Dolly whined and licked his ear.

"Oh no, you don't." Seth yanked the quilt up and over his shoulders.

"Good morning, Irish Falls." The nasally, singsong male voice came from somewhere to Seth's right. He staggered out of bed and took the quilt with him, but the disembodied voice came from the radio, not inside the apartment.

Dolly barked again and bounced from one end of the bed to the other, like her paws were on springs.

"You're listening to KXIF, the voice of the Adirondacks. If you're heading out of town, I had a call that a herd of cows is blocking the road at the bottom of the mountain." The man, who also sounded as if he had a heavy cold, dropped his final t's so "out" became "ou" and drew out his vowels so "cows" sounded more like "caows."

Seth dug in his duffle bag for a T-shirt and pulled it on then sat back on the edge of the bed and dropped his head into his hands. This wasn't a nightmare. It was real. Almost twenty-four hours later he was still here, so the train wreck that was the rest of his life and he had to dig himself out of was here, too.

He flipped off the radio to silence the guy in mid-sentence and raised his head to eyeball the dog. "I need a shower and an extra-large coffee, after which you and I are going for a walk to figure a way out of this mess."

Dolly whined and thumped her tail, leaving clumps of white hair on the navy comforter.

"Okay, breakfast for you as well." A heaping scoop from the big bag of dog food propped in a corner of Jake's hall closet. "I'm still finding you a good family, but I can see why Jake liked you." Seth rubbed one of Dolly's silky brown ears. "But no more sharing this bed, you hear?"

Three hours later, Dolly, the hairball in his bed, was the least of Seth's worries. A takeout coffee in one hand and Dolly's leash in the other, he stood on the narrow pedestrian walkway on the bridge that spanned the Black Duck River in the middle of town.

Not that he'd doubted her, but the lawyer had confirmed what Annie had said. The station was only his to sell if he ran it for six months. Jake had also added a long list of conditions to ensure Seth couldn't skip town and appoint an interim manager.

He pulled out his wallet and flipped to the dog-eared photo he kept in the plastic space at the back. Five-year-old Dylan beamed at him from behind a birthday cake decorated with racing cars and, as always, the love and trust in his son's gaze pulled at him and reminded him of what he'd lost. In what seemed like the blink of an eye, Dylan had grown up and into a life of his own, and now he was at college in New York City and Seth was a bystander relegated to the sidelines.

Dolly nudged his leg, and he stooped to pat her soft head. He stared into the silvery water bubbling against the dark rocks below the bridge. Sticks caught in the current drifted toward the falls. It wasn't too late to start over with his son. If only his ex-wife had been able to be a mom, maybe she'd have known what to do. But if Amanda had been around for all those years of raising Dylan, maybe he and his son wouldn't have gotten into this mess in the first place.

"Seth?" Footsteps clattered on the wooden bridge slats, and he started as Annie stopped beside him. "I hope you aren't going to jump in the river. The story here is that a guy did that on a dare back in the nineteen forties. The current's stronger than it looks, so he drowned. Some folks believe his ghost still haunts this bridge." Although her smile mitigated her words, it didn't quite mask the concern in her eyes.

He snapped the wallet shut and slid it back into his pocket. "No. I lost track of time." And got caught between a past he didn't want to think about and a future he couldn't yet imagine.

"There's a storm moving in. Didn't you notice? We'll get rain for sure, maybe even late-season snow."

Annie's gaze locked with his. Something he didn't want to put a name on sizzled between them.

"Snow? It's the third week of April. What kind of climate is this?"

"The Adirondack kind. Here, even when it's milder like this year, winter gets a grip and doesn't want to let go." She gave him an impish grin. "Dolly hates wet weather."

"I . . . uh." Seth glanced at the dog then back to Annie.

She wore a dark blue rain jacket and above it, her pretty hair was windblown.

"Are you okay?" Her eyebrows drew together as she frowned. "The first time I called your name you didn't answer. I'm on my way back from the bank. Pretty much anywhere you want to go in town, you have to walk or drive across this bridge."

"I'm fine." The lie rolled off his tongue with ease.

He turned to follow her off the bridge and, below the hem of the jacket, her butt swayed in a pair of sculpted jeans. Seth jerked his head up. *Whoa.* She was the executor of Jake's will. He could be friendly to her, but no more than he'd be with any professional colleague.

When she reached the bakery side of the bridge, Annie stopped and dug a dog treat out of her pocket for Dolly. "The attorney said you talked to him."

"News travels fast here." Seth fell into step beside her, along the sidewalk that led up the hill to the bakery on Malone Street in the center of Irish Falls.

"Karl's office is three doors down from Quinn's." A half-smile played around Annie's mouth. "He drops by morning and afternoon for coffee and one of the German spice cookies Tara makes from his Oma's recipe. You could set your watch by him."

"I asked him about Jake's will." Seth moved closer to her as a red pickup rattled by on the street beside them, leaving bits of straw and mud in its wake.

"What did he say?" She stepped away and maneuvered Dolly between them.

"I want a second opinion." The truth might be staring him in the face, but he still had to try. He flinched as an icy raindrop landed on the end of his nose.

"Karl's practiced law here for almost thirty years. He's smart and Jake trusted his advice. If you don't want the station, though, the charities Jake nominated if you said 'thanks, but no thanks,' could sure do a lot of good with that money." Annie picked up the pace and Seth broke into a jog to keep up with her.

"If Jake was big on charity work, why didn't he leave the station to those groups in the first place? And why did he insist I come here in person to find out the terms of his will?" Seth's stomach hardened and he stared at the colorful century-old buildings that lined Malone Street. "Since he left me the station with the caveat of running it for six months, he must have had a reason."

"I'm sure he did." A gust of wind tossed Annie's hair around her face, and she yanked up the hood of her jacket as misty rain blew in on the wind.

"It sounds like you were close to Jake. Why didn't he leave the station to you?" Seth lurched forward as Dolly pulled on the leash.

"I'm not Jake's family. You are." She fixed him with a steely gaze. "His only living family." Her left hand closed over Seth's right and tugged on the leash. Dolly stopped straining.

Her touch warmed him. Then Annie took her hand away and stuck it in her jacket pocket before striding ahead of him.

"I . . . hey . . ." Seth's hand tingled with the imprint of

hers, and feelings he was certain he'd left behind years ago churned in the pit of his stomach.

Annie stopped beneath the bakery's green and white-striped awning. Inside, two women stood behind the counter and stared out the big front window at them. One was Tara and, given the bright red hair, as well as what the lawyer had told him about the Quinn family earlier, the other one must be the third sister, Rowan.

Seth turned his back on the window and the two pairs of curious eyes boring into him. "I'm sorry. I'm not usually so . . . abrupt." He swallowed as the words stuck in his throat. "Jake's death hit me out of nowhere. I hadn't thought of him in years, and then, all of a sudden, I got a phone call from some lawyer in a place I'd never heard of who told me I'm the sole beneficiary of Jake's estate. If I'd known he was sick, I'd have come to see him. I should have been here for the funeral. It was only last week."

"Jake left instructions about that, too." Annie's gentle voice was like a healing balm to his soul. "He didn't want you here then. He wanted you to remember him as he was when you were a kid, not the sick old man he was at the end. He told Karl to not contact you until after the funeral. We had to wait a few weeks until the ground thawed enough for burial." Her voice hitched and she half turned away from him.

Seth glanced at Dolly huddled against the bakery wall. Her eyes were two brown pools of sadness and her small body quivered. He scooped her up and tucked her into the crook of his arm. "I care about what Jake wanted, but I've got commitments and responsibilities." Most of which were either broken or tenuous. "How can I stay here for six months?"

"I don't know, but, at the end of the day, family is all you have." Her expression was wistful and her tone implied she didn't like him a whole lot right now.

"Sure, but . . ." Seth's heart punched his ribs. Apart from Dylan, he didn't have any family to speak of.

"My dad died when I was twelve, and when Jake turned up here, he filled a big gap in all our lives." Annie blinked and her voice was halting. "He didn't replace my dad. Nobody could ever do that. But he helped my mom with fixing things around the bakery, and he was there for my sisters and brother and me if we needed him. We didn't know he had a family of his own, but he did. You."

"I'm sorry about your dad. I . . ." Seth's throat got raw. There were parts of himself he didn't like a whole lot either, but in the last few weeks he'd vowed to hit refresh on his life. Could he do that here? At least for a little while? Maybe running the station could work to his advantage. A family inheritance would be a good reason to stay away from LA, and six months would be more than enough time for him to clear his head and launch back into work with a great game plan. And Irish Falls was in the same time zone as New York City so it might be harder for his son to push him away when Seth tried to reconnect.

The silence lengthened between them as he studied the street, charming even in the rain. Storybook storefronts like Quinn's Bakery marched up the hill toward a water tower with "Irish Falls" painted on it in green letters surrounded by shamrocks. Halfway up, a pocket-sized square had a white-painted bandstand at its center and beyond it, children's voices echoed from a schoolyard, with yellow buses clustered out front like a convoy of covered wagons.

"Dad passed a long time ago. My mom remarried nine years ago, and my stepdad's been great for her and all of us," Annie said, her shoes hitting the flagstones in a quick staccato as she moved to the bakery door.

"But your dad's still important to you."

Annie stopped by the door and her shoulders slumped.

"Of course he is. He always will be. My dad was my hero and . . ." Her mouth worked and she stared at the sidewalk.

Seth's stomach lurched. How would his life have been different if he'd known his dad, or if his mom hadn't passed so young? "I need to think about all this. I'm not making any promises, but you're right, Jake was my uncle and I owe him." For his mom's memory and for how Jake brought fun and laughter into both their lives. "I want to go through the station's books, take another look at the studio and equipment, and talk more with you and the staff."

"Sure. That's great." Annie's tone was flat, her lips got tight, and then she fumbled with the rolling pin door handle.

Seth took a step back. His initial impression was wrong. It wasn't dislike of him he'd heard in Annie's voice earlier. It was something more akin to distrust or even fear.

Chapter 3

Maureen McNeill, who still sometimes thought of herself as Maureen Quinn, came into the front of the bakery from the kitchen. Tara sat behind the counter making notes in the order book and tapped her foot in time to Hannah's favorite Taylor Swift song on the radio. "I thought I heard Annie's voice out here."

"You did." Her daughter looked up. "She's in the office." Tara lowered her voice. "With Jake's nephew, Seth Taggart." Tara glanced at the hall door as if Seth lurked outside it.

Maureen rested both hands on her cane. Her son and daughters ran the bakery as well as she had, but she missed being a real part of the business. "Was Rowan here, too?" She stared out the window onto Malone Street, where tendrils of mist hung low and mellow light from the Victorian-inspired lamps illuminated the slick pavement. A few hardy pedestrians scurried between stores half-hidden under umbrellas.

"She only dropped in for a few minutes to pick up cupcakes for the PTA meeting." Tara's laugh was forced. "You know how busy she is with her kids, work, and well . . . everything."

Maureen bit back a sigh. Like Tara's sadness, and Annie's too brittle cheerfulness, Rowan's almost frenetic busyness worried her. "It's quiet this afternoon."

"Would you want to be out in this weather?" Tara's mouth curved into a soft smile.

"As your Nana Gerry would have said, April showers bring May flowers." Maureen chuckled. "Despite the weather, I like this time of year. Every other season, we have to share Irish Falls with tourists, but for these few weeks, it's all ours. Not that I mind the tourists. They're good for the town and help keep us in business. But I cherish these weeks between ski season and Memorial Day, when we're watching spring come. And when there aren't any strangers in town so I know everyone."

Except this year. Maureen bit her lip. "There's something about Seth that's got Annie upset. She won't talk to me. Has she said anything to you?" The fact Annie had avoided talking about Jake's nephew told Maureen something was up.

"No, she won't talk to Rowan or me, either." Tara's tone was protective.

Maureen found a pair of tongs and reached into the bakery case. "It was Hannah who told me he showed up early." She took out two thick slices of apple cake and popped them into a paper bag.

"Here, I'll help you." Tara reached for the bag, but Maureen waved her away.

"I've got it." Her daughter meant well, but couldn't she understand how it hurt to be helped? How it hurt when people asked about her hip, as if the pins and plate holding the fractured bone together had fundamentally changed who she was? She opened the door to the hallway with her good hip and followed the low murmur of voices to the small bakery office.

The voices stopped as Maureen rounded the corner. Annie sat behind the cluttered desk, and a man, who must be Seth Taggart, was in the armchair across from her. Dolly was curled up on his lap, wrapped in a pink bath towel. In one corner, a heater fan whirred and pushed out warm air to mix with the smell of wet dog.

"Mom." Annie jumped up.

Seth got to his feet too, but kept hold of Dolly. "Please take my seat, ma'am."

Maureen shook her head. Someone had taught him manners, but that respectful ma'am made her feel even older than she already did. "I'm not staying." Tension crackled in the small room. "I only came by to introduce myself. I'm Annie's mom, Maureen McNeill."

Seth set Dolly on the floor and took the hand she held out. "My pleasure to meet you." His handshake was warm and firm, and he had a look of Jake about him. The same dark brown hair, defined cheekbones, and deep-set eyes that had women falling at his feet when Jake turned up in Irish Falls more than twenty years earlier. "The attorney told me what you did for my uncle when he was sick. I surely appreciate it."

"Jake was like family to us." Maureen looked him up and down. "That makes you as good as family, too."

"Mom, you—" Annie's voice held a warning note.

"What?" Maureen pinned her daughter's gaze. "I raised you to be neighborly, didn't I?" She turned back to Seth. "I brought some of my apple cake for you to have with your supper. Jake was real fond of this cake. He said it reminded him of one his mother made."

She held out the bag, and Seth took it.

"Thank you." A smile started at his mouth and reached deep into his magnetic blue-gray eyes.

Despite her sixty-five years, Maureen caught her breath. She glanced at Annie. Her daughter's hair tumbled around her flushed face, and she stared out the office window at the steady rain, away from Seth. "Jake's radio station is the heartbeat of Irish Falls. I heard you do something in the music business. Will you be taking on Jake's legacy? We all miss hearing him on the morning show."

"I . . ." Seth flicked a glance at Annie, who continued to avoid his gaze. "I'm a songwriter, not a radio announcer or station manager."

"You look like a smart man, so I bet you could pick things up real fast. That station isn't the same without Jake. When he got too sick to work, he and Annie had to hire someone to fill in. Maybe you heard Steve? He's also doing Jake's show. He's got a voice like a cat with its tail caught in a door. Not the kind of voice you want to wake up to, whereas you—"

"Seth hasn't made any final decisions yet." Annie broke in, moved around the desk, and took Maureen's arm. "He only got here yesterday. He hasn't even seen the station properly or met all the staff."

Maureen shook Annie's hand away. She wasn't so old or infirm she needed to be held up, and she wasn't about to let any of her kids boss her around, either. "That station was Jake's life. He'd be mighty proud to have his nephew take it over."

"Mrs. McNeill." Seth smiled at her again, and this time there was an edge of steel behind the charm.

"Maureen, please." That smile told her he had backbone. She liked backbone.

"Maureen." His smile slipped. "Like Annie said, I haven't made any decisions yet."

A mix of rain and sleet pattered against the window. Dolly howled and scooted under Seth's chair.

"Life often catches you while you're making decisions." Maureen fixed him with her firmest gaze. "I read somewhere that more people in this country listen to the radio than watch TV or use computers or fancy phones or what have you. It's not just old folks, either. A lot of those Generation Xers and Millennials are big radio listeners too. It's like that with Jake's station. Everyone in this town depends on it and listens every day."

"Of course, I'll figure something out for the station. The least I can do is not leave the people of Irish Falls in the lurch." Seth gave her an easy smile.

"Thank you." Maureen didn't smile back. Instead, she glanced at Annie, who had a worried pucker between her eyebrows. She didn't know much about what went on in

Annie's head. Her daughter had been a mystery to her since she'd come back from college pregnant with Hannah. Even though, on the surface, she seemed happy with her life, there was a restlessness there, as well as a wall Maureen had never quite managed to break through.

Come to think of it, it was a lot like the wall that had grown up between her and her husband. Duncan had brought new love into her life when she'd expected to die a widow, but lately things had changed between them. And like Annie, he'd shut her out too.

All winter she'd looked for a sign. She'd even wished on the wishing tree, in secret, because her kids didn't hold with the old ways. She glanced between Annie and Seth. "Annie didn't say how long you're intending to stay in town, but we'd be pleased if you'd join us for Sunday night supper."

"Mom, I'm sure he has other plans." Annie's voice went up an octave.

"That's real kind of you, but I couldn't impose," Seth said.

"Nonsense. You're a stranger here, and we want to get to know you better. We'll see you around five." The only advantage to growing older was folks couldn't argue with you like they once did. "Not that there's enough of Irish Falls to get lost in, but Annie will give you directions."

Maureen tightened her grip on her cane. Before another season turned, she had to start driving the changes she wanted to see in her life, as well as with Annie. Maybe Seth was one of the signs she'd wished for.

~ ~ ~

An hour later, Annie pasted what she hoped was a bland smile on her face and took Seth past the studio, Jake's cubbyhole office, and the galley kitchen where Jake's "Boss" mug still sat on the shelf above the sink. "I'm sorry about my mom. She always speaks her mind and Sunday dinner with my family . . . you don't have to come. If you don't want to, I mean." Her stomach got tied in knots, along with her tongue.

"It's only dinner. Your mom was being hospitable." Seth backed out of the kitchen with Dolly at his heels and stopped in front of the glassed-in studio where the late afternoon talk show, "North Country Voices," was in full swing. "Unless you don't want me to come to dinner." Seth's voice was expressionless.

"Of course not. You're welcome to join us." Annie smiled harder. "Like you said, my mom's hospitable." But she had something on her mind, and it was something related to Seth that went beyond neighborliness to Jake's nephew. Dinner was neighborly and so was that apple cake, but there had been a gleam in her mom's eyes Annie didn't trust.

"I wasn't expecting the station to be so modern." Seth nodded at the "North Country Voices" host through the window, and the guy tipped his John Deere ball cap in response. "Like I said before, I don't know a lot about radio, but I'm impressed. All that digital equipment, streaming so people can listen on computer, and Jake even subscribed to a service to cover overnight and some weekend programing. It's also a much bigger operation than I thought." Seth's eyes narrowed. "And although I haven't looked at the books in detail, it seems pretty profitable too."

"Jake never talked much about his life before he came here. I never asked either, but he wanted to make a go of this station, so he hired good people to help and everybody who works here does a bit of everything. He was smart about business too. Although he had investors to start the station, he bought them out years ago." Annie rubbed her bottom lip and her body got heavy. Even though a part of her wanted Seth to go right back to LA, she couldn't stand by while Jake's life's work was destroyed. She had to try and save the station.

Seth raised one dark eyebrow. "Why can't those good people keep doing what they've been doing?"

Annie's jaw got tight. "Jake's cancer was diagnosed four months ago, and it was only two months ago he told us he was sick. Everybody wanted to keep things going for him. Now he's gone . . ."

Seth let out a heavy breath. "Change, I get it."

"He was the lynchpin that held this station together." Annie glanced through the studio window and then at the empty reception desk. "Without Jake in charge, things are falling apart. Even Sherri . . ." She gestured to the desk. "She called in sick today, and she once came to work with a temperature of one oh two. Her sister was in the bakery earlier and she said Sherri's scared of losing her job."

"But why?" Seth frowned. "Anybody who bought the station would still need a receptionist and cleaner. I made sure to tell Sherri that when I met her yesterday."

"A cleaner yes, but maybe not a receptionist like her. If a big company took over, they might want somebody different. Jake gave Sherri a job after her husband was killed in a snowmobile accident. She'd been home raising her kids for years and she learned fast, now she even helps out with sales and she's great, but . . ." Annie's throat worked. "If she loses this job, all she might be able to find is cleaning work. She has a family to support."

"I see." Seth half raised a hand then dropped it. "And the morning show your mom mentioned?"

"Steve, the guy we hired, isn't a good presenter, or a good people manager, either." Annie swallowed the lump in her throat. "I feel responsible because I made the final decision to give him a try, but when I talked to him about his performance on Monday . . ." She blinked. "He said 'didn't think anybody could make a success of this station.' Jake had his own way of doing things. It worked for him, but without him, the staff are lost. I haven't been able to find anybody around here with the skills or personality Jake had." She moved into the reception area and pointed to the row of awards that hung on the wall behind the desk. "Jake earned those, but they're the past. Nobody else here has the vision he did, or the business savvy."

Or the charisma, either. Annie took a step away from Seth, as if it would protect her from the same charisma that emanated from him. Age had mellowed Jake's charm, but on Seth that raw masculinity was still potent—and dangerous.

"Even if I took on the station for six months, like Jake wanted, wouldn't it have to be sold in the end anyway?" Seth stared at his palms as if he didn't see them.

"Maybe, but if someone like you gave it a shot . . .the staff and I could help you learn the ropes." From where she stood, and maybe where Seth did too, it was an impossible situation but somehow, she had to help him see what this station meant. Apart from Jake's legacy, the staff counted on their jobs here, not only for the money they earned but for a sense of community that couldn't be measured in dollars and cents. "This station is like a family. I know you have a whole life back in LA and Irish Falls is a small town. There's no comparison but if you could even consider . . . for a little while . . . take some time to get to know the place and the people before you sell."

Seth crossed his arms, and his eyebrows drew together. "You said Jake updated his will a week before he died. Do you know why?"

"No. That was his business." And like Jake had always respected her privacy, she'd respected his and hadn't asked questions when the lawyer turned up at his hospital bed.

Seth uncrossed his arms and leaned against a filing cabinet beside the desk. The casual pose was at odds with his grim expression and dark intensity of his eyes.

Dolly lay down by the desk and looked from Seth to Annie.

"I only found out the details of how Jake had changed his will after he passed. That's when I found out about you." Annie fumbled for the tiny key she'd worn on a chain around her neck since Jake's funeral. "He gave me an envelope the night he passed." She unclasped the chain, and the key slid off and into her palm. "He told me not to open it until after, but when I did, there was a note for me, along with this key." Tears burned the backs of her eyes, and she curled her hand around the small piece of metal.

"After?"

"He knew he was dying. He knew it would be soon. I promised him I'd do as he asked and then we—my mom, my sisters, and I—although we wanted to stay with him, he made us go and get something to eat. The nurse called my cell half an hour later. He'd slipped away."

Seth leaned forward and squeezed her hand. "You told me he was a private guy. Maybe he wanted to leave on his own terms and spare you."

"Maybe."

His warm hand lingered on top of hers. The skin on his fingertips was callused, like a guy who played a lot of guitar.

Annie stiffened, jerked her hand away, and took a deep, steadying breath. She wasn't eighteen anymore, and she was immune to masculine charisma, no matter how potent. "This key is for the chest of drawers in the living room of Jake's apartment. Except for a safety deposit box at the bank, he kept any private stuff he had in those drawers. In the note he left me, he said you were his nephew and asked me to give you the key after I showed you around the station."

As he took the key from her, Seth's expression gave nothing away.

"Apart from his guitar, he always said he didn't have anything valuable to steal, but maybe there are family papers or stuff about his life." Hyperaware of Seth beside her, and the heat radiating off him, she took a step back.

"Maybe." Seth's mouth was pinched.

"As my mom said, Jake was like family to us." Annie blinked away the tears that threatened to spill out and roll down her cheeks. "We all cared about him. Any one of us would have done anything he asked to help him pass easier."

Seth's cell rang with the melody for Dolly Parton's "Nine to Five," and Annie started. "Sorry, I have to take this." His voice roughened.

"Sure." She gestured to Jake's office next to the reception area. As the door closed behind Seth, she sat in Sherri's chair and turned to a stack of unopened mail. She'd given him the key as Jake had asked. And like why Jake had suddenly updated his will, whatever was in that chest of drawers was none of her business.

"I guess Seth's a Dolly Parton fan, too." She reached down and patted the top of Dolly's head.

"You can't be serious. None of this was my fault so why—" On the other side of the closed door, Seth's voice rang out.

Then there was silence again, and Annie dipped her head and tried to concentrate on separating junk mail from invoices and payments.

Five minutes later, the door swung open and caught the wall behind it with a bang. Annie jumped and looked up as Seth jammed his phone into the front pocket of his jeans. Anything she might have said died on her lips at the expression on his face. It was Jake at his most pissed off.

"Sorry, that call . . . I had to take care of some . . . stuff." Seth came to a stop in front of the desk and grabbed the key he'd dropped when his phone rang.

"Of course." She kept her tone neutral and tossed the junk mail into the recycling box.

"About the station," he said, then paused for a heartbeat and gave her a strained look. "I still haven't made any decisions about what I want to do long-term, but if you can handle an amateur, I'll run it for a while. It sounds like it's important to you."

"It's important to all of us." Annie's chest hurt.

"I'll start tomorrow." Seth's expression was shuttered.

"Really?" Annie's mouth fell open.

"Yes." His voice was curt, and his brows drew together, but instead of looking pissed off, his expression was bleak. "If Steve has a notice period, he can show me how to work the equipment. Broadcasting technology has gotten a lot more computerized since I worked in a radio booth.

"Steve's a freelancer. I hired him for two months at first and then from week to week until I found out what you planned. If I call him now, he can show you the ropes tomorrow before he leaves."

"Great." Seth's tone was decisive. "Since Sherri's off sick, can you help me and get the staff together for a start-of-day meeting here? I wouldn't ask except I'm guessing you know most of them." A stiff smile creased one corner of his mouth.

"I know all of them." Annie linked her hands together to stop them from shaking. "And I'm happy to help."

"Thanks." His voice rasped. "How hard can it be to do better than a guy with a voice like a cat with its tail caught in a door?" Something that might have been amusement flickered in Seth's eyes before it was snuffed out.

"Not hard at all." Annie cringed.

Seth had remembered what her mom had said.

"Steve was the only one I could find on short notice."

"Then maybe you did me a favor. Things can only get better, right?" Seth's smile was tight. He fingered Jake's key, and Dolly got up and nuzzled his hand.

Despite her relief, there was a sinking feeling in the pit of Annie's stomach. Why would a guy like Seth want to bury himself in a place like Irish Falls, even for a little while?

That phone call had changed something, and, while it might be good for the station, she wasn't so sure it would be good for her.

She stared at the mail without seeing it. She'd have to work with Seth on the estate paperwork. And while he got up to speed with the running of the station. But after that, she wouldn't have to be around him very much. Besides, she was taking charge and figuring out what she wanted in this new stage of her life. She'd dealt with all her old fears long ago, learned from her mistakes, and moved on. It didn't matter that Seth was in the music business. Except as a hobby, that part of her life was over.

"Annie?" Seth's voice curbed her thoughts. "Jake was lucky to have you and your family. Nowadays . . . that kind of loyalty, it's not . . . it's rare."

Her throat clogged. "We were also lucky to have him. He was a good friend to us." And Jake had been a friend to her especially. After she'd lost Nana Gerry—the woman who'd healed her heart—Jake and the bond she'd shared with him through music had helped heal her soul.

Seth turned and looked out the window. "What I don't get, though, is why Jake ended up here. From what I remember, he liked the bright lights, cities, clubs, and checking out a new group every night when he wasn't on stage with one of his bands."

"I guess he found something here he needed." Like her. When her dream had turned into a nightmare, she'd come back to the place where she had roots and felt safe. Annie stood and walked around the desk to join Seth at the window. Outside, lacy snowflakes drifted from a soft gray sky.

Seth pointed toward the waterfall. "Why are things tied to that tree over there?"

"It's the Irish Falls wishing tree." And she'd been telling newcomers about it her whole life. "It's supposed to be magical. If you write your wish on a piece of paper and tie it to one of the tree's branches, your wish will come true."

"You're kidding me, right?" He tilted his head and pursed his lips.

"Nope." If anything, she'd kidded herself back when she was one of the ones who'd wished on that stupid tree. As if a tree had the power to make wishes come true, even wishes with plans and talent behind them. "The wishing tree helps put Irish Falls on the tourist map. Every July, the town holds a wishing tree festival that draws visitors from all across the northeast and Canada too. The radio station and bakery are both big festival supporters."

Seth made a sound somewhere between a snort and a laugh. "But what happens when it's raining and snowing, like now? All those wishes must be a big, soggy mess."

Annie stiffened. Although she didn't believe in the tree, an outsider had no right to mock it or what it meant to people. "Volunteers harvest the wishes every week or so. When the weather is bad, they do it more often. See that guy?" She pointed to an older man in a black rain jacket who stood at the far side of the tree with a basket under one arm. "He's taking the wishes off the tree. There aren't a lot there now, but in summer, it gets so busy the wishes sometimes have to be collected two or three times a week so the branches don't get too heavy and break. If the wishes are wet, they're dried in the conservation room at the county museum before they're archived."

"Is it a religious thing?" Seth's expression softened and became curious, not disrespectful.

"Spiritual, but not associated with any organized religion." Annie rubbed a hand across her temple, where the start of a headache throbbed. "Each wish is a story, part of a beginning, a middle, or an end. People wish for their hopes and dreams. Some wishes are happy and others are sad." And once upon a time, she'd made both those kinds.

"You said the wishes are archived?" His smile was boyish and crinkled his eyes.

"Yes, now they're stored in an online database, but the museum has a collection of written wishes going back to the eighteen eighties. They did an exhibition about it a few years ago." And although the world had changed, people's wishes had remained remarkably similar over the years—desires for world peace, to reconcile with family or friends, to cure an illness, or to find a lasting love. Annie's chest constricted.

"Do you believe the tree is magical?" Seth asked, his tone careful.

Annie shook her head. "No, but don't try to convince my mom that tree isn't special. She won't hear anything against it. I go along with her because it's good for business. Quinn's sells wishing tree boxed picnic lunches from the Memorial Day weekend through to Labor Day. They're very popular."

"I don't believe in wishes." Seth's voice was low and threaded with pain.

"Me neither, but a lot of folks are real attached to that tree." She cleared her throat, and the pain in her chest got worse. "Maybe you don't know much about small-town life, but around here it's supposed to bring bad luck if you say anything against our wishing tree."

The bitterness in his laugh made her flinch. "Did Jake believe in it?"

"He never came right out and said so, but I know he wished on it." Although he hadn't told Annie what most of those wishes were for. "Jake said the tree brought him Dolly."

The dog gave the guttural whine she made whenever she heard Jake's name, and a familiar lump rose in Annie's throat.

"I don't know anything about dogs, but Dolly seems like a good one." Seth glanced at the mutt, who gave him an expectant look. "Your mom doesn't want to adopt her?"

Annie shook her head. "Now she's mostly retired, she and my stepdad, Duncan, want to spend a few months in Florida each winter. They bought a motorhome last year so they can travel around in the summer, too. Mom says it's time for her to spread her wings. She doesn't want to be tied down by a pet, work, or anything else."

Her heart squeezed. Along with finding some new dreams, getting Hannah launched successfully into adulthood was her focus. There would be time enough to spread her wings once Hannah left home. Annie pressed a hand to her throat. She'd made her choices and, until a few days ago, she'd never questioned them but now she was questioning almost everything about her life and who and what she thought she was.

Seth stepped away from her and turned his back on the window, the falls, and the wishing tree. A shaft of spring sunshine poked through the clouds and burnished his brown hair with gold. "I don't want to be tied down, either."

Annie swallowed as his words echoed and came to rest beneath her breastbone near her heart. Long ago, she'd heard those same words from another guy with an easy smile and slow Southern drawl. A guy who wouldn't ever have stuck around a small town like Irish Falls, no matter how picturesque and friendly. And a guy who'd never have blended into the fabric of the town, either, with its slower pace, interconnected relationships, and a wishing tree as its claim to fame.

Suddenly, her body was too hot and her breathing sped up. She closed her eyes and then opened them again as the room seemed to sway around her.

"Annie? What's wrong? You look like you've seen a ghost." Seth's voice reverberated near her ear, and his warm breath brushed her cheek. "Here, let me." He took one of her arms to steady her, and she fought the urge to lean into him and stay there.

She blinked, and his strong jaw and chiseled cheekbones swam into focus again. "Nothing. I'm fine." She gave him her best fake smile. "With the stress of Jake's illness and death, it's been a tough time. I don't know what came over me."

But she did and her mind was playing tricks on her. Seth might remind her of her past, but he wasn't that past. And apart from the accent, his voice was nothing like Todd's. Except in the most superficial way, he didn't look like him, either.

She had nothing to worry about. And if she said it often enough, she'd make herself believe it.

Chapter 4

That evening, Seth slumped in a chair at a table in a corner of the Black Duck, the roadhouse on the outskirts of town. He stared into his glass of diet soda, but there were no answers there, either.

Usually a savvy guy, he'd been so focused on what had gone wrong with his son he'd missed the signs with work. Or maybe he'd ignored them because he'd trusted the guy. On the phone earlier, his attorney's message had been unmistakable. Seth's business partner had cheated him, lied, and stolen from him. And, along with the big contract they'd been about to sign, the collaboration they'd built together was officially in ruins.

A group of older men in checked shirts and jeans played darts in one corner of the low-ceilinged room. Above the bar, the TV showed an NHL hockey game with the sound turned off. On the small stage along the back wall, a young guy strummed a guitar and a platinum blonde in knee-high boots, tight jeans, and an even tighter top sang an old Vince Gill hit. Seth winced as her voice warbled up and down the scale and the guy plucked chords seemingly at random.

"Seth?"

He raised his head. "Hey."

Annie stood beside his chair. His gaze slid to the teenage girl at her side. An inch or so taller than Annie, she had curly red-gold hair and dark eyes that stared back at him with undisguised curiosity.

"This is my daughter, Hannah." Annie's voice held a warmth he hadn't heard before.

"Pleased to meet you." He held out a hand, and the teen took it and grinned.

"Go tell Grandpa Duncan to get a move on," Annie said to her.

"Sure." She gave another quick glance at Seth before moving toward the darts players, where she spoke to a man with thick white hair.

"Duncan, my stepdad, plays darts here every Thursday night. Until he has cataract surgery, he's not supposed to drive after dark." Annie fidgeted with her purse strap. "Mom is babysitting my sister's kids, so I'm picking him up."

"Hannah looks like you." He got to his feet to stand beside her. He'd chosen a table with only one chair because he hadn't wanted company. He still didn't. And Annie had a daughter, so she likely had a husband. For both those reasons, he needed to keep this conversation as short as politeness allowed then make his excuses and leave.

Annie gave him a brief smile. "She's taller, but Hannah also looks like my mom did at the same age."

And like her daughters and granddaughter, Maureen was a fine-looking woman. "I bumped into your mom at the grocery store earlier. She told me almost your whole family comes to Sunday dinner. How many people should I be expecting?"

"Hannah and I, my mom and stepdad, Tara, my other sister, Rowan, and her two kids, and my brother, his wife, and two of their boys. Twelve, if everyone can make it." She paused. "I'm a single parent."

"Me too." Seth's heartbeat sped up. She didn't have a husband. Despite his better judgment, maybe he didn't want to head out right away. "My son's finishing his freshman year of college. He's studying animation in New York City." And apart from a few stilted text messages, Seth hadn't heard from Dylan in four long weeks. "My wife and I split up when Dylan was a baby, so since then it's only been the two of us."

"It's hard raising a child on your own." Annie's eyes softened in compassion, as well as understanding.

"I . . . thanks." He swallowed the unexpected lump of emotion and took an involuntary step back. He never talked about Amanda, but something about Annie soothed him. At the same time, though, being around her made his stomach flutter in an unfamiliar way. He hadn't been celibate since Amanda walked out, but until now, he'd never met a woman he wanted to get close to in a way that went way beyond anything physical. "I'm not used to big families."

"I've never known anything *but* big families. My mom's one of eight kids, and my dad was one of six. When the whole clan gets together, it's almost as big as the church picnic." She laughed then worried her bottom lip. "Hannah's an only child. As far as producing kids goes, I fell way short of the family standard."

Seth winced at the sadness in her voice. Somebody, sometime, had hurt her bad. Both that tone and the pain lodged deep in her gentle blue eyes came from more than grief over Jake's death. "There's nothing wrong with only children. I'm one and so is Dylan."

A sweet smile tugged one corner of her mouth. "If your son comes to visit while you're here, Mom will want to invite him over for a meal, too. She loves feeding people."

"Dylan's busy at school." Seth dug in the pocket of his jeans and curled his fingers around his truck keys until the metal dug into his palm.

"It's good he's focused on college. Hannah needs to think more about college and her future." Her expression tightened as she glanced at her daughter, who stood by the side of the stage with a rapt expression on her face. "I have to get Duncan home, and if I don't drag Hannah out of here, she'll want to listen to that music for the rest of the night, and she has school tomorrow. I'll leave Mom's address under the door of Jake's apartment. She and Duncan live three streets over from the bakery beyond the Catholic church. Their place is easy to find."

"The Catholic church?" From what he'd seen so far, Irish Falls had an abundance of churches, most of them historic.

"The one with the statues of saints out front." She gave him a small smile.

"Thanks." His hands got damp. He couldn't have feelings for Annie. He'd only met her yesterday. Besides, he wasn't at the right place in his life to have feelings for any woman, especially not one who lived here. Irish Falls and everything about it was temporary. "I didn't know about Jake's funeral, but where was he laid to rest? I'd like to pay my respects."

"Of course." Annie's face went pink. "I'll take you. What about tomorrow afternoon? I get off work at two. The cemetery's a few miles out of town."

"I don't want to bother you. I'm sure I can find it on my own if you point me in the right direction. My GPS works fine." Besides, if he limited the time he spent with her, he'd limit that prickle of attraction toward her too.

"Not in this area it won't." Amusement tinged her voice. "You might find yourself in the middle of a creek or halfway up a mountain." The pink on her face deepened, and she cleared her throat. "It's no bother. Now the snow's gone, I want to go out there to tidy up and . . . you know . . . visit. My dad and my grandmother are buried there, too. I haven't done anything about a headstone for Jake. I thought you'd want to organize that."

"Of course." He stared at his feet. The rituals of death were familiar and yet foreign, especially for a man he barely remembered.

"I'll see you tomorrow." The sympathy in Annie's tone made him feel like he'd known her for years. "And good luck with the show. We'll all be listening." She touched his arm, then, with a little wave, she was gone. A fresh floral scent lingered in her wake and masked the stale roadhouse smell.

The blonde singer shook her curvy hips and squeaked out a high note. The guitarist glanced at Seth, raised his sandy eyebrows, and shrugged.

Under the cover of the music, Seth choked out a laugh. He'd messed things up with his son, and even though it hadn't been his fault, his career was messed up, too, and his creative muse was missing in action. But although he might be down, he sure wasn't out.

He shrugged into his jacket and straightened his shoulders. Nobody, not even Dylan, would ever have to know the real reason he'd decided to stick around Irish Falls. Jake's station was in surprisingly good shape and, although he didn't have anything to prove, maybe running it for a while was exactly what he needed. If anybody back in LA ever asked, it was a business opportunity. And when he did return to the City of Angels, he'd have cleared his name, and found respect with himself again, and, most importantly, from his son.

~ ~ ~

"Seth sure has a sexy voice." Tara inclined her head toward the radio on a shelf in the bakery kitchen and sliced a log of chilled cookie dough in a smooth rhythm. "It's the kind of voice you could get used to waking up to." She winked at Annie. "On a pillow next to you."

"Stop it." Annie's stomach lurched and she glanced at Holly, her brother Brendan's wife, making scones on the other side of the big table.

She only had to pretend it was a morning like any other and Seth doing the show was the same as when Steve did it, or even Jake. It wasn't anything to get worked up about. When Monday rolled around, she'd be more used to Seth's voice, warm like hot fudge sauce on cold vanilla ice cream, and how it made her feel.

"No need to hush her for my sake, honey," Holly said. "Tara's right. Seth Taggart is exactly what that morning show needs. He's got a face and body to match his voice, too. The word at yoga last night was he sent Lisa Drysdale into a hot flash when she bumped into him in the produce aisle at Nolan's grocery. I can sure see why." Holly grinned and fanned herself with a pot holder.

"Says the woman who's been married for almost twenty-five years to my big brother, no less." Annie went to the sink and ran cold water over her floury hands. "Brendan better not hear you talking that way. He's out front checking a delivery."

Holly's throaty laugh rippled out. "Brendan has nothing to worry about. Like a fine wine, he's only gotten better with age." She turned the dough onto a floured surface in a deft motion. "Although, these days he's getting to be more of a silver fox, he's still my red-hot redhead and he knows it."

"We don't know how long Seth will stay here. We can't get used to him doing the show," Annie said. She took a shaky breath. It would be all too easy to get used to him, and, after waking up to Seth, nobody in Irish Falls would want to go back to waking up to Steve. Her fingers tingled as she dried them with a kitchen towel. Even when he talked about something as ordinary as the weather, Seth's voice reached deep inside and made her feel like his words were for her alone.

"We have to convince him to stay." Tara slid a sheet of cookies into one of the commercial ovens and set the timer.

Annie got out the ingredients for the date and walnut loaf, Quinn's Friday special. Apart from the specials of the day, the morning routine, comforting and predictable, never varied. "Why would a guy like Seth stay in a place like Irish

Falls? He's a high flier. Look at his clothes and that new truck parked out back."

But it was more than what was on the outside. Even from the little Annie knew about him, Seth's attitude was big city, not small town. Whether walking down Malone Street, or sitting in the Black Duck, it was obvious he didn't belong around these parts. And that was before he opened his mouth and that liquid Southern drawl spilled out to turn her insides to putty.

"Seth's not as successful as you might think." Even though the three of them were alone in the kitchen, Holly lowered her voice. "When I got home after yoga, I looked on the Internet. I couldn't find out exactly what happened, but it sounds like something went wrong with a guy he worked with. Anyway, even though it wasn't Seth's fault, he still lost a big contract and had to close down his business."

"How awful." Tara glanced at Annie.

"It is." Holly frowned. "I don't know how some people sleep at night. Up until a month ago, Seth had no idea what was going on. I guess his business partner had been cheating him for ages."

"A month ago?" Around the time Jake had updated his will. Annie's heart thumped and adrenaline jolted through her.

"That's what the article said." Holly's brown eyes softened. "If it's true, Seth needs a break."

Annie turned to look out the window above the counter. The branches of the wishing tree swayed in the spring breeze, and sunlight danced on its new green buds. Jake had never mentioned Seth to her or any of them, but he must have kept tabs on him.

"We better not say anything. Seth wouldn't want folks talking about him." Tara's voice yanked Annie back to the present.

"Of course not." Maybe the will update was a coincidence. Or maybe not. "But Holly likely won't be the only one in town to Google him." If Hannah's destructive kitten hadn't taken Annie offline, she'd have done so late last night when she'd lain awake thinking about that sadness in his eyes she'd glimpsed at the Black Duck. Not to mention that unexpected tingle in her fingertips when she'd touched his arm to wish him luck for the show.

"Seth's taking requests." Holly's voice rose above the radio, and she tucked several strands of brown hair back under her hairnet. "Shush."

"Holly, this song comes to you from Brendan because you'll always be the love of his life." Seth's melodic voice rolled into the sudden silence of the kitchen, and Annie caught her breath. "It's an oldie but still a goodie. John Michael Montgomery, 'I Love the Way You Love Me.'"

"Ooh, ooh, he . . . Brendan . . ." Holly squealed. "That's our song. We danced our first dance to it at our wedding."

"Who knew my brother could be so romantic?" Tara grabbed a spoon and swayed in time to the music.

Annie chopped walnuts, and her hand tightened around the handle of the knife. It *was* romantic, but what would it be like to have somebody love you enough to announce it to the whole town? To have that somebody still love you as much as he had when you were eighteen, even after four kids, a mortgage, and all life's ups and downs.

She glanced at Holly, who stared at the radio with a besotted expression. Then at Tara, who had her eyes closed as she swayed to the music. Both of them believed in happy ever after—Holly because she still had it, and Tara because she'd had it once and would always carry the memories in her heart. Annie dumped the walnuts into a bowl and tore open a package of dates. Seth had sounded so sincere when he'd talked about love. What had happened between him and his ex-wife? And why had he raised his son alone?

The song ended, and a beep signaled the news. It was already eight and they were behind schedule. "Are you two going to do some work? The cake for that fortieth anniversary party won't ice itself." Annie's voice came out sharper than she intended so she forced a smile.

Tara smiled back and tossed the spoon into the sink. "It's sweet. I wish . . ." Her voice hitched, and guilt smote Annie. "Holly's lucky."

"Yeah, she is." And all that sweetness and luck had Annie tied up in knots. Holly wasn't only her sister-in-law, she was another sister. And Brendan helped her with something around Nana Gerry's old house at least once a week. Her ringside seat to their happy marriage had never bothered her before.

"I've got fresh cinnamon buns to take up to the station. Annie?" Holly slid a basket along the counter toward her. "Friday's your day."

"Can't you or Tara do it?" Seth's voice had already unsettled her enough for one morning. She didn't need to see the man, too.

Holly gave her a cheeky grin. "Nope. As soon as I finish these scones, I want to help Brendan out front. After that song, my hubby needs to know how much I love him. Maybe he can finish early. The guy starts work at four every morning and gets up at three. I think he needs some R&R, don't you?"

"Please. No more information. That's my brother you're talking about." Annie made a face. "Tara?"

"I can't leave these cookies." Tara sliced another log of dough and avoided Annie's gaze.

"But . . ." Annie stopped. She couldn't let her sister or Holly guess how—or why—Seth had her all worked up. "Fine. I'll do it." She untied her apron, took off her hairnet, and smoothed her hair.

"You look beautiful." Tara's voice was soft.

"I'm only going upstairs." Annie picked up the basket covered with a blue-checked napkin.

Tara reached over to give Annie a one-armed hug. "It's exactly the same as when Jake and Steve were up in that radio station, isn't it? Not." Her soft chuckle was way too smug. "Go on, Annie-Bella." Her steady gaze met Annie's across the pungent cinnamon buns. "All you have to do is walk up those stairs." Her sister's tone was loving.

Tara was right, except, a few minutes later, looking at Seth through the familiar studio window, Annie pressed a hand to her all-of-a-sudden fluttery stomach. He wore a black, long-sleeved Henley, and his jaw was dark with beard stubble. He sat behind one of the microphones, with headphones over his ears, and his expression focused.

"This next song is for Annie Quinn and her family." His voice came through the overhead speakers. "I want to thank them for what they did for my uncle, Jake Kerrigan. He was a good man, and I know he was a friend to many of you." Seth's voice cracked, and he hesitated for a fraction of a second. "It's a classic Alabama tune I found on one of Jake's playlists and fits what I'm feeling."

The haunting notes of "Angels Among Us," a song Jake had played on his Gibson many times, melded with the lyrics Annie knew by heart.

She couldn't tear her gaze away from Seth. As if he sensed her gaze, he looked up and half rose from his seat to give her a smile as sweet as it was tender.

"Thanks," she mouthed through the glass.

"No problem," he mouthed back.

She took a step toward the closed studio door. Dolly was curled up on the carpet in front of it, the picture of a peaceful and happy dog. She couldn't go in there. Seth was live on the air. She put the basket of cinnamon buns on top of a filing cabinet and gestured toward it before backing away.

Seth still looked at her through the window as the music rose and fell, like an invisible thread linking the two of them. She pressed her hands to her face. No matter how much she might want to, she couldn't pretend to herself this morning was like any other. As long as Seth did the show, weekday mornings would never be the same.

Annie went out the door and down the wooden stairs to the bakery. It was no good to want something she couldn't let herself have. Not even if it was big and sexy, and had a voice hot enough to melt even her ice-like resolve. She'd buried any regrets deep, and she had no intention of digging them up again now.

Chapter 5

Seth nudged the pile of fresh black dirt with the toe of his boot. A small wooden cross with Jake's name on it was stuck into the end of the plot farthest away from where Seth stood.

The cemetery was three miles outside Irish Falls, down a series of what were, to him, identical tree-lined gravel roads. Without Annie's help, he doubted he'd have found it. She stood with her back to him, in front of a headstone several rows over. Wrapped up in the blue duffle coat she'd worn the night before, her bright hair glinted in the wintry afternoon sun.

"It's me, Seth." He looked at the pile of dirt again. He was here to pay his respects, not obsess about the meaning of life. The wind whistled through the bare tree branches, and he shivered as he stuck his hands into his jacket pockets. "I thought of you a lot over the years." His throat tightened. "I wondered why I never saw you again."

The last time had been at his mom's funeral. Jake had sat at the back of the church, and in his black jeans and black dress shirt with the silver studs down the front, he'd stood out amongst the other mourners in their conservative suits and dresses.

Afterward, he'd drawn Seth close for a bear hug and whispered, "Take care of yourself, little buddy. And promise me you'll keep on singing. Music can be a powerful comfort. It'll get you through hard times when nothing much else will."

Then his grandmother had pulled Seth away from Jake. Her blue eyes were icy and, although Seth hadn't heard exactly what she said, her tone was unmistakable. And Jake hadn't ever dropped by his grandparents' house again. Sometimes, in the years that followed, Seth wondered if he'd imagined him. His grandparents had never spoken of Jake, at least not in his hearing, and it was like he'd never existed.

Seth crouched beside the dirt. "You were right, Uncle Jake," he murmured. "Music *has* been a comfort. But you see . . ." He took a shaky breath of cool air. "I made some mistakes. I want to fix them, but I don't know how."

In the tree beside Jake's grave, a crow cawed, a hoarse grating on Seth's ears.

"I did your show this morning. I wanted to do you proud." He picked up two small white stones and stacked one on top of the other. "Thanks for leaving me your Gibson. I'll take good care of it. I learned to play guitar when I was fourteen."

And his grandmother had hated it. Seth's mouth tipped into a half-smile. Despite the piano lessons she'd insisted on, guitar was the instrument he loved. "When I was seventeen, I snuck into a club and heard you play. You were good." More than good, but Seth had only recognized that much later. "I wanted to talk to you after the set, but I didn't know what I'd say, or if you'd even remember me."

Seth had been with friends, and he also hadn't wanted to look stupid in front of the other guys. Then he'd got caught up in life and never thought to try to contact Jake again. Now it was too late.

"If I'd known you were sick, I'd have come to see you." He found a third stone, smaller still, and balanced it on top of the other two. "From what Annie said, I know you didn't want that, but I'd have liked to have been there for you. Like you were there for Mom and me when she got sick and you lived with us for a few months." Before then, Jake had dropped in and out of their lives, a mostly phantom presence, apart from a jean jacket hanging on a hook in his mom's closet and a framed picture she kept on her dresser.

"Remember when you came to visit Mom and me for Christmas the year it snowed? We made the biggest snowman I'd ever seen. It was bigger than me." His mom and Jake had laughed, and Seth had laughed, too. It was one of the rare times in his childhood when he'd been happy and untroubled and felt completely loved—as light in himself as the snowflakes that dusted his mom's dark hair and melted in Jake's beard.

"I missed you after you left." His grandparents had been elderly and remote, and there were no cousins or aunts and uncles to visit at Thanksgiving and Christmas.

"I can't be around for you, little buddy. I hope you'll understand why when you're older, but if you ever need my help, I'll be there." Those last words Jake had whispered in his ear had blurred with time and, until now, Seth had almost forgotten them. He stared at the heaped dirt. He should have brought flowers. Or from what he remembered about Jake, maybe a bottle of Jack Daniel's finest Tennessee whiskey, except that would shock the good people of Irish Falls.

"How are you two getting on?" Annie's voice came from behind him.

Seth swung around and stumbled to his feet. "Two?"

"You and Jake." She inclined her head to the grave. "I'm sure he can hear you. I chat with my dad and Nana Gerry all the time."

"They can't answer back." Seth had never thought much about the afterlife. Only that people disappeared. If not through death, like his mom and grandparents, then they left for some other reason, like his ex-wife and now his son. His stomach knotted.

"That doesn't mean they aren't still in my heart. Jake is too, along with Tara's husband. He's with his family over by that big butternut tree." Her voice quivered.

Seth looked where she indicated. "I'm sorry." His throat got tight. "That's rough."

Annie's chin jerked. "Adam was in the marines. We all went to high school together. He was killed on active duty in the Middle East eighteen months ago. Tara's had a hard time. She came back here after . . ." She paused and cleared her throat. "She doesn't like to talk about him. I wouldn't have said anything, but since you're coming to dinner, I thought you should know." She stared at the mass of dirt.

"Thanks for telling me." Seth swallowed and moved to stand beside her. "I get why you come here. You have a lot of loved ones in this place."

She hunched her shoulders. "Too many, but it's peaceful. It's also a good place to think. I've solved lots of problems sitting on that bench." She inclined her head toward a wooden bench beneath another tree. "Jake wasn't a church-going man, but he said he felt closer to God here than anywhere else." She bent to pick up several twigs and gave Seth a tentative smile. "Since he didn't have any family we knew about, we put him in our family plot."

"He'd have liked that." Seth's eyes burned, and a heavy lump of loss lodged beneath his breastbone. If only his mom could have been laid to rest in a tranquil place like this, instead of beneath a marble family monument in a cemetery where the graves were laid out in precise manicured rows and rigid class distinctions were maintained in death as they had been in life.

"This cemetery is pretty much an extension of Irish Falls. If you can describe a burying ground as friendly, this one is." Her smile slipped and, as she fashioned the twigs together with a few bits of dead grass, her brow furrowed in concentration.

"What are you doing?" He tilted his head to take a closer look.

"Making a guitar." She balanced the twigs against the stones he'd piled up. "The snow we got yesterday melted, but it looks like you've made Jake a snowman. It's not complete without a guitar." She added a fragment of a brown leaf for the strap.

"How did you guess?" He forced a laugh, because the moment—and her unexpected understanding—was too intimate.

"I saw how you looked at Jake's Gibson." Her mouth curved into a sweet smile. "You should bring it on your next visit here and sing to him. You have a great voice for radio, and my brother . . . he said . . ." She stopped, and her cheeks went pink.

"Brendan caught me singing along to some tunes before the show today." He grinned at her, the tension broken. "I thought I was alone in the studio at five this morning, but when he brought me coffee and a donut, we got talking."

"He said you were good enough for a recording contract." Annie grinned back. "I should warn you, he mentioned it when there were half a dozen people in the bakery, including the priest from St. Patrick's and a couple of Baptists. Don't be surprised if all the clergy in town ask you to join their choirs."

Seth raised an eyebrow. "You're joking, aren't you?"

"Nope." Laughter edged Annie's voice. "Men who can sing are thin on the ground here."

"I haven't sung in a church choir since I was twelve." Seth gave her a wry smile. "Back then, ditching choir was one of the few ways I had to defy my grandmother."

"She mustn't have been anything like Nana Gerry." Annie gave the stone snowman a gentle pat and got to her feet. "I wanted to sing in the choir because she did. I was happy to be around her."

"You were lucky." Seth straightened too. Would things have turned out differently for him if he'd had a Nana Gerry in his life? Or a big loving family like the Quinns? "My mom died when I was seven. My dad was never in the picture, so Mom's parents took me in. Although they gave me everything I needed, they weren't what you'd call warm." His body went cold, together with a sick feeling in the pit of his stomach. Private school and Key West vacations hadn't compensated for the loss of what was most important of all—unconditional love.

The tenderness in Annie's eyes almost undid him, then her warm hand reached out to clasp his. "It sounds like you've had a bunch of losses in your life, too."

"Yeah." Seth shook the dirt off his boots as the imprint of her hand seared his soul. Annie meant well, but he couldn't let her or anyone else into the guarded fortress of his heart. "It looks like it's going to rain again." He gestured to the gun-metal gray sky.

"Like you said in the weather report." Annie dropped his hand and turned away. "April showers and all." Her tone was distant. "A guy in the next town does monument work. I can give you his number if you want to talk to him about a stone for Jake."

"That would be good." Seth glanced at the dirt mound again.

He'd been rude to this woman who'd been nothing but kind to him, and Jake wouldn't have liked that. His mom would have called him on it, too. "I never talk about when I was a kid, but I shouldn't have taken it out on you."

"It's okay." Annie's voice softened. "Seeing Jake's grave must be hard. We all have stuff we never talk about—stuff we don't want to think about, either."

His ex-wife had called it baggage, and he pictured it as a big old trunk he dragged around behind him but never opened. And in the past six weeks, that trunk had gotten even heavier. "Yeah, well." He cleared his throat. "We should head back to town."

"Of course." Annie moved beside him, along the path to where they'd left the truck. "Half the town called the bakery earlier. After hearing your show this morning, they want you to stay."

Seth's insides quivered. No matter how hard he tried, he couldn't write songs like he used to, and he didn't have anything else to do, but Annie didn't know that. He sucked in a harsh breath. "I've decided I don't want to sell the station, at least not right now." He pulled open the truck's passenger door for her, and Dolly bounced over to them, her tail in propeller mode.

"You're staying for six months?" Her clear blue gaze met his, and the expression in her eyes was like a punch to his gut. Somehow, she'd found out what had happened in LA.

"Yeah." And right now, six months seemed like an eternity. "I don't want Jake's business to fail." Seth worked moisture into his dry mouth.

She exhaled. "That's good news. I guess." She didn't look at him as she slid into the truck.

He closed the door before walking around to the driver's side to get in. "I . . ." He shifted behind the wheel. "Thanks."

"For what?" She clicked her seatbelt into place then rubbed at her hands.

"For not . . ." He stared at the raindrops that dotted the windshield and sweat trickled between his shoulder blades.

"Even though Irish Falls is a small town and people talk, your business is your business." Her voice was gentle. "You're a part of this community now, and we look out for our own. Jake was well-liked so, because of that, a lot of people here have your back. You're not only part of my family, you're part of the town family, too."

Family. Although the word brought a familiar pain, mixed with it was a new warmth. "I don't know what to say." His tense muscles relaxed, and his body seemed lighter than it had for weeks.

Annie gave him a cheeky grin, and there was a sudden flutter in Seth's chest. "You don't have to say anything, but not knowing what to say must be real hard for someone who'll be talking on the radio from now on."

"You have a smart mouth, you know that?" A mouth he'd like to get better acquainted with. The hairs on the back of his neck raised as he fumbled with the key to start the truck.

"Takes one to know one. I listened to your show this morning, remember?" Annie teased him back. "Are you going to drive us back to town? If you haven't noticed, city guy, there's a lot of rain in those clouds, and the road by this cemetery borders a creek prone to spring flooding." She looped an arm around Dolly, and her gorgeous hair fluffed out around her face.

"City guy?" His fingers tingled as he put the truck in gear, flipped on the wipers, and backed out the grassy path to the main road—if a gravel track bordered by a split-rail fence and woods could be called such.

"You're a city guy, in a city truck, but you're Jake's nephew, so that gives you brownie points." Her musical laugh pealed out and made him laugh, too. "When you come for dinner on Sunday, bring Jake's Gibson."

"Why?" Seth kept his eyes on the road, where water had already begun to puddle.

"I already guessed you play." She flicked on the radio, and Dean Brody's voice singing "Time" swirled around them. "And my mom likes music."

Rain pattered against the windows, and the small cab cocooned them from the rest of the world. He maneuvered around a pothole. "I'm not a professional, but playing helps me unwind. I have a guitar of my own back at the apartment."

"I like music too." She paused, and her breath hitched. "Music is something Jake and I had in common. I don't share music with my sisters." Her voice was tentative. Like she'd told him something important she maybe didn't share easily.

"Having something for yourself is important." Music had saved his soul a lot of times and maybe it was still saving it. "I'd be honored to play Jake's guitar for you and your family."

Dolly thumped her tail against Seth's thigh, and he took one hand away from the wheel to scratch her velvety ears.

When he'd come to Irish Falls, he'd expected to be gone in a few days. Instead, in those few days, the place, its people and, most of all, the woman beside him, had given him comfort and a sense of security he hadn't anticipated or thought he'd ever need.

He made his living writing hit songs, but somewhere along the way, he'd gotten caught up in the glitz and glamour and forgotten about the people with hopes and dreams and sorrows who listened to those songs—the kind who also listened to Jake's show.

The condo he'd moved into when Dylan left for college was a place to sleep, not a home. With a couple of phone calls—one to the property management company, the other to the woman who cleaned for him—he'd arranged for the place to be checked every forty-eight hours and the clothes and a few other things he needed boxed and shipped to him here.

He hadn't come to Jake's grave to figure out the meaning of life. But maybe this visit, along with doing the show this morning, had helped him figure out who he used to be. A guy who didn't want to disappoint himself or Jake, either. And a guy who wouldn't ever let his son slip away.

~ ~ ~

On Sunday evening, Annie took the rinsed plates from Seth and slid them into the dishwasher in her mom's kitchen. She hadn't wanted to like him. Everything about him—from his boots, to his truck, to his polished smile and easy patter—reminded her of the man she didn't want to be reminded of. But the more time she spent with Seth, the more things she found to like about him. And the more everything she thought she knew about herself and what she wanted got turned upside down and inside out.

He respected her mom and stepdad. He got along well with her brother and sisters, and he'd joined the regular before-dinner card game with Hannah and her niece and nephews as though he'd done it for years. He'd bowed his head for the blessing before the Sunday meal, and he'd admired the collection of beer steins that were the pride of her stepdad's heart.

Then there was how he'd talked to Hannah. Seth's casual comments about the music business had made her daughter's eyes widen and meant more than anything Annie could have said about why Hannah needed to stick with school.

Seth dried his hands on a towel. "It's been a long time since I had a home-cooked Sunday dinner. I didn't know people still had Sunday dinners with roast chicken and apple pie and all."

"In Irish Falls they do." Annie turned on the dishwasher and moved away from him. This whole setup was too cozy and domestic. And it wasn't accidental that after Brendan, Holly, and the boys left, Tara made everybody else go into the living room to play more cards, leaving she and Seth alone in the kitchen to finish cleaning up.

"Your family's welcoming. I like them." Seth's voice had that mellow intimate note that wrapped around her heart and squeezed it tight.

"They like you, too," Annie said as she stared out the kitchen window into the backyard at the treehouse her dad had made in the big maple for her and her sisters. The heavy rain had barely let up in two days. Water pooled at the base of the tree and ran down the driveway in an ever-growing stream. "What you said to Hannah was great. She doesn't listen to me, but maybe she'll listen to you."

"Since when did teenagers ever listen to their parents?" Seth gave her a wry smile. "You're right to be worried, though. The music business *is* tough. Among other things, staying in school will give Hannah discipline. You need that so you don't throw in the towel the first time things don't go your way."

Annie stiffened. Had she thrown in the towel all those years ago? No, back then she hadn't had a choice. She was pregnant, and Todd hadn't wanted the baby. *Except, I let fear shape my choices ever since, and I never tried again with music.* There was that little inner voice again, louder and more insistent. Could part of changing her life involve doing something with her music too?

"Mom's counting on you giving us some music tonight." She pasted on a bright smile. "She misses Jake's music almost as much as she misses him."

"I'm afraid she'll be disappointed." Seth stood back to let Annie go through the kitchen door first. "I'm an amateur compared to him." He picked up the guitar case from where he'd left it in the hall and ran his fingers over the worn leather. "I'll do my best, though."

Half an hour later, Seth set the guitar down, and Annie pressed a hand to her chest. He wasn't an amateur any more than Jake had been. He might only be playing to her family, but he was a consummate entertainer with a voice to match. He'd even gotten Duncan to clap along, and her stepdad didn't have a musical bone in his body.

"Hearing you play all those old songs is such a treat." Her mom's cheeks flushed with pleasure and her eyes glowed. "It takes me back to my high school days and when my kids were small, too. When we could get a sitter, my first husband and I used to go dancing on Saturday nights at the Black Duck. Mick was such a good dancer."

"That's so romantic," Hannah said. From where she sat cross-legged on the floor with Rowan's boy and girl, Hannah clasped her hands together. "These days, guys don't know how to dance. All they do is shuffle around and call it dancing."

Duncan grunted and flicked a button on his recliner.

"It *is* romantic," Annie said. What was wrong with Duncan? He'd been a widower before he'd married her mom and spoke about his late wife with the same warmth and fondness as her mom spoke about Annie's dad.

"Of course, I can't dance anymore, not with my hip." Her mom's expression was sad.

"You will soon." Annie made herself sound encouraging. "The doctor said you're doing great and healing like a woman of fifty."

"Except, I'm not a woman of fifty." Her mom glanced at Duncan again and bit her lip.

"Anytime you want me to play for you, let me know." Seth got to his feet. "It keeps me in practice. But next time, the rest of you have to join in. I'd like to hear you sing, Hannah. You too, Annie. You mentioned you used to sing with your church choir."

"She still does and she's—"

"Not going to be able to get up to be at work at five thirty tomorrow morning if she doesn't get a move on." Annie cut Tara off and picked up her purse from beside the chair.

"Hannah?"

"Mom." Hannah did her eye roll.

"You have school tomorrow," Annie said.

"My kids and I do too." From the far side of the living room, Rowan got out of the club chair that had belonged to their dad.

Hannah and her cousins groaned in unison.

"Shouldn't things ease off now the school play is over?" Annie studied her sister.

Rowan was the youngest sister and worked as a fifth-grade teacher at the local elementary school.

"I wish." Rowan's laugh had a bitter note. "But I got roped into helping organize the end-of-year carnival and I've picked up some outside tutoring too. Somebody has to put food on the table."

And that somebody wouldn't be Rowan's ex-husband. Annie bit back a sigh and glanced at her mom, who had a worried pucker between her eyebrows.

"I also have a radio show to do early tomorrow morning." Seth's smile was directed at Annie's mom. "It's been a pleasure, Maureen, Duncan." He included Annie's stepdad. "Thanks for your hospitality."

"Our pleasure." Duncan smiled. "Jake was a fine man. You've got big boots to fill."

"So I hear." Seth picked up the guitar case. "But I hope people come to respect me for myself, not only as Jake's nephew." When he turned to Annie, his smile changed. Although the warmth was still there, it was shaded with a darker, more sensual edge. "And not hold being a city guy against me."

Annie tried to smile back, even as her stomach flipped. When she'd been Hannah's age, she'd had her life planned out. She'd make it as a singer, and she'd find a city guy who'd be her passport to a bigger and more exciting world than Irish Falls. She'd found the guy, but, thanks to him, she'd lost her singing career, her college education, and a father for Hannah. Then, just like a homing pigeon, Annie had ended up right back in the small-town world she'd started from.

She already liked Seth way too much for comfort. Only by thinking of him as that kind of city guy could she stop herself from liking him even more.

Chapter 6

"You still look rough, buddy." Just after noon the next day, Brendan met Seth outside the studio door and handed him a black coffee. "If you aren't used to it, getting up so early can be a real killer, especially on Mondays. It gets easier, I swear."

Seth took a sip of the piping hot brew. "Compared to when you start your morning, four thirty is late." Even when he'd slept, he wasn't used to getting up at four thirty but this morning, all he wanted was to get through the show, close the door on Jake's apartment, and get out of town. Except he couldn't do either of the last two because he and half the town were stuck on one side of the flooded Black Duck River, and the road out of town was on the other side and also flooded.

"I'll cover for you for a few hours if you want." Brendan still studied him. "If you can handle the afternoon talk show, the other guys should be able to get in for the suppertime and evening slots."

"I appreciate the offer, but you run a bakery. You're not a radio announcer." Seth set the coffee mug aside and stared out one of the windows into the pouring rain.

"And you are?" Brendan quirked a red-blond eyebrow. "I'll make you look even better, won't I? I dabbled in radio back in high school. Jake showed me the ropes. I covered slots before when he was short-staffed and nobody complained." He flashed a masculine version of Annie's smile. "At least not too much."

"Is anybody listening in this weather?" He'd been on the air for more than six hours today and wondered more than once if he was talking to himself.

"This is when people listen to local radio most. The power's off outside town, and this station's a lifeline. They can manage without me at the bakery for now. Get some sleep. You look like you could use it. I'll keep Dolly here so she doesn't wake you. She's already real attached to you."

Like he was already real attached to the mutt. "Thanks." He gave Brendan a thumbs-up. "I owe you."

"No, you don't." Brendan's smile broadened. "My wife likes hearing me on the radio. It makes her real affectionate. She sent me up here to help you out. You're doing *me* the favor."

"Rub it in, why don't you? I'm single, remember?" Seth slapped Brendan's shoulder. "I'll be back by three, unless we slide into Irish Falls before then." A distinct possibility, given the river of mud behind the station and the rain that still pounded against the windows.

He moved down the short hallway and opened the door to Jake's apartment. His chest tightened. To the right of the sofa, the pine dresser was as he'd left it with the bottom drawer half open. And Jake's letter still sat on the dinette table. He bit his lip and stood in the small foyer, shifting from one foot to the other.

"Seth?" Annie's voice came from the half open door behind him, and he jerked his head around. "I brought you some food. You were on the air for hours so you must be starving."

He moved toward her and took the tray she held out. "Thanks, I—"

"What's wrong?" Annie took one look at him, shut the door, and came into the apartment. "Have you had bad news from your son?"

"No." Because Dylan wasn't talking to him. "He's fine." He had to be. Somebody would have called Seth if he wasn't. He set the tray on the dinette table with a hollow thud.

"Then what is it?" Annie pulled out a chair and pushed Seth into it.

"Nothing." Only that as soon as he'd started to get a handle on things, the world had caved in on him again.

"Yeah, right. I live with a teenage girl. I know when someone is lying to me." Annie took the cover off a bowl and fragrant steam rose off it. "I made my stick-to-your ribs chicken soup with dumplings. You might not want to talk, but you still need to eat."

"You must be real busy at the bakery." Although Tara had come up first, followed by Holly, and then Brendan, he'd missed Annie—even though he didn't want to consider why.

"It's quieter now, but we had people lined up outside the door earlier." She slid a plate of thick-sliced soda bread next to the bowl of fragrant soup. "Thank goodness Tara and my mom live on this side of town so they could come in. Since Rowan's school is closed, she's here as backup. I even called Hannah to help because her school bus didn't run."

Seth scooped up a spoonful of soup, and the warm broth soothed his throat, raw from emotion, as well as all those hours he'd been on the air.

"So apart from what some folks are calling the flood of the century, what happened between last night and this morning?" Annie sat across the table from him. Instead of a Quinn's apron and her hair tucked up in a net, she wore jeans and a blue sweater, and her hair tumbled in loose waves on her shoulders—a wholesome, fresh-scrubbed look he hadn't expected to find so appealing.

"Why do you think something happened? I did the show and more, didn't I?" He flinched as the building shook in the wind.

"You're a pro, city guy. Like Jake. He'd be proud of you." The tenderness in Annie's smile ripped at Seth's heart.

He dropped his spoon with a clatter, and soup splashed onto the table. "You all think Jake was so perfect, but he wasn't."

"I don't understand." Annie's smile slipped. "He had some rough times before he came here. Maybe he did things he wasn't proud of, but—"

"He sure did." Seth shoved the soup bowl away and grabbed Jake's letter from beside the tray. "Last night after I came home, I went through the drawers of that dresser over there you gave me the key to. The top one was full of music stuff. Songs he wrote and information from clubs he must have played at. The middle one had bank statements and bills. But the bottom drawer . . ." He let out a harsh breath. "Along with a bunch of pictures of me as a little kid, I found this." He waved the single sheet of white paper toward her. "He must have written it right before he went into the hospital."

Annie twisted her hands together. "He was dying and maybe—"

"Don't excuse him." He spat out the words because what Seth had read in that letter made him want to die too, except he wouldn't give the lying bastard the satisfaction. "Read it." He dropped the letter on the table between them.

She picked it up and fingered the heavyweight paper. "It's private."

"Not anymore. Go ahead. Read." Seth swallowed the anger that rose up in his throat and threatened to choke him. It wasn't Annie's fault. All she'd done was give him the key to unlock something he might have been better off not knowing. The anger was at Jake and even himself. Deep down, maybe he'd always known the truth, but he'd avoided it.

When Annie looked up from the letter, the shock and

sadness in her eyes hit Seth like a kick to the belly. "I swear, I didn't know. None of us did. That you're not . . . you're his—"

"I'm Jake's son, not his nephew." His voice cracked, right along with his heart. "I told you my dad was out of the picture. The truth is, I never knew him. My mom never mentioned him, and I was too young to ask many questions. When I got older, I asked my grandparents but if they knew something, they wouldn't tell me. There's always been this big hole in my life, as if a part of me was missing." He tried to steady his raspy breathing.

"Your mom . . . she didn't . . . on your birth certificate?" Annie reached for Seth's hand and curled her stiff fingers around his.

"Nothing on my birth certificate. Nothing anywhere." Except for that big aching emptiness where his dad should have been. "Maybe my mom thought she had more time and she would have told me eventually, but she didn't. And her folks were her only family."

"I'm sorry." Her hand was warm on his, and he was glad she didn't say anything else.

"How could Jake do it? When my mom died, he left right after the funeral. He said he couldn't stick around and that I'd understand when I was older, but he was my father. I was seven."

Annie's grip on Seth's hand tightened. "I can't imagine," she said, her voice thick. "You must have felt so lost and alone."

More than he could ever tell her or anyone else. And part of him still felt like that seven-year-old boy in the black cowboy boots. Those boots had been his mom's last birthday gift to him, before leaving him all on his own in a big and scary world.

"In this letter, Jake says that after he got his life together, maybe he should have fought for me and insisted on a paternity test, but at the time, he thought Mom's parents could give me the good home he couldn't. He didn't even try, though." And so, he'd relegated Seth to a loveless upbringing—the kind he'd been determined to not replicate with Dylan. His heart clenched as new pain rolled in to mix with the old.

"Was your mom close to her parents?"

"No. She left that so-called 'good' home as soon as she turned eighteen. They must have reconciled before her death—she wouldn't have granted them guardianship of me otherwise—but there wasn't a lot of love for her there. Or me, either."

His eyes stung, and he crumbled a piece of bread and tried to eat it. This kind of pain went beyond anger and superficial hurt to go deep into his bones and become part of who he was. "Mom waitressed and sang in clubs because she didn't want to live on her parents' money or be who they wanted her to be."

The wind buffeted the building again, but Annie's gaze never left his.

Seth rubbed the back of his free hand across his burning eyes. "Your family was like his family, but all along he had his own family. Me. Dylan. He never even bothered to get to know his grandson."

Annie disentangled her fingers from his, got up, and came around the table to sit beside him. "Why didn't he say something to us? If he had, maybe I could have—"

"What? Tried to make it right? What would you have said?"

"I don't know." Her eyes were troubled. "The Jake I knew wasn't the kind of man to abandon his child. I loved him. I trusted him." Her voice was as raw as his. "What would you have said to him if he'd come back into your life when you were a teenager? Or if he were here now?"

"I don't know." Seth dropped his head into his hands. Right now, he'd be more inclined to take a swing at the guy than talk to him.

"He says he loved your mom. Do you think that's true?" Her words were halting and laced with pain.

Seth raised his head. "I was only a kid, but from the way he looked at her . . . yeah, I guess so, at least whatever love meant to him. And Mom, she . . . I never remember any other guy in her life but Jake. I knew he wasn't her brother because she didn't have siblings. I guess I thought Jake had something to do with my dad's family."

"Did he dump her because she was pregnant?" Annie slumped in her chair. "If he did . . ." Her voice broke.

"Not that I know of. Jake always seemed to be there when we needed him. Before my grandmother came on the scene, he even lived with us for a while after Mom got sick." Seth's chest tightened and it was hard to breathe. "I found a picture, it must have been around the time I was born because it looked like it was taken in a hospital, and it was of Jake, my mom, and me. He was holding me wrapped up in this blue blanket and together they looked happy . . . like they were like a—"

"Like a family?" Annie's voice was almost inaudible.

"Yeah." He spoke around the lump of grief and anger in his throat. "I found a bunch of other pictures with the three of us together, too. Jake came in and out of our lives, but he always came back." Except for the last time when he hadn't.

"From the little Jake told us about his life, he was mostly on the road before he ended up here. He wasn't exactly a drifter, but from a few things he let drop, it sounded like he was drinking a lot, maybe even doing some drugs." Annie looked at Seth's uneaten food. "He was never a drinker when I knew him. He wouldn't even have a glass of wine at Christmas, but he once told my mom that Irish Falls was his second chance." She exhaled slowly. "Sometimes he'd get this sad, almost defeated look in his eyes. Certain times of year were hard for him, like early July and Thanksgiving.

Most years he'd go off for a week around then and not tell anybody where he'd been."

"My mom passed on Thanksgiving weekend." Seth's tongue was stiff and made it hard to shape the words. "And my birthday is right before Independence Day. Do you think . . .?" He blinked.

"I don't know, but he still left his child. No matter what a mess his life was in, what kind of man does that?" She pressed a hand to her stomach.

"Someone I don't want to call my father." Seth's voice was flat.

A tear rolled down Annie's face. "He must have had regrets and a whole lot of guilt. Why would he have written this letter for you to find if he hadn't?"

"Too little, too late." A bitter taste infused Seth's mouth.

"Still, he must have wanted you and loved you once. He wouldn't have kept tabs on you all these years if he hadn't." She gulped. "I know it's not much, but at least you have that."

"But I also have to live the rest of my life with a bunch of questions I can never get answers to." He rubbed a hand across the back of his neck.

"I'm not defending Jake, and I can't know how you feel because it hasn't happened to me, but what comes next is up to you." The warmth in Annie's voice seeped into his frozen heart and thawed some of the ice that had encased it since he'd read Jake's letter. And along with indignation, the steadiness in her expression gave Seth hope.

"You won't tell anybody about him being my dad? I need some time to process all this." Starting with a profound sense of not only disorientation, but betrayal.

"Not a word." She patted his forearm, her touch consoling.

"Thanks." The word came out in an embarrassing croak

like a boy whose voice was changing.

"You're welcome. I'm guessing you also need some space, so I'll go. Just promise me you'll reheat this soup and eat." As Annie pushed back her chair and got to her feet, her smile was more nourishing than the home-cooked food. "It sounds like the rain is letting up so the emergency crews will be back at the bakery to refuel with caffeine and sugar. I'm related to most of those guys, so I know what they're like."

Seth stood and gave her a wooden smile. Jake could have gone to his grave and Seth would never have been any wiser, but instead, Jake had given him both the station and his paternity. And Annie was right. It was up to him what he did with both those things. "You're a big part of this town, aren't you?"

"All those hours you spent on the radio today makes you a big part of Irish Falls, too." She closed the small space between them and wrapped her arms around him in a hug.

Without thinking, Seth hugged her back. She was soft and warm and smelled of gingerbread cookies. The top of her head fit under his chin, and the soft wool of her sweater brushed his forearms below the rolled-up sleeves of his shirt.

She stepped away and a faint flush tinged her cheeks. "We're staying open late because of the weather. Let us know if you need anything. Holly's making pizza later."

Seth needed something, but it wasn't pizza. He blinked and opened his mouth but nothing came out. Last night, while he'd tossed and turned on Jake's uncomfortable mattress, he'd been set to forget about the station and leave Irish Falls as soon as the water receded. But he couldn't because this place held part of his past and, no matter what he thought about Jake, he needed to deal with that past instead of dragging it behind him.

Moreover, Irish Falls also held a woman who intrigued him and who he wanted to get closer to, even as logic warned him to stay away.

~ ~ ~

As usual, Annie had acted first and thought later. Even a week later, she still cringed at the memory of that moment in Jake's apartment when she'd hugged Seth and how right it had felt, how safe.

She stared out the window of the bakery kitchen and as she washed dishes she hummed the song she'd worked on the night before. She had too much time on her hands. That was the only reason she thought about Seth so much. And now she knew why she was doing it, she could stop. For her, musicians were off limits—now, always, and forever.

"It's sure a pretty day out there."

Annie jumped and stopped mid-note. "Mom." She turned away from the window, where the early afternoon sun danced off newly-budded leaves. A roguish spring wind ruffled the honeysuckle bushes lining the path toward the falls. "You scared me."

"You knew I was out front in the store. Maybe you expected someone else?" Her mom's expression was quizzical as she propped her cane against one of the counters and sat on a three-legged wooden stool.

"Of course not. Tara's delivering the cake for that baby shower." Annie dried a clean mixing bowl with a tea towel, avoiding her mom's scrutiny. "And Holly is still at the dentist, which is why you should be out there serving customers."

"There haven't been any customers in twenty minutes, and I wasn't talking about Tara or Holly." Her mom gave her a meaningful look. "I hear Seth spends a lot of time with you."

"So? He works upstairs. Jake spent a lot of time with me, too." Except, Jake had never made her heart beat faster and her mouth go dry or looked at her like Seth looked at her. "Seth has questions about Jake's estate. There's a lot of paperwork for us to go through."

"I'm sure there is." Her mom's tone was dry. "But you have to admit, he's a good-looking man."

Annie dried a set of measuring cups. "I'm not looking for any man, good looking or not." She had to get her life together and figure out what *she* wanted first.

Her mom exhaled and, in the bright light from the window, she looked older and so weary that Annie's heart shuddered. "Don't let life slip past you, honey. You've never wanted to talk about Hannah's father, but—"

"Todd's not part of my life." That was all her mom needed to know. It was all Hannah needed to know, too.

"So why won't you go out with anyone beyond one or two dates?" Her mom's lips tightened. "I'm not getting any younger, and I want to see you settled."

"I *am* settled. I don't need a man for that." From the little she knew about Seth, he was exactly the kind of man to unsettle her. Annie clenched her jaw. "Shouldn't you go back out to the store? Somebody could come in and—"

"If they do, we'll hear them. That's why there's a bell over the door." Her mom covered one of Annie's hands with hers. "I worry about you being alone."

"How could I ever be alone with all our family?" She forced a smile. "My life is good, really." And she was working on making it even better. She'd signed up for a pottery class at the community center and next fall she planned to take a college course through online learning.

"Good enough?"

"Mom." Annie took her hand away and her face got hot. Her mom had always been way too discerning. "You and Dad had the perfect marriage, and now you and Duncan do too. You set a high standard for me, that's all."

"There isn't any such thing as a perfect marriage." Her mom's voice faltered. "Your dad was my soulmate, but we still had our differences. And now Duncan . . . maybe it looks . . ." She stopped and pulled a tissue out of her pocket.

"What is it?" Annie left the dishes and crouched beside where her mom sat. "I don't want to pry into your life, but lately you haven't seemed like yourself."

"I have almost enough hardware in my body to outfit Duncan's workshop. Of course, I'm not myself." Her mom's voice held a sob, and she ran a hand through her silver-white hair.

"I know your hip fracture set you back but—"

"Set me back?" Her mom got to her feet, and the stool wobbled before overturning with a thump. "It set me back, knocked me flat, and turned my whole life upside down." She grabbed an apron from a drawer and looped it over her head.

"It was an accident." Annie found another apron. If her mom wanted to bake, she'd help. "You slipped and—"

"I slipped on a sidewalk I've walked on since I was a child. One minute I was in front of the church thinking about trying a new meatloaf recipe, and the next I was flat on my back convinced I was about to meet my maker." She flung open a cupboard door and pulled out a mixing bowl with a clang. "You girls have reorganized everything in here. Where are the raisins? How am I supposed to make my carrot cake if I don't know where things are?"

"The raisins are right here." Annie slid the canister along the counter. Carrot cake was her mom's signature recipe, and she didn't trust anyone else to make it. "The doctor can't explain why you broke your hip. Remember what she said? It just happened."

"Do you think that makes it any better? Knowing I could have some kind of turn like that again . . ." She scrubbed a hand across her face.

"What does Duncan say?" Better to tackle the problem head on, or at least what Annie thought might be the problem.

"He doesn't say anything." Her mom's chin trembled. "He hardly talks to me. After I lost your dad, I never thought I'd find another man to share my life with, but now I don't know Duncan at all."

"What makes you say that?" Annie's breathing sped up. "You've only been retired a few months. It's a big change. Everybody says retirement takes time to adjust to."

"It's more than that." Her mom measured raisins with an unsteady hand. "Duncan and I haven't slept in the same bed or even the same room since I came home from the hospital. He says he doesn't want to disturb me or hurt me or some other such nonsense."

"I'm sure he wants to give you enough time to heal." Annie busied herself getting out carrots, walnuts, and spices. Thinking about the absence of her own sex life was bad enough. She didn't want to think about her mom's.

"I don't need to give you the details." Her mom's face flushed. "But we used to do so many things together like dinners out and movies, but now he makes excuses. All winter it was his darts league and bowling. Now he can't wait for the golf course to dry out and his softball league to start up again. Even when he's home, he as good as lives in that basement workshop."

"What if you took a special trip? A cruise would be great. You could travel from New York City so you wouldn't have to fly. Once you were on the ship, the two of you could relax and spend time together." Annie patted her mom's back. "A long motorhome trip might still be too hard for you with all the driving, but—"

"No." Her mom scooped flour into the mixing bowl with jerky motions. "You remember how Duncan loved to travel? A few weeks ago, I printed out a bunch of information about resorts with fishing because he likes to fish, but a few days later, I found it beneath the store flyers for recycling. I don't think he even looked at it. It must be me. He doesn't want to be with me anymore."

"I'm sure that's not right. Duncan loves you." At least Annie hoped he still did. "I see the way he looks at you. And remember how he likes to tell the story of how you met? If his car hadn't broken down, he'd never have come in here. He saw you, and then he ate a piece of your carrot cake, and that was it. Love at first sight." Despite the leaden feeling in her stomach, she made her voice bright and encouraging.

"Duncan hasn't told that story in ages." Her mom sniffed. "And he doesn't look at me much these days, either. It's like I'm part of the furniture. He pays more attention to his fancy recliner than me."

"Have you talked to a friend or one of your sisters? Or Tara and Rowan, even?" Annie stared at the tub of brown sugar without seeing it.

"No." Her mom made a noise somewhere between a sob and a snort. "I can't talk to anybody, especially not your sisters. Tara's still grieving Adam's death, and Rowan is so angry about her husband leaving."

Annie's heart was heavy. "Maybe talking it out would help and—"

"Like you, everyone thinks Duncan and I have the perfect marriage. I can't admit anything is wrong. It might get out, and he's such a proud man. He'd never forgive me for sharing our private business."

"Hey." Annie wrapped her arms around her mom's heaving shoulders. "Do you want me to talk to him? It's probably a big misunderstanding."

This was why she'd steered clear of relationships after Hannah's dad. They brought complications she didn't need. Even if you found a man you were sure was "the one," people changed—even Duncan, one of the most rock-solid men she'd ever known.

And then Jake. She thought she'd known him, but she hadn't. Her stomach quivered. Maybe he'd been there for Seth's mom, but he'd still abandoned his son like Todd had abandoned Hannah. The only difference was in the details.

"You can't say a word to Duncan. I shouldn't have said anything to you or stuck you in the middle. You're my daughter." She gave Annie a watery smile.

"I also hope I'm your friend." Annie breathed in the faint scent of roses from her mom's perfume—the fragrance she always associated with home, love, and security.

"You are . . . but—"

"Then I can help. Tara and Rowan will, too. Even Brendan and Holly—"

"You can't say anything to anyone." Her mom stepped back. "And you have to forget I ever mentioned this. Promise me? If anybody talks to Duncan, it has to be me."

"Of course I promise, but are you sure?" Annie's chest ached.

"I'm sure." Her mom gave her a tight smile. "Maybe like you said it *is* retirement. I'm home more now than I was before. And Jake's death hit Duncan hard, not that he'd ever say so. It was so soon after my accident, too. You know, Seth could be exactly what Duncan needs. That night he came for dinner, Duncan was almost like he used to be."

Annie grabbed a cutting board, peeler, and several carrots. "Although he's decided not to sell the station right away, Seth won't stay here permanently. I bet he'll be gone by Halloween at the latest."

"A lot can happen in six months." Her mom's expression brightened.

A lot Annie didn't want to think about. "Why wouldn't he go back to LA? That's where his life is." It wasn't her place to nose into that life, but the look on Seth's face when he talked about Jake's letter was seared on her mind and heart. He wasn't the man she'd first assumed and, like her, he'd known a life-changing hurt.

Her mom rummaged in another cupboard and avoided Annie's gaze. "He might find a reason to stick around. Jake stayed. Why shouldn't his son do the same?"

"What?" Annie dropped the peeler. "How did you—?"

"Seth's the spitting image of Jake when he was younger." Her mom's steady gaze met Annie's. "He's got the same mannerisms, the same way with music, and he has a little heart-shaped birthmark on the inside of his right wrist, almost the same as Jake had. I noticed it when he played for us."

Annie shook her head. "I can't . . ."

"It's not your secret to share. I haven't mentioned it to anyone else, and I won't, either."

"Seth doesn't want anyone to know."

"He told you, didn't he?"

"Mom, please—" Annie stopped as the bell over the bakery door jangled.

Her mom exhaled. "It's good to keep yourself safe, but don't forget to be happy, too, Annie-Bella." Her smile was tender, then she patted Annie's arm and was gone. Her voice drifted out from the store as she greeted a customer.

Annie's eyes smarted. She *was* happy. Or at least she had been before Jake died, Seth turned up, and everything— who and what she thought about, and even the stories she told in her songs—had changed.

Chapter 7

"You know your way around a toolbox." Brendan clambered down the ladder propped against the back of Annie's house. "Thanks for helping me."

"No problem." It wasn't as if Seth had anything else to do on this Saturday afternoon. "I always liked carpentry work. I helped a friend's dad out, back in high school. The guy owned a construction company, but he said even if you were the boss, you still had to get your hands dirty."

Seth followed Brendan down the ladder and hopped off to stand beside a cleared patch of ground that, in the summer, must be a garden. He'd never understood what people meant when they said they could smell spring. Now he did. It was in the water of the Black Duck River rushing below the bridge in the middle of town and swollen with melted snow that had come down from the hills. It was in the winter-brown grass where green shoots poked through patches of dark mud. And it was on the warm breeze that swooped across Annie's backyard and snapped the sheets on her clothesline.

"From what I saw up there, that roof needs re-shingling in a bad way." Seth breathed in the fresh air and tilted his face to the sun.

"It does, but money doesn't grow on trees. Still, compared to a lot of folks, our family got lucky. None of us were flooded out." Brendan tossed Seth a water bottle, and Seth caught it. "My sons and I, as well as a bunch of guys I play hockey with, are getting a work party together to help a few folks with some repair jobs. You on board?"

"Sure." Seth's chest expanded. Brendan respected him, and he'd never asked about what had happened in LA—or why Seth had decided to stay here.

Seth uncapped the water and took a long drink. The house was shaded by big trees, but on the roof the hot sun blazed out of a cloudless blue sky. It was a crisper blue than that he knew in either LA or the South, and the air had a hint of spicy pine. "Do all your boys live nearby?"

"Apart from the two you met at Mom and Duncan's who are still in high school, the older two live on their own nearby. One's an electrician over the mountain, and the other is finishing his sophomore year at SUNY Adirondack." Brendan's eyes gleamed. "I'm real proud of my sons. They're hard workers and smart too, but they know family always comes first. Anything they can do to help out, they're there. The don't expect to be paid, either."

"You raised them right." Seth scrubbed a hand across his face. He'd tried to raise Dylan right too, but somehow it had all gone wrong.

"Not only me." Brendan gave a self-deprecating smile. "I have the right woman sharing the load and most of the town, too. You know that saying 'it takes a village to raise a child'? Folks in Irish Falls take that one to heart."

Seth stared at Annie's garden, the soil turned over in preparation for spring planting. He hadn't had the right woman, or any woman. And he hadn't had a town. He'd only had himself. He'd done his best, but it hadn't been enough. "I have a son, too. Dylan's eighteen. He's at college in New York City."

"You guys close?" Brendan gathered up the tools scattered across Annie's back porch and tucked them into his toolbox.

"We used to be." Seth's stomach knotted. "But now . . . he has his own life."

"He'll come back." There was surprising understanding in Brendan's smile. "Some guys need to be their own person for a while. My oldest was that way. When he first moved out, he talked to Holly all the time, but me, not so much. It's like he needed to learn how to become that last bit of a man without me." He shrugged. "My mom says it's in God's time."

"I guess." But from what Seth remembered about God, it didn't hurt for a guy to move things along on his own. He rolled his shoulders and winced.

"You're going to hurt tomorrow." Brendan's smile broadened.

He already did, but it had been worth it. Hanging out with Brendan and working in companionable silence, he'd gotten a part of himself back he hadn't even realized was missing. "You want to grab a beer and shoot some pool at the Black Duck?"

"Sorry, no can do." Except, Brendan didn't look sorry. "Now the kids are on their way to being launched, Saturday's my date night with Holly."

"Yeah, sure." Seth sat on the porch step and took off the work boots he'd borrowed from Brendan. It was no big deal. He'd spend another evening on the sofa in front of Jake's old television or read one of the thrillers he'd found in the bookcase.

The screen door behind him squeaked open, then Annie moved past to lean against one of the porch pillars. "Even though I can't see what you did up there on my roof, if you got Brendan's approval, you must be good."

His heart skipped a beat. "Thanks."

"I'd never have guessed you knew what to do with a hammer." Her mouth tilted into a smile. "There are a few things around the station that need fixing, too. Jake was a good carpenter but he liked working on special projects, not basic maintenance." She stuck her hands in the front pocket of her jeans.

"Happy to help." At least there was something he didn't share with his old man. Seth tried to concentrate on tying his sneakers and not on how Annie's fitted white T-shirt outlined curves usually hidden by her Quinn's apron or a bulky sweater.

"Seth's a pro." Brendan picked up his toolbox. "See you at Mom's tomorrow?" His gaze swiveled to Annie.

"Sure." She smiled at her brother then watched him walk to his truck at the end of the driveway.

Seth got to his feet. "I should head home, too." Except, he didn't want to. He sucked in a breath. He wanted to stay here with her.

"Of course." She crossed her arms in front of her chest. Red-blonde hair tumbled around her shoulders, and her skin was almost translucent in the soft light of the shaded porch.

"You probably have plans with Hannah or . . .whatever." His heart thudded and his voice echoed in his ears. "But it's almost suppertime. If you're free, do you want to grab something to eat with me?" It was a friendly gesture because he didn't know many people in town, but that didn't explain why his breathing sped up and he was a whole lot warmer than the temperature warranted.

"Hannah's watching movies with friends tonight, so I guess so." Annie nibbled her bottom lip. "We could go through more of the estate papers." She fiddled with the silver bangle on her right wrist. "I'd have to go to Quinn's first and pick up some stuff from the office though."

"No problem." He swallowed and let out a breath. "I need a shower and have to let Dolly out."

"Shall I meet you at Jake's apartment in an hour?" She backed toward the door and put a hand to her mouth.

"Sure . . . great." Seth moved closer, then stepped back.

This wasn't a date. He and Annie would get a meal and talk about estate paperwork, nothing more.

Yet, as he walked to his truck, his legs trembled and not from the manual labor. The estate paperwork was an excuse, and they both knew it.

~ ~ ~

It was only dinner. Annie tucked the folder under one arm and locked the filing cabinet in the bakery office. And if she talked about the bequests in Jake's will, she wouldn't be drawn into any personal conversational paths.

She moved down the hall and into the bakery kitchen, singing the song she'd been working on. Through the half-open window, the fresh spring wind whispered in the trees, and water tumbled over Irish Falls with a muted roar. She didn't have to meet Seth for another fifteen minutes, and nobody was around. She set the folder on a counter, drew in a deep breath, and let the music spill out.

The kitchen disappeared. Irish Falls disappeared. And she was in that special place where only music ever took her.

A dog barked.

Annie stopped mid-note. Her heart pounded, and her stomach went rock hard.

"Dolly, no." Seth lurched past the window. "What do you think you're—" The outside door banged open, and Dolly skidded across the floor with a chorus of excited yips.

Seth stopped beside Annie. His chest heaved beneath an open-necked white shirt above a pair of dark jeans. "I'm sorry. She heard your voice. The door was ajar and . . . hey." He gestured to Dolly to sit. "You're an incredible singer."

Annie flinched as images of what might have been flashed through her mind. A stage, bright lights, and an expectant hush. She held back a cry. "It . . . it wasn't me. It was the radio." She bent to pat the dog and her stomach heaved.

"I see." Seth glanced toward the shelf where the radio sat, silent.

"Yes. I turned it off before you came in." She straightened and pressed a hand to her chest.

"I didn't recognize the song, but whoever was singing has perfect pitch. Her voice has a special quality. I've heard a lot of good voices, but that was a great voice. The song was great, too. Even from the little I heard it has hit written all over it." His tone was casual—deceptively so. "What station were you listening to? I want to contact them so I can play that song here."

Annie licked her lips. Could she trust him with the truth? "It wasn't the radio." She gulped. "It was me." She picked up the folder from the counter and gripped it so hard her knuckles went white. "I said I'd meet you at the apartment. What were you doing out there?"

"Dolly had to do her business." His blue-gray gaze seared her. "Do you sing like that in your choir?"

"No." Her shoulders sagged under his penetrating gaze. "You know that when you sing in a choir, your voice has to blend with everyone else's." And over the past sixteen years, she'd gotten good at blending in. She'd blended into her family, Irish Falls, and her job at Quinn's and, until a little while ago, she'd convinced herself she liked it that way.

"Who wrote that song?" He took a step closer, and she backed up against the counter.

"I did." She gave a high laugh. "It's a hobby."

"I haven't heard that combination of melody and lyrics in a long time, maybe ever." His expression softened. "You had me working out harmonies and backing vocals right there on the path. I didn't mean to sneak up on you, but your voice and that song . . . you shouldn't hide your talent."

"Lots of people sing." She hugged herself.

"Not like that. They don't write songs like that, either."

The gentleness in his voice cranked her panic up another notch. "Whether you admit it or not, you have a big talent."

She froze, rooted to the spot as his words hit home. Why had she let what Todd had done become such a part of her that she was afraid to share her music in case it jeopardized her hard-won safety? "You wouldn't understand."

"Try me."

Her head spun and time seemed to slow. "When I was Hannah's age, I wanted to make it in music like she does."

"And?" Seth's voice was soft.

"I left for Nashville after I finished high school. I had a scholarship to study music at Belmont University." She shivered and reached across the counter to shut the window.

"Then what happened?" His voice held no censure, only warmth.

She swallowed hard. "A week after I got there, I met Hannah's dad. His name was Todd. He was a studio musician and songwriter, and I met him at a gig I went to with some girls from my dorm. I had stars in my eyes." She bit her lip as her stomach heaved again. "I believed everything he told me, but it turns out I was another small-town girl with dreams bigger than herself."

Seth let out a long breath. "It's not too late. Your voice and—"

"Look at me." She raised an arm and dropped it by her side. "I'm almost thirty-six. How many women my age make it in Nashville or anywhere else? The music business is a young person's game. There are lots of girls with great voices. And they're young, more beautiful, and hungrier than I'll ever be."

"Even if everybody else writes you off, that doesn't mean you should do it, too." His tone was serious, like he was talking about more than her music.

"I'm being realistic. I had my chance, and it didn't work out. I got pregnant with Hannah, gave up my scholarship, and came back here." Even if she had regrets, that part of her life was over.

"Maybe you wouldn't make it as a singer, but what about songwriting? Would you sing your song for me the whole way through?" His expression was hopeful.

She tensed. "I don't sing in public."

"I'm not the public." His tone cajoled her. "You already sing in church and you help out with the school music program. You must sing with the kids."

"That's different, but how do you know about the school? Tara?"

He shrugged and gave her a teasing smile. "She loves you."

And if she didn't love her sister so much, she'd kill her for blabbing to Seth. "What else did she tell you?"

"That you sucked your thumb, still sleep with a bear called Mr. Snuggles, and you're the best mom and sister ever." His grin almost split his face in two.

"I've never had a bear called Mr. Snuggles." Her face heated because she had a stuffed rabbit named Flopsy who still sat on her bedroom dresser. "As for the thumb sucking, I stopped in kindergarten."

"Two out of three, and I guessed the most important one, didn't I?" His chuckle was more appealing than it should be. "Will you at least think about singing for me? I promise I won't bite."

That was the least of her worries. "Okay." She put a hand to her mouth. What had she done?

"Great. While you think about it, let's get some food. The Black Duck?" His smile was also much too intimate.

"I . . . okay." It was only dinner at the local roadhouse, not the top of a slope that might prove way too slippery. "We'll have to take your truck, though. I walked here because my car wouldn't start. It's probably the battery but my cousin who's a mechanic can't check it until tomorrow."

"No problem. I'll take Dolly back to the apartment and meet you at the truck in five."

She nodded, unable to speak around the tightness in her throat. Seth wasn't Todd, but, despite the desire that tugged in the pit of her stomach, and the unexpected warmth stealing through her body, she couldn't let herself get close to him. Maybe someday she'd meet another man—one outside the music business who she could trust with her heart—if not her songs. And one who couldn't break her, along with her music.

Chapter 8

"I didn't expect to see you here tonight." Holly fluffed her hair and grinned at Annie beside her in front of the mirror above the row of sinks in the ladies' restroom at the Black Duck. "What happened to get you out from in front of the TV with Tara? Or maybe I should say *who*?"

"I needed to talk to Seth about Jake's estate paperwork. Tara's helping a friend with some sewing tonight, and he and I were both at a loose end." A tingle spread from the back of Annie's neck and across her face. "The Black Duck has the best burgers in town."

"Indeed." Holly's smile widened.

"It's not like that. I told you, we have to talk about estate stuff." Yet, although the conversation had been entirely businesslike while they waited for their meals, as soon as the food arrived, they'd talked about a lot of other things, and Seth didn't seem in any hurry to leave.

"Who knew estate paperwork could be so interesting?" Holly winked and picked up her clutch purse from beside the sink. "The way the two of you were leaning toward each other, I thought you were on a date for sure."

"We're not—" Annie stopped as the restroom door banged shut behind her sister-in-law. She rested her palms on the narrow vanity and stared at her flushed reflection in the mirror. This wasn't a date. If it were, she'd have dressed up and freshened her makeup.

Except, maybe she hadn't done either of those things because she'd been scared it could turn into a date. When Seth heard her singing, and had gotten part of the truth out of her, it had taken every ounce of her willpower to come here with him tonight—and pretend what he'd heard, and what she'd shared with him, wasn't a big deal.

As much as she'd tried to hide the old Annie who'd been set on getting out of Irish Falls and making it in Nashville, she was still there. And after talking to Seth in the bakery kitchen earlier, that small flame of self-belief that had never truly died flickered back to life. She wasn't sure where it would take her yet, or if it could take her anywhere, but she needed to try. And a pottery class or online college course would always be second best.

She pulled open the restroom door and stepped out into the soundtrack to a Black Duck Saturday night—a buzz of conversation, the clank of dishes, and a medley of country tunes.

"Hey." Seth waved as she wended her way through the crowd to sit at their table. "Are you okay? I was about to send somebody in after you."

"I'm fine." Annie plastered a smile on her face and tried to ignore the flutter in her stomach. "There was a line."

"Do you want to get another drink or more dessert?" His face creased into attractive lines as he smiled. "That pie was great, but Brendan told me the Black Duck buys cheesecake from Quinn's."

"No thanks. I should get home."

He couldn't be flirting with her, could he? What she'd said about that Nanaimo Bar Cheesecake being better than sex the day he arrived in town still made her cringe.

"Sure." Seth signaled their waitress for the check. "No." He shook his head when Annie reached for her purse. "Let me take care of this one. I invited you out."

"We should split it." If she paid for her own meal, there couldn't be any misunderstanding about what this evening was—or wasn't.

"You can get it next time, okay?" Seth pulled his wallet out of the back pocket of his jeans.

Next time? Even if she wanted to, she couldn't let herself go down that path with him.

"Hey, it looks like they're setting up for some live music." Seth glanced toward the stage then handed the waitress several folded bills and nodded at her to keep the change. "Why don't we stay and listen?"

"Hannah will be home soon. I need to be there before she is." Her hands shook as she looped her filmy scarf around her neck and buttoned the jacket he had held out for her to slip into. Once, she'd been a regular at the Black Duck's live music nights.

"Of course. Sorry. I forgot." His smile was wry. "Parenting is a twenty-four/seven job."

"Yeah." Annie's breathing eased. She'd never faltered or forgotten her responsibility to her daughter, and she wouldn't start now.

"You need to direct me from here to your place." Seth jingled his keys as they walked to the door of the restaurant and out into the night. "I'm fine going back to the station once I'm at your house, but I'm still finding my way around town, and I'm not used to how dark it is here at night."

"Sure, but it's pretty easy once you figure out the street pattern, even in the dark. I don't usually bother with my car. I can walk from home to the bakery and almost everywhere else I need to go." Annie tucked her hands into her jacket pockets. It might be spring, according to the calendar, but the nights were still chilly.

Seth opened the passenger door of his truck, and Annie slid in. Nana Gerry would have said he'd been raised right, the way he took care of doors, coats, and things. It was more than politeness, though. Although he was a big guy, he had an innate gentleness and care in how he treated others.

The truck engine roared into life, and Seth stared ahead as he navigated the pothole-filled lot, where vehicles were parked three deep. "It's a whole different world for me here." His profile was a lighter silhouette against the dark interior of the cab.

"We're pretty far off the beaten track, but the tourists like it that way." And until recently, she'd been fine with that isolation. "I've never been to LA." Annie clasped her hands together on top of her purse on her lap.

"It's a fun city. Lots of people, sunshine, and excitement. Traffic, too." The truck bumped over the railroad tracks, and the water tower loomed in front of them, ghostly in the moonlight.

"Here, a traffic jam is a lineup of three cars waiting to get out of the grocery store parking lot at closing time."

Seth laughed as he signaled right onto Malone Street, where Annie indicated. "That sure beats sitting in freeway traffic for hours."

"Why did you move to LA?"

Seth took another right and then a left as he followed Annie's hand gestures. "Why any kid does. Dreams of fame and fortune. I was a guy with a guitar who played in a band and LA was where everything happened—or so I thought." He slowed the truck to a stop in front of her house. The two-story blue clapboard with white trim was hugged by a wide porch, and window boxes waiting to be filled with spring blooms.

Like why she'd gone to Nashville. "Here we are." Her voice cracked, the sound loud in the sudden silence.

"Thanks for keeping me company tonight." Seth unclipped his seatbelt and turned to face her.

"No problem." Annie undid her belt and pushed the truck door open.

"Wait." Seth jumped out and came around to her side.

"My grandmother had her faults, but she taught me to walk a woman to her door."

"Thanks." The path to her front door had never seemed so narrow, but Seth had never walked up it with her before, either. "Thanks for dinner, too." She stopped on the bottom porch step and dug in her purse for her keys.

"You're welcome." Seth held out his hand. "The board on that step creaks like it's loose. I'll swing by tomorrow afternoon and take a look. It probably only needs a few nails. I don't want you to slip and fall."

Her hand disappeared into his bigger one. The board *was* loose, and she'd slid off that step more than once. She never seemed to have enough time to take care of things like loose porch boards and damaged roof shingles. "Brendan talked to you." She tried to laugh and ignore the sense of safety and security of his hand in hers.

"Only a little bit." His voice was slow and soft, with long vowels. He fished a small flashlight out of his jacket pocket with his other hand. "Your brother looks out for you."

The light went on and illuminated the key ring in the depths of her purse. She took her hand away from his and fumbled for the house key.

"Here." He gave her his arm as they went up the rest of the porch steps, took the key from her, and unlocked the door. The trees near the house cast dark shadows, and a light wind rustled the branches. He flicked off the flashlight with a soft click. "I had a good time tonight."

"Me too." Annie gulped in air heavy with the scent of spring earth. "Hannah, she'll be home soon."

"Teenagers never get home when they say they will." His voice rumbled above her.

Teenagers like Hannah didn't. "Still, I should . . ." The moon peeped out from behind a cloud and illuminated his face. The words she'd intended to say died at the heat in his eyes.

"Annie?"

"Yes?" Her voice stuttered.

He dipped his head, and his warm lips brushed her cheek in a whisper of a kiss. Then he stepped back and, except for the lingering spicy scent of his aftershave, she might have imagined the intimacy of the moment. "Thanks for having dinner with me."

"I . . ." She swayed toward him.

His phone played a guitar riff and shattered the stillness. "It's my son. I have to take this." He backed down the porch steps and groped in his jacket for his phone.

"Of course. See you." Annie pushed open her front door and stumbled through it then slammed the door behind her and sat on a hall chair. Her heart pounded and she dropped her head into her hands. If Seth's phone hadn't rung, would he have kissed her again? Or would she have kissed him instead?

~ ~ ~

"Dylan, I . . ." Seth slid into the driver's seat of his truck and gripped his phone, his palm sweaty. Kissing Annie hadn't been part of his plan, not even an innocent kiss on the cheek that really wasn't all that innocent, but he couldn't think about that right now. He'd almost given up hope his son would call him back, but maybe this was the bridge he'd looked for. "It's great to hear from you."

"You said in your message you wanted to talk to me." His son's deep voice held wariness. When had talking to Dylan become like talking to a polite stranger?

"I wanted to let you know I'm sticking around Irish Falls for a while. I've got a great business opportunity here. I texted you, but I thought . . ." His chest tightened. What had he thought? That one phone call would make everything better between them? He stared into the night. Beyond Annie's house, a light from a neighbor's garage cast a faint gleam across the tree-lined road, and through the half open truck window, the mournful howl of a dog echoed.

"Oh." Dylan's tone was stilted.

"Maybe you could come visit me once you're done with exams. It's real nice here. There's lots of nature and hiking. We could go camping." Even though Seth hated the hopefulness in his voice, he pressed on. "You always liked camping, and you've never been this far north. I've got an apartment so you could stay and—"

"I've already got a summer job lined up in Manhattan." His son's voice was flat. "I'm renting a place with friends."

"That's great." And it was. Dylan was hardworking and ambitious, what a man like Seth's grandfather would have called a self-starter. "Well, maybe you could come for a long weekend. What about for Memorial Day or over July Fourth? Independence Day is probably a big deal in a small town like this one."

"Thanks, but I'm spending the holidays with Mackenzie and her family in the Hamptons. Her parents have a beach house there. Her dad's the one who gave me the job, and he says he'll take me golfing. He wants to introduce me to some guys he works with. He might be able to help me get an internship next year."

The excitement in Dylan's voice was palpable, and Seth drew in a pained breath. Some other guy would help his son in a way he couldn't. "Are things serious with Mackenzie?"

"Dad." Seth didn't miss the sarcasm.

Okay, the girlfriend was still off limits. "How is school going?"

"Fine." Dylan's tone was clipped. "Look, I should go. I need to study."

And since when did his son study on Saturday night? "Sure." Seth rubbed the back of his neck with his free hand. "If your plans change, let me know. I could come and see you. Even if you're busy, we could still hang out for a few hours—get a meal or catch a baseball game." The stuff they used to like to do together.

"Right." Dylan hesitated. "I heard what happened with your work. I . . . I hope stuff works out for you up there." There was a slight warmth to his voice that hadn't been there previously.

"Thanks." Seth stared at his lap. Despite that glimmer of warmth, he wouldn't get his hopes up. "If you need anything, money or whatever, let me know." His company had bitten the dust, but he still had savings—and a robust investment portfolio. But he wanted to give his son more than money. And he wanted to have what they used to—a real relationship instead of this unnatural exchange.

"I'm good."

"I know you are. And I . . . I'm proud of you." No matter what, he'd always be proud of Dylan. "Not that you need it, but good luck with your exams and the job. Text or message me. It would be great to hear how things are going."

"Okay." A burst of noise erupted on Dylan's end of the phone—male voices, rap music, and the bang of a door. "I really gotta go."

"Sure, I . . ." The phone went dead. "I love you, son." Seth rested his forehead on the steering wheel and whispered the words into the night.

He put the key into the ignition and glanced at Annie's house. Warm yellow light gleamed from several downstairs windows and spilled out onto the porch. It was cozy, homelike, and welcoming—exactly like her. His heart clenched and he put the truck in gear.

Maybe his grandparents had loved him, but they'd never showed it. And Jake . . . bile rose in his throat as he drove down the narrow street and hung a left and then a right back toward the station. He couldn't change the past, but he wouldn't repeat its mistakes, either. There was no way he'd abandon his son or ever give up on him. He'd have to find another way to connect with him. And if Dylan needed him, he'd always be there.

Seth pulled into the empty lot behind the station and parked. Dylan's call hadn't been the bridge he'd hoped for, but that didn't mean there weren't other bridges.

The roar of the falls made a counterpoint to his thoughts and, beyond the water, the wishing tree glinted silver in the moonlight. From across the years, his mom's sweet voice resounded in his head. Every night when she'd tucked him into bed, she'd sung "A Dream is a Wish Your Heart Makes." Back then, he didn't know *Cinderella* was a girls' movie. It was only a movie she liked to watch, so he'd watched it with her, tucked into the gentle curve of her body as the two of them sang along with the characters.

It didn't take a shrink to tell him if his mom hadn't died, his life would have been a whole lot different. He got out of the truck and stared at the velvety blackness of the night sky hung with a canopy of stars. Were his mom and Jake together up there in that vast ever after and had they found the happiness that had eluded them on earth?

His fingers tingled and a song fragment drifted through his mind, a new idea, the first one he'd had in months. He pulled out his phone and made a note. Maybe his dry spell was over, and maybe he still had lots of chances to make a fresh start with his son, his career, and even with a woman like Annie. Although he didn't know where things were going between them, one thing was certain. The next time he kissed her, it wouldn't be a chaste peck on the cheek.

Chapter 9

"I'm worried about Annie." Maureen sat in the easy chair in the living room of the house she'd shared with Duncan since they'd gotten married. Nine years ago now, and where had the time gone?

Across from her, Duncan stretched out in the multi-speed recliner the whole family had given him for his sixty-fifth birthday. It had more features than her first car, and she never sat in it for fear of breaking something.

"You're always worrying about one or more of the kids." Duncan's gaze never left the television screen.

"Like you don't worry about your two? Would you turn that TV off and listen to me?" Maureen tried to keep the irritation out of her voice.

He picked up the remote and muted the sound. "It's Saturday night. I always watch hockey on Saturday night. And this is a playoff game."

"You don't follow either of those teams." Maureen's breath hitched. She'd been replaced by whatever was on TV. "Annie's unsettled. Haven't you noticed?"

"No." Duncan's gaze flicked back toward the TV.

"I said off." Maureen snagged the remote and the screen went dark. "Ever since Seth turned up, she hasn't been herself. She won't talk to me, but maybe if you sort of laid the groundwork, I could—"

"No." The chair flipped forward, and Duncan's sock feet hit the carpet with a muffled thud.

"Why not? You two get along so well, and all I need is

for you to introduce the subject. Like you're looking out for her as her stepfather."

"Annie's not twelve. She's a grown woman. She'd tell me I was interfering and rightly so." The table light shone on Duncan's thick white hair. On him, the color was distinguished, whereas on her, it just looked old. "What makes you think anything I could say would make a difference?"

Maureen exhaled. "I don't know, but she won't talk to anyone else in the family. We've all tried."

"That should tell you she doesn't want to talk to anybody." Duncan's voice softened. "Most of us don't wear their heart on their sleeve like you. I may not be related to her by blood, but Annie's a lot like me."

Maureen curled her toes inside her slippers. Like her daughter, her husband still shut her out. She'd told Annie that if anybody talked to Duncan, it had to be her. But now he'd given her an opening, she didn't know what to say. She cleared her throat. "Lately you've seemed . . . is there something you aren't telling me?"

"No." His laugh was strained.

"Don't you think I know when something's not right?" Maureen reached across the side table between them for Duncan's hand. "For better for worse, remember what we said in front of the priest?"

His hand stiffened, and he looked at the blank TV screen, not meeting her gaze.

"Is there . . .?" She stopped then made herself say the words. "Have you met someone else?"

"What?" Duncan's normally placid blue eyes blazed into her. "Since I came into Quinn's and saw you behind that counter, I've never looked at any other woman. You have my heart, and you always will. How could you even think something like that?"

She wrapped her fingers around his cold hand. "I don't know what to think. You don't seem to want to spend time with me or talk to me, and we . . . well . . . since I came home from the hospital after my hip, you've slept in Rowan's old room."

"I don't want to disturb you." He stared at their joined hands with the matching yellow gold bands on the fourth fingers.

"I miss you." Maureen swallowed the lump in her throat. "I miss us and who we were together."

"We're still us." Duncan's smile didn't reach his eyes. "You've put up with me for a good few years, haven't you?"

"I love you." Her voice wobbled.

"I love you too, Reenie." He squeezed her hand before he released it. "The only thing I want for Annie is to find the kind of partner you are to me. From what I've seen of Seth, he's a decent man. The way he looked at her that night he came to dinner, he wouldn't treat her wrong."

"You can't be sure of that." Maureen suppressed a sigh. Seth had a wariness almost as great as Annie's.

"Stop fussing, woman." Duncan reached for the remote control. "You stew about everything and most of it will never happen."

Maureen took a deep breath. "I'm not tired yet. Why don't I run a bath and we—"

"You need your rest." Duncan's words were too quick. "You can't climb in and out of that high tub yet, either."

"I guess not." Maureen's stomach tensed as she studied his bent head.

"Why don't you make us some cocoa? That always settles you before bed. And I'll get out the chess board. We haven't played chess in ages. What do you think about starting a game?" His tone was too bright.

"What I think is you're avoiding something. If it isn't me, it's something else." She smoothed the cover of the library book she hadn't been able to focus on. "I bumped into Dr. Nguyen's nurse at the garden center this afternoon. She said she'd see us on Monday, but when I got home and checked the calendar, neither of us has an appointment then."

"She must have been mixed up. It's easy to make a mistake with all the folks who go through that clinic every day." Duncan cleared his throat, pulled open the table drawer, and dug through several packs of playing cards and loose scrabble tiles. "Where did the chess set go to?"

"It's on the shelf in the hall closet where it always is." Maureen shivered and rubbed her arms.

Duncan got out of his chair and grunted. "Why don't you add marshmallows to the cocoa? Let's live a little."

Maureen stared after him as he disappeared into the hall. He'd never given her cause to doubt him, and she'd never thought he'd lie to her. But he was lying to her now, and if it wasn't another woman, maybe it was something that would still take him away from her.

Her stomach contracted, but she sat straighter, filled with fresh determination. First thing Monday morning she'd call Dr. Nguyen's office to confirm the appointment. If it was for Duncan, she'd be there beside him and wouldn't take no for an answer.

~ ~ ~

After Seth fixed the loose board on Annie's porch steps, she seemed to have done her best to avoid him over the past week. If Tara or Holly didn't come up to the station with coffee and a muffin or some other sweet treat, Annie scuttled in and left the tray on a table outside the studio before darting out again.

He shut Jake's closet and eyed the bags he'd packed for the thrift store in the next town. There were no clues about the man who'd been his dad in the nondescript shirts and pants. More conservative than Seth expected, the clothes could have belonged to any guy in his early sixties. All except for the worn cowboy boots and black Stetson, and he'd left those in the boxes where he'd found them, at the back of the closet behind a trio of battered suitcases.

Seth turned away from the clothing, and the unanswered questions that went along with it all, and looked out the bedroom window. On this sunny Sunday afternoon, downtown Irish Falls was bustling and people spilled out of O'Connor's country store down the street. He traced a treble clef on the bedroom window with an index finger, then grabbed a jacket from the chair beside the bed. If Annie wouldn't talk to him, he'd have to find a way to talk to her.

Five minutes later, he parked his truck in front of her house beside a lilac bush filled with tight purple buds.

"Seth?" A shock of red hair appeared from around the other side of the bush, followed by Hannah in a pair of ripped jeans and a white T-shirt with "Nap Queen" on it in pink letters.

"Hey." He grinned at the teen. "Is your mom around?"

"I left her up on the mountain." She jerked her head in the direction of the hill at the end of the street. "I have to get ready for a gig, and she's pretty pissed off about something."

His heart sank. "Where up on the mountain?"

"There's a lookout with a bench about ten minutes along the trail. It's Mom's favorite place. There's a creek up there, too. You can't miss it." Hannah grinned back. "Mom might have cooled down by now, but if I were you, I'd take chocolate just in case."

He dug in his jacket pocket for the bar he'd bought from the kids at the grocery store who were raising money for sports equipment at the school. One of the little boys looked so much like a young Dylan that Seth had ended up buying a dozen bars to see his freckled face light up in a gap-toothed smile. "Will this one do?" He held the bar up for Hannah's inspection.

"Awesome. Mom loves those." Her grin broadened, and she gave a musical little chuckle.

Seth's heart pinched. Dylan used to be as easy with him as Hannah. "What kind of gig do you have?"

"A kids' birthday party. I dress up and sing Disney Princess songs. This afternoon it's to a bunch of six-year-old girls. Singing is singing, no matter how young the audience. The kids love it, and I make good money, too." Hannah sobered. "I don't know what's up with Mom. She's usually pretty chill, but this past week something's sure got her riled up. She skipped choir practice and then church this morning, and she hasn't sung at all, not even in the shower."

Seth pushed away the much-too-tempting image of Annie in the shower. "Your mom usually sings a lot?"

"All the time." Hannah's voice filled with pride. "She has a great voice. My grandma says Mom could have made it big if she hadn't quit when she got pregnant with me."

"What about your dad?" He made his tone casual. Part of him hated himself for prying, but if he wanted to convince Annie to sing for him, he had to know what he might be up against.

"I never met him."

"I'm sorry." Inadequate, but what words were there for the kind of absence he knew too well?

Hannah shrugged. "Mom and him split up before I was born. He didn't want a kid."

"He didn't know what he'd miss." There was a bitter taste in Seth's mouth. Despite everything, and even though he'd been a kid himself when Dylan was born, his son was the best thing to ever happen to him.

"Yeah, right." Hannah's eyes glinted too bright.

"I mean it. A child not only makes your life worthwhile, but they teach you what really matters." Which was why he'd never understand why Jake had abandoned him, or why Amanda didn't want to be a bigger part of Dylan's life.

"Whatever." Hannah stuck her hands in the front pockets of her jeans. "If you want to talk to Mom, you better get going. It's already mid-afternoon. In an hour or so, the black flies will eat you alive. The closer it gets to sunset, the more those things come out."

Seth glanced at the sky where the sun already tilted toward the west. "Thanks."

"No worries, but don't say I didn't warn you. You might want to lead with the chocolate." She gave him a little wave before setting off at a jog toward the house.

Seth walked to the end of the street then followed a steep, dirt path uphill through the trees where tree roots stuck up through the soil. Five minutes in, he took off his jacket and rolled up his shirt sleeves. When the hill finally plateaued out, he stopped. To his left, a creek bubbled out of a stand of trees, and Annie sat on a stump with her back to him. Her floral top made a splash of color against the early spring landscape, and her bright hair gleamed like copper in the sun.

Seth picked his way around a rocky outcrop and pile of brush then pulled out the chocolate bar. A branch snapped beneath his feet, and above his head a bird let out a raucous cry.

Annie swung around and her gaze locked with his. He'd told himself he wasn't at the right time and place in his life to get involved with her or any other woman, but maybe he'd been wrong. And maybe what was in his heart was more important than what was in his head.

~ ~ ~

Annie lurched to her feet and brushed twigs and soil from her jeans. How had Seth found her here? And, more to the point, why had he come looking for her?

"Hi." In jeans and a blue shirt, with a jacket looped around his waist, he walked across the log bridge that spanned the narrow creek and met her where one side of the hill dropped off into the valley below.

"Hi, yourself." Her hiking boots squelched on the muddy ground.

"I brought chocolate." He held out a bar, like some kind of peace offering.

"Did Hannah tell you where I was?" She hesitated, then took the chocolate from his outstretched hand and gave him a small smile.

"I dropped by your place and met her out front." The corners of his mouth crooked upward in that heart-melting smile. "I hope I'm not barging in."

"You know you are." Annie tried to keep her expression aloof, stern even, but it was no use. The combination of that smile and mellow drawl got her every time. Plus, he had chocolate. She unwrapped the paper and foil and broke off several squares then handed it to him to share. "I come here when I want to be alone." She gave him a pointed look. Maybe he didn't know how sexy his smile was. Or maybe he did and used it to get to her and any other woman who crossed his path.

"I'm sorry." Except, he didn't sound sorry. "You're a hard woman to pin down."

"I've been busy." Since the radio station was upstairs from the bakery, avoiding Seth took some doing, as did trying to make herself forget that fleeting kiss. But she'd also been busy worrying about her mom and Duncan. Why had her mom asked Annie to drive her to the doctor's office on Monday afternoon, but wouldn't tell her why? And why was the car her mom and Duncan drove already parked in the lot?

"I hope I didn't make you uncomfortable when I said good night last Saturday." He looked at his mud-blackened sneakers.

"No, it wasn't even a real kiss." Annie made herself laugh, the sound false, even to her ears. "Forget it."

"It might not have started out that way, but if my son hadn't called, it sure might have become a real kiss." Seth's voice had a sensual timbre, and Annie's stomach fluttered.

"We don't know that." Her skin prickled.

"I do." He stared into the hazy blue distance instead of at her. Below them, the Black Duck River meandered across the valley floor, and the town of Irish Falls clustered at its heart, like a toy town from this height. "Maybe I can forget the kiss, but what I can't forget is that voice of yours."

Annie's face went hot. Why hadn't she shut the kitchen window? And knowing Seth was upstairs, why had she sung in the first place? Rhetorical question. She sang all the time, not only when she was happy, but also when she was upset. If he'd turned up a few minutes earlier, he'd even have caught her singing here.

"I already told you, I don't sing for anyone these days except for the kids at school and in the choir."

"You didn't sing in the choir this morning." He gave her a lopsided smile.

"You went to my church?" She sucked in a quick breath.

"Yep." His eyes twinkled. "A lot of my listeners go to St. Patrick's. It's important for me to be visible in the community."

"You . . . you . . ." Her jaw got tight. Not only was Seth persistent but, as Nana Gerry would have said, he had more nerve than a canal horse.

"There's nothing wrong with a man going to church on Sunday morning." His tone teased her. "A couple of sweet old ladies invited me to sing in your choir. They said I had a beautiful tenor."

"Don't be fooled by appearances. Those 'sweet old ladies' are as smart and wily as they come." She briefly clenched her hands. "They think if they get to you first, you won't darken the door of another church in this town again.

faiths listen to your station, too. A bunch of non-believers as well."

"See, that's why I need you as a friend." He gave her a wide-eyed, much-too-innocent look. "I don't know anything about small towns, but you do. I guess I can't be seen to take sides, even when it comes to church going. In this morning's announcements, though, your priest mentioned a fundraiser night at the Black Duck on Memorial Day weekend. It's to help folks who got flooded out. A couple of local singers are doing sets. You should sign up."

"No." Annie tensed.

"But it's for such a good cause." He paused. "I thought you were more civic minded."

Seth was smooth, she'd grant him that, and he knew how to get to her.

"I'll write a check." She set off across the log bridge and back to the trail. "Quinn's is donating three cakes for the raffle. One is a wedding cake and those are expensive."

"I thought you'd want do to something more personal. If you lived a few blocks closer to the river, you might have lost everything, too." Seth's expression was sad. "If it's singing alone that's the problem, I'd be happy to sing with you. Or I could accompany you. Whatever you want. When I spoke to Father Michael earlier, I promised the station's full support. All the churches and service clubs in town are working together to organize the event, but they need help with advertising and promotion. That's where I can step in."

"You never give up, do you?" Annie stumbled over a tree root, and Seth grabbed her arm to steady her.

His laugh was a soft rumble at her side. "When I want something as much as I want to hear you sing again, I don't."

Annie stopped and turned to face him on the narrow trail. "Okay. I'll sing one song for you." Even as the words came out of her mouth, she regretted them, but there was something about Seth that wore her down. "I'll come up to the studio before work tomorrow morning." She jerked her arm away from his hand.

"Great, that's—"

"You'll make sure my brother isn't around to listen." She picked up the pace, and her boots sprayed dirt and gravel across the path. "Since you started doing the morning show, Brendan pops up to the station all the time. I don't care what you tell him, but you can't tell him I'm singing for you."

"Done."

"I'll see you at five fifteen tomorrow morning." She coiled her toes inside her boots. She couldn't let Seth guess how much he rattled her.

"That's only fifteen minutes before you start work." His eyes narrowed.

"Fifteen minutes is all I can give you." She strode down the hill, away from him as fast as the almost vertical incline allowed.

"If I only have fifteen minutes, I want you to sing one of your songs." His voice reached her from the other side of a large sugar maple tree.

"Fine." She flung the word over her shoulder.

"Terrific." His tone was smug.

When the path levelled out, she broke into a jog to put more distance between them and sprinted through the last clump of trees to come out at the end of her street. When she stopped by Seth's truck, she had a stitch in her side and a sore spot where one of her boots had rubbed against a heel. She walked across the lawn to her front porch, all the while conscious of his gaze boring into her from the bottom of the mountain.

She took several deep breaths. She didn't have any reason to panic. It was only one song and fifteen minutes. She'd promised herself she'd try to do something with her music and maybe singing for Seth would be the first step on that path. And once she'd sung for him, her life would still be as comforting, familiar, and safe as it had been before. Nothing could happen to change it in only fifteen minutes.

She opened her front door and went into the hall. Hazel the cat and little Olivia the kitten were curled up together in Nana Gerry's favorite armchair. In the kitchen, the chicken and vegetable pie she'd made earlier was tucked in the fridge and ready to put in the oven. And when Hannah came back from that birthday party, they'd pick a movie to watch together like they did every Sunday night.

Hannah. She flinched and hugged herself. It had taken a lot less than fifteen minutes for her to get pregnant with her daughter and then to tell Todd he was going to be a father. Her fingers instinctively sought the places on her forearms where the purplish-red bruises had been. Although the marks had faded in a few weeks, the memories they'd left behind were still fresh. And that had all started with one of her songs, too.

Chapter 10

Would Annie turn up? Or would she bail on him? Seth dragged one of the dinette chairs into the studio and set a glass of water on the desk.

His phone display said five fourteen a.m. Nobody had ever sung for him so early in the morning, but nobody with a voice or a song like Annie's had ever sung for him before, either.

Dolly thumped her tail and cocked her ears toward the outside door.

Footsteps thudded on the stairs, and then Annie came through the door and into the studio with a guitar case. "I have to be quick. Brendan might have seen me come up." She glanced behind her, as if her brother might already be in pursuit.

"He won't have, not unless he can see through a floor and a flight of stairs." Seth smiled to try to put her at ease. He shouldn't have doubted her. Annie stuck to her commitments. "I messaged him to ask if he had any of that coffee cake you keep in one of the basement freezers. He said he'd go down and check. He also said he has a batch of bread in the oven so, between both of those things, he won't be coming up here anytime soon."

"Thanks." Her voice trembled.

"I brought Jake's guitar if you want to—"

"No need." Her face was as white as the sweater she wore above a pair of worn jeans that molded to her curvy hips. "I can accompany myself." She heaved the guitar case onto the desk and opened it.

"I got you a chair and water." For a second, he felt bad about pushing, but if he could help her make something of her music, it would be good for her.

She sat and clutched the guitar like a life raft.

"I'll take Dolly back to the apartment and—"

"I want Dolly to stay." She pursed her lips and eyed him up and down. Evidently, she preferred the dog's company to his right now.

"Okay, whenever you're ready." He moved behind the broadcast desk and sat in the announcer's chair. He had to take it slow. Otherwise, she'd be back down those stairs to the bakery faster than Dolly when she spotted a squirrel.

Annie strummed a few chords and shifted on the chair. Then she stood and tapped one sneaker-clad foot against the carpet. The seconds ticked away, and he held his breath. Finally, she fixed her gaze on a point above his head and started to sing.

Quiet at first, her voice then rose in tandem with the music she coaxed out of that old guitar. Even without the words, the simple tune reached straight into his chest and wrapped itself around his heart, but the words made it something more than he'd ever thought possible. Seth leaned forward and the hairs on the back of his neck lifted.

A lot of country songs were about love and loss. Except, Annie had taken that theme and made it her own. She drew him in because, although her song was about heartbreak, it held hope too, together with a raw honesty that stirred hidden parts of his soul.

As the last chord died away, Dolly, who'd stayed silent, barked and nosed Annie's knee.

"That was . . ." Seth stood and cleared his throat. "Great." Such an ineffectual word for what he'd heard, but he couldn't seem to get his mouth to shape any others.

"Thank you." Annie's voice was soft and, as she bent to pat Dolly, a curtain of hair half covered her face.

Adrenaline rushed through Seth and, for an instant, the studio spun. Not only did she have the voice of an angel, she looked like one, too. But this was about so much more than her voice or her looks. "Have you written any other songs?"

"Sure. I've fooled around with songwriting since I was younger than Hannah." Her tone was hesitant, maybe even fearful.

"Have you kept them?" He held his breath, almost giddy. If any of her other songs were even half as good as the one he'd just heard, she had the whole package. There were a lot of good singers out there, but ones who could write music and lyrics like hers were rare.

"Except for the songs I'm still working on, the others are in boxes in my attic." She straightened and put the guitar back in its case.

Seth made his tone casual to keep his excitement in check. "With the right packaging and promotion, that song could be a big hit."

Her gaze drifted to her small, understated watch. "This is Irish Falls, not Nashville. How could my little song ever be a hit?"

"It could be Nashville." His heart pounded. "A few parts of the melody are still a little rough, but I can help you with that. I also know where we can access recording space and backing musicians. Trust me, if you make a demo, once word gets out, you'll have people lining up to produce that piece for you."

"No." Her face got a grayish tinge and she backed toward the studio door. "I said I'd sing one song for you. That's it. I'm not ready for anything else. I have to get to work and—"

"Wait. Maybe you don't understand. This could be huge for you." He came around the desk to her side. "I want to help you. You're talented. Why are you hiding that talent? You need to share your songs, as well as your voice. Why not start by singing at the fundraiser?"

"It's . . . I can't." She bumped into the door, and tears glistened in the depths of her amazing eyes. "Except for my family, choir, and the kids at school, Jake was the only other person I sang alone for. At least since . . ." She hugged herself. "He got me singing again after . . . well, before I sung for you, I didn't realize I missed it so much. When you got caught up in my music, it did something to me."

It had done something to Seth too, although, right now, he couldn't analyze what. "Something bad?" He stepped around Dolly and looped a careful arm around Annie's tight shoulders.

"No, it's something I needed to face, but . . ." She gulped and covered her mouth with one hand.

"Music can heal. Jake said that to me when I was a kid." Seth squeezed her arm, and she flinched—imperceptible, but an unmistakable little quiver through her thin sweater. He took his hand away, and her body relaxed.

"He said that to me all the time, too." She gave him the ghost of a smile. "He was full of sayings, but he never gave me advice, even when I asked. He said I had to figure life out for myself."

Seth's heart constricted with a mixture of bitterness and regret. Even though he'd told himself it didn't matter, he'd missed having a dad who, even if he hadn't given advice, would have been part of his life.

"I have to go. I'll be late for work." Annie reached past him to grab the guitar case, and her light breath fanned the hair at the nape of his neck.

Seth stood rigid. If he let himself touch her, he'd be pulled into her warmth and softness like quicksand. Yet, his hand curved around her waist. Her sweater was smooth beneath his fingers, and she was so close he could—

"Annie?"

Seth jerked his hand away, and Dolly yelped.

Tara stood in the half-open studio door. "It's Duncan." Her mouth worked. "He's having chest pains. Mom called an ambulance, and he's at the hospital." She flicked a glance at Seth, her expression strained. "Brendan and Holly have to take care of the bakery, and Rowan can't leave her kids this early, but Mom needs us."

"Of course." Annie's voice shook.

Seth spoke past the tightness in his throat. "Do you want me to call anyone? Father Michael maybe?" The Quinns seemed like a family who'd appreciate the support of a man of the cloth.

"That would be great." Annie's face was pale. "Our dad . . . he died from a massive heart attack. Mom must be so scared." She propped the guitar case against the studio wall with unsteady hands.

"Duncan's got a lot of fight in him. Mom said he told the paramedics there was no reason for him to go to the hospital since he wasn't sick. He made her promise she wouldn't even call his kids yet." Tara's voice quavered. "But Mom. she's . . ."

"All alone." Annie reached her sister in two strides and held her tight.

"What's Duncan's favorite song? I'll play it on the show for him." Annie and her family had helped Jake, and they'd helped him. Even if only in a small way, he wanted to be there for them.

"He'd like anything by Johnny Cash," Annie said. "He once told me 'I Walk the Line' was the first record he bought." Her scared gaze caught his and held.

Seth's breathing quickened. "You got it. Tell Duncan I'm pulling for him. And if there's anything else I can do, text me."

"I will. Thanks." She gave a nervous laugh and turned away with Tara.

After the station door shut behind them, he moved to a computer and glanced at the show's playlist file without seeing it. He wanted to take away that desperate look in Annie's eyes—comfort her and care for her in a way he hadn't wanted to do for any woman ever. Maybe it didn't matter too much that they were both working on Jake's estate, but how could he get involved with her if he only planned to be here for six months? There was her music, too. Would she think he only wanted to get close to her because of it? He rubbed a hand across the back of his neck where the muscles were taut.

"You wanted a slice of coffee cake?"

"What?" He looked up as Brendan came through the door his sisters had just left through.

"You messaged me earlier?" Brendan held a plate in one hand with a coffee mug balanced on the edge.

"Right." He moved back around the desk to take the mug.

"I met Tara and Annie on the stairs. Scary stuff for Mom and Duncan. All of us, really." Brendan set the plate on the desk, his usually easygoing expression guarded. "What was Annie doing up here with her guitar?" He flicked a glance at the case still propped against the wall.

"Nothing important." Seth's stomach knotted. "Look, I'm going on air soon and—"

"Annie's never said much about Hannah's dad, but he hurt her." As Brendan studied him, Seth drew back. "She's never been the same as she was before she went to Nashville. When she came back here, I vowed if any guy ever hurt her again, he'd have to deal with me."

"Understood." Seth set the mug down and toyed with his headphones. He wanted to help Annie. Why would Brendan think he'd ever hurt her?

"Good." Although Brendan's tone was conversational, it also held a warning. "You should play a song for Duncan. Folks will want to wish him well."

"Already covered. Johnny Cash, 'I Walk the Line.' But I wasn't going to mention Duncan's name. He won't want folks knowing his business."

Brendan snorted. "Ten minutes after the ambulance left the house, half the town would already know where he was going. Lizzie Driscoll lives next door to Mom and Duncan, and she never misses anything, day or night. She's also the biggest talker between here and the Pennsylvania state line. If you don't mention Duncan's at the hospital, folks will think you don't like him. Small-town radio's part information and part public service, all with a personal, down-home touch."

And that was why Seth had no intention of being a small-town radio announcer or station manager any longer than he could help. Except, like Johnny Cash, he was walking a line—one between his head and his heart, and the more time he spent here and around Annie, the more that line got blurred.

~ ~ ~

Even the hospital lobby had an antiseptic smell. At this time of the morning the place was quiet, the gift shop and flower kiosk shuttered, and only one security guard sat behind the reception desk. Annie tucked her phone in her purse, glanced at the overhead signs, and tugged Tara's arm. "Mom's text said she's in the family room. It's this way. If you want to wait here, I'll find her and—"

"I'm fine." Tara dropped Annie's arm.

"No, you're not. I'm not, either." Thanks to the stomach-churning ride in Tara's Jeep, they'd made the twenty-minute drive to the district hospital in under fifteen. "But there's nothing so bad we can't face it together." Actually, there was. But Annie wouldn't let herself go there right now.

"Should we should call one of Mom's sisters?" Tara's anxious gaze met Annie's.

"No." Annie tempered the word with a smile. "If we do, before we know it, the whole family will be here. Besides, you told me Mom said Duncan didn't want her to call his kids, remember?"

"Yes, but that's different." Tara worried her bottom lip. "It's still the middle of the night on the West Coast."

"He'd have said the same even if it was afternoon. Duncan's a private person." And that was one of the reasons Annie liked him so much. He never pried into her life. She let out a breath and pushed open the door to the hospital's family waiting room. Her mom sat in a chair near the window huddled into her spring coat.

"Thank God, you're here. Duncan . . ." Her mom's voice faltered. "I lost your dad on a gurney through those doors. And now, Duncan . . . I can't . . ." Her body shook with suppressed sobs. "Do you think the nurse put me in here by myself because he's dead and they haven't told me yet?"

"Of course not." Annie slid into the chair next to her mom and rubbed her cold hands to try to warm them. "I'm sure she thought you could use a quiet place to sit, away from everyone in the emergency waiting room. She was being kind."

"Maybe." Her mom's voice broke.

"You did the right thing to call the ambulance." She glanced at Tara, who hovered inside the doorway. "You aren't going to lose Duncan. He's an active, healthy guy."

"I thought your father was, too." Her mom stared at her feet.

"You told me Duncan talked to you all the way here." Tara moved into the room and crouched by their mom's other side. "That has to be a good sign."

"Tara's right. Once the doctor checks Duncan out, I bet he'll be fine." Annie tried to make her smile encouraging.

Her mom's hands tightened around Annie's. "Maybe there's something wrong with his heart, and maybe there isn't. I told him it was too late to eat that spicy chili after bowling last night, but he insisted." She gulped. "It's not . . . this isn't all. He went to his own doctor last week, but I only found out about the appointment by accident."

Annie's muscles tensed. "Is that why you asked me to drive you to the clinic?"

Her mom gave a jerky nod. "We don't know for sure, but Duncan might have prostate cancer."

The dreaded C-word. Annie's insides clenched, and Tara sucked in a ragged breath.

"Duncan didn't want me to tell anyone, but I didn't promise. I have to talk to someone. Who else but my daughters?" Her face was gray and pinched. "We had so many plans for our retirement, but with my hip and now this . . ."

"Those plans are only delayed a bit." Annie hoped she was right. She stroked her mom's arm. "I'm sure I read somewhere that prostate cancer's really treatable these days."

"It's still cancer." Her mom bent her head and her shoulders sagged.

"It is and that's why if you tell people, they'll want to help. If Duncan knew how upset you are, he wouldn't want you going through it alone. Like when Dad passed, you need the support of your family and friends."

"Duncan doesn't want anybody to know because he's a man and, well . . ." Her cheeks went red. "He'd be uncomfortable with people, family even, talking about his . . . equipment."

"I understand but . . ." Annie stopped. She didn't understand, not really, and nothing she could say would make things better right now.

"I shouldn't even have told you two. You can't say a word." Her mom's expression was pleading as her gaze darted between Annie and Tara. "Not until we know something for sure, anyway."

"Okay." Annie exhaled. She disagreed, but getting Duncan riled up wouldn't do anybody any good, least of all him.

"Thank you, honey." Her mom forced a smile. "I don't know what I'd do without all of you living so close by. Along with Brendan, you're my comfort and joy. And after losing my babies, you three girls are an extra special blessing."

Annie's throat closed. Her mom rarely spoke about her miscarriages, or the baby boy who'd died two days after his birth when Brendan was three, but the pain of those losses still ran deep. Whenever Annie thought about leaving Irish Falls, she knew she couldn't. Even if she hadn't gotten pregnant and finished her college degree, she probably wouldn't have stayed in Nashville. Family would have pulled her back to northern New York state like a fish on a line.

"Of course we're all here for you, and Duncan, too." It was no good thinking about the paths she could have taken.

"I'm sure not going anywhere." Sadness clouded Tara's face. She patted her mom's knee and got to her feet. "Why don't I see if I can find you a cup of tea and a blanket? You're freezing."

"Thanks, honey." After the door closed behind Tara, her mom slumped back in the chair. "Some days I think she's doing better, but then the grief closes in again. I know what she's going through, but at least when I lost your dad, I had you kids as a part of him. If Tara and Adam had been able to have a child, maybe . . ."

"Yeah." The knot in Annie's stomach tightened. She wasn't the only one with paths not taken. "Tara needs time." At least she hoped that was all she needed. "She's focusing more on the positives than she used to. Like she didn't get flooded out so she still has her keepsakes."

"Compared to a lot of others, our family is blessed." Her mom glanced at the floor, where half the tiles had been pulled up. "There's even flood damage here. That fundraiser will help folks all across this valley. I heard Seth's giving free advertising spots to help spread the word."

"So he told me." She'd sung for him less than two hours ago, but it seemed like a lifetime.

"We need to do more." Her mom's expression turned thoughtful. "What do you think?"

"About what?"

"What would get younger people to take part? Every fundraiser we have is more of the same. A raffle, a dance with a few people doing karaoke, and a community garage and bake sale. Let's shake things up a bit." Her mom's voice had new strength. "Memorial Day is the first big tourist weekend of the year. What would interest visitors too?"

Her mom didn't know she'd sung for Seth. And she wasn't asking her to sing at the fundraiser. However, singing for Seth had made Annie wonder what it would be like to sing on a stage again. She was older. She didn't have stars in her eyes. She was also smarter and nobody could take away what she wouldn't give. "We don't have a lot of time to plan but maybe we could get the school involved. What about a talent show with different age groups?" Unexpected excitement coursed through her. "We could make it a real showcase for the town."

"That's a great idea." Despite her worry over Duncan, her mom beamed. "I bet Seth would be on board. He could be one of the judges or the host. It would be like 'America's Got Talent' here in Irish Falls. Not only would we raise money with entry and admission fees, but it would be fun. Maybe Seth knows someone who could headline a show. That would draw a crowd, don't you think?"

"Hang on." Annie blinked. While she'd been thinking baton twirlers and cute pet tricks, her mom envisioned an Adirondack version of the Grand Ole Opry. "For anything like that, we'd need to start small—and much earlier."

"Mrs. McNeill?" The family room door swung open. A dark-haired man wearing a white coat came in.

Aaron. Annie dredged up his name from the recesses of her memory. President of the science club in high school, a senior when she was a freshman and, based on an article in the local newspaper, he'd returned to Irish Falls last month.

"You can come through to sit with your husband. We're still running a few tests, but he hasn't had a heart attack."

"Then what?" Annie glanced at her mom.

"I'm thinking anxiety and maybe indigestion from something he ate." Aaron, now Dr. Aaron Lafontaine, according to the name tag pinned to his coat, smiled. "Do you know if he's worried about anything? He won't tell me."

Her mom exhaled with what sounded like a mix of relief and frustration. "What isn't Duncan worrying about? He seems like such an easygoing guy, but underneath it's a different story." She raised an eyebrow at Annie. "When Tara comes back with that tea, you drink it. You're as big a worrier as Duncan and me put together, and right now you look real wound up. A nice hot drink will settle you right down."

If only it was so easy. After her mom had left with Aaron, Annie sat back in the chair.

Until now, the ties that held her to Irish Falls had never been a burden. But instead of bonds she cherished, and almost without her noticing, they'd begun to chafe and pull her tight. If she sang on a stage again, would it set her free, or would it only be a poignant and painful reminder of what she missed most and had let slip through her fingers?

Chapter 11

"So, what's going on with you and the hot radio guy?" From the treadmill beside Annie's at the Valley Fitness Center, Rowan puffed out the words.

"Nothing." At least that was what Annie wanted her sisters and everyone else to believe.

"We won't push you if you don't want to tell us." Rowan slid her the kind of sideways glance that usually got Annie to open up.

"It didn't look like nothing to me that morning Duncan went to the hospital." Despite having her treadmill set to an incline and at jogging speed, Tara had barely broken a sweat. "Those were some sparks you and Seth were giving off in the station."

Annie pressed her lips together because it'd been over a week since she'd sung for him, and whenever she was around Seth—and she was around him a lot—she was hyperaware of those same sparks. "Seth asked me to sing at the flood relief fundraiser. We're friends, and we both like music." *I don't believe that so why should my sisters?* She kept to a steady walk, and the even vibration of the treadmill beneath her feet grounded her.

"That's a great idea. You should go for it. There's nothing to be scared of." Rowan's tone was encouraging.

"I'm not scared." Scared was too mild a word for the terror that engulfed Annie at the thought of singing in public again. "I don't even sing solos in church. Why would I sing at the fundraiser? Now we've added a talent show, the whole town and a lot of visitors will be there." Although the event wasn't the Grand Ole Opry, it had nevertheless quickly taken on a life of its own and seemed to get bigger by the day.

"We know you can do it. Besides, it will also help the hospital and, with Duncan's biopsy, it's a great time to show your support." Even when she exercised, not a hair on Tara's head was ever out of place.

"I'm already showing my support in lots of ways." Annie shoved her sweat-dampened hair off the back of her neck. "Who's organizing the talent show, for a start?"

"You." Rowan slid her that glance again. "And the hot radio guy."

"Why don't you and Seth sing together?" Tara jogged faster and gave Annie a cheeky grin. "A guy like him would have women throwing bills at the stage as soon as he opened his mouth. Mom told you she thought the town should have something fun, didn't she?"

"Please. This fundraiser started out as a church event." Except, Tara was right. Seth was the most exciting man to land in Irish Falls in years, maybe ever. And he had offered to sing with her or accompany her if she wanted him to.

"It's not like Seth would be taking his clothes off. Mind you, from what I've heard around town, a lot of women wouldn't complain if he did." Tara chuckled.

Rowan reached over and patted Annie's shoulder. "We're only teasing. Forget about Seth. Maybe you need to sing at that fundraiser for you."

Annie stared at her purple running shoes. Her sisters understood her inside and out—both the blessing and curse of their close bond. "Maybe I do, but . . ." She studied her reflection in the gym's mirrored wall. If she was going to get up on a stage, and even though it would only be at the Black Duck, she'd have to get a haircut and find something to wear to hide that extra ten pounds she couldn't seem to shift, no matter how many miles she walked on this machine.

"But what? You're gorgeous." Tara sobered. "All you have to do is believe it."

And that was the hard part. Her confidence had taken a big hit all those years ago, and she'd never truly gotten it back. "Singing in front of all those people would be way out of my comfort zone." Annie stepped up the pace until her lungs burned.

"What's the worst that could happen?" Rowan's gaze sharpened. "It isn't about the singing, not really. It's about facing your fears." She took several gasping breaths. "I should know. I'm not there yet, but you are."

"I should be." Annie's stomach tightened. She'd kept herself hidden away for so long that maybe the fears had gotten bigger. "I appreciate you both care about me." She raised her voice above the noise of the exercise equipment. "But I swear, there's nothing going on between Seth and me." Even though she couldn't stop thinking about him.

"Annie?" Tara's usually soft voice was almost shrill.

"What?" She flipped the treadmill dial to a higher setting. "Seth's a friend, that's all. I'm not having sex with him or anyone else." There had to be an easier way to burn fat and get in shape. The treadmill noise on either side of her stopped, and her breath was loud in the sudden silence.

"Hey, Annie."

That deep Southern voice was the same one she heard on the radio every morning. Her head jerked up. Seth stood in front of her treadmill, wearing black gym shorts and a white T-shirt. He had a gym bag slung over one shoulder, his dark hair curled against his neck, and his skin had a healthy flush.

"Hey." She hit the treadmill dial again and staggered to a halt. Her face burned. "What are you doing here?" Her and her big mouth. He must have heard what she'd said, right down to the fact she wasn't having sex with him—which might give him the idea she'd thought about it. She cringed.

"I use the weight room here. This is the only gym in town." He nodded at Tara and Rowan before his gaze slid back to Annie.

"Tara and I were about to hit the showers." Rowan gave Annie a speculative look. "Tara?"

Tara glanced at Annie, too. "Right. See you at work in the morning."

"But you said you wanted . . ." Annie's stomach fluttered, and she scratched a black fly bite on the inside of her wrist.

"Change of plans." Tara grabbed her water bottle from the holder and raised her eyebrows. "Rowan and I have to make tracks."

And where was her sisterly support when she needed it? Annie took the towel she'd hung over the treadmill and wrapped it around her shoulders. Although her workout gear—a gray tank top and black leggings—wasn't revealing, in front of Seth, she felt as exposed as if she'd been naked.

She slugged water to ease her dry throat. "Rowan and Tara mean well, but they can, you know, get involved in stuff that's none of their business." She'd lived with that mixture of love and interference her whole life, but despite how it sometimes irritated her, she couldn't imagine being without it.

"That sounds a lot like small-town life, too." Seth grinned, and the twinkle in his eyes eased Annie's tight breathing.

"You're new in town, and there's not a lot going on, so people like to talk. But it's also part of being sisters. Tara and Rowan always have my back and that's great, but, before you know it, closeness can turn into nosiness."

"It's okay." At the tenderness in his expression, her knees went weak. "But just so you know, you may not be having sex with me, but I'm glad you're not having it with anyone else right now, either." His lips tilted into a smile that could have melted her into a puddle right there on the treadmill.

Annie tried to smile back like what he'd said was a joke, instead of something that could change everything about their relationship that wasn't a relationship. "I should . . . uh . . ." She gestured in the direction of the locker room.

He studied her for a moment, then detachment replaced the tenderness. "Before you go, have you thought any more about singing at the fundraiser? If you're going to do it, I can help you work on your song."

She took a shaky breath. Seth was as persistent as Dolly following a scent, but Rowan was right. She had to face her fears, and if she did, it would help her daughter, too. "I'll do it, but only if Hannah sings backup vocals and you accompany us." She needed to sing for herself but having Seth and Hannah there too would give her courage.

"You . . . I'd be honored." He leaned toward her and took a step closer. "It's a deal."

"My mom said we needed to find something fun. That's why I thought of the talent show, but if the three of us do a special number, we could close the evening." She stepped off the treadmill, and her legs were like jelly. "Folks love your radio show, and Hannah's pestered me for months to let her get up on the Black Duck stage. She's already entered the talent show, but she wants to do more. If she sings with me, she can." She made herself give him an impersonal smile. "What do you think?"

"It's great." His voice hitched. "You won't regret it."

Sweat not from her workout trickled between her breasts. "You don't know that." And she already regretted too much.

"No, but what I do know is I don't want anybody or anything to hurt you, or Hannah, either." His eyes darkened to a smoky blue-gray. "If you two are sharing that stage with me, I'll have your backs. Not like your sisters do, of course, but as much as I can."

She didn't doubt his sincerity, but she also needed to make sure he understood. "It's more than being on stage."

The silence stretched between them, and she had to force her mouth to shape the next words. "It's Hannah. She's young and impressionable, and she has big dreams." Her eyes smarted. Her daughter also had stars in her eyes, and when she talked about the future, it always came up roses with no thought of thorns lurking amidst those beautiful bright blooms. "She's a lot like I was at her age. I don't want anybody to give her false expectations so I . . . I need your help."

"You got it." Seth's voice was rough.

"Thanks." Annie pushed her shoulders back, realizing too late the gesture also pushed out her breasts.

"Tell me what you need." His gaze drifted to her chest then slid back to her face. "And what you're thinking." He leaned even closer and trailed an index finger across the curve of her cheek.

Even though she might want to, she couldn't. The blood pounded in her ears, and she stared mutely at him before she mumbled something unintelligible then turned away and headed to the locker room.

~ ~ ~

Something about Irish Falls had crumbled Seth's defenses. Or maybe it was Annie, the woman he'd barely stopped thinking about since she'd almost run from him at the gym two days before.

To keep himself from looking at her yet again, he glanced around her living room instead. Blue and green pillows were piled on a taupe sofa, and a wooden rocking chair, holding a rag doll, sat in a sunny corner by a set of French doors. A leafy potted palm stood beside an upright piano, and several red and white geranium plants perched atop a low bookcase stuffed with books and music. From the two cats snuggled into an armchair in the front hall to the rustic wicker furniture on the porch, Annie's home was more storybook adorable than designer sleek, and it suited her.

He straightened the penciled sheet music on the stand in front of him. "Do you want to take it from the top again?" If he focused on music, his mind wouldn't wander to other things, like how comfortable he was not only in this house, but also with Annie and her daughter.

Hannah gave a little skip, and her red hair bounced around her shoulders. "Whatever you say." She glanced at Annie. "Mom?"

"Sure." Annie's expression was guarded, and there was a worried crease between her eyebrows.

Seth adjusted the strap on Jake's Gibson and tapped out the beat with his foot. Annie's voice rose in the first notes of her song, and he drew in a breath. She was a dream to accompany, with an instinctive feel for the music. And each note that had come out of her mouth since they'd begun rehearsing had confirmed his first impression. She had a huge talent, and it was wasted in Irish Falls.

His fingers caressed the guitar strings like Jake's once had. He might not have any time for the man who'd fathered him, but whether he liked it or not, holding the guy's Gibson made an intangible, but irrevocable, connection between them. He nodded at Hannah, and she grinned before her voice joined Annie's. He'd worked out a new arrangement so Hannah could sing backup vocals, leaving Annie's melody unchanged but adding depth, or what he thought of as light and shade, to the deceptively simple tune.

He concentrated on the music and a tricky bit of harmony as Hannah's voice blended with her mom's. The teen was an alto, not mezzo-soprano, and her singing had a different timbre. But, like Annie, Hannah had a spark. And although only sixteen, she already had the looks and personality to light up a stage.

He'd promised Annie she wouldn't regret singing at the fundraiser, and he'd promised himself he wouldn't push her, or Hannah, either. But he couldn't stand by without at least trying to help and if he opened the door, opportunities would surely follow.

Annie held the final note, and her powerful voice resonated in the quiet room until he played the last chord.

"Did I sing that last part like you wanted?" Hannah's eyes sparkled and she bounced on her bare feet.

"You were fabulous." Seth gave her a high five. "Both of you are going to be a big hit at that fundraiser."

Hannah hugged Annie. "You're the best mom ever to let me do this. It's a dream come true." She turned to Seth. "I don't know what you said to my mom to convince her to do this, but thanks."

"I don't think I said anything." Except, maybe he'd helped her begin to believe in herself again, if only a little. But no matter why Annie had changed her mind, he was glad she had.

"It was okay, really?" Uncertainty and vulnerability mingled in Annie's voice.

"More than okay. The two of you are terrific."

He had a lot of reasons to be pissed off at Jake, but he was grateful to him for at least one thing. Without his legacy, Seth would never have come to Irish Falls and met this woman with a talent that blew him away, even as it humbled him. And if she sang at the Black Duck like she had today in her living room, she couldn't go back to only singing on Sundays in the church choir or helping out with music at the school.

Annie flushed. "Thanks."

"What's your song called? It's not on the music I'm using to accompany you and since I'm hosting the show too, I have to announce you."

"It's . . ." Annie glanced at Hannah, whose fingers darted over her phone's keypad. "I call it 'My Hometown Heart' because, in a way, it's about Irish Falls."

And the song was as natural and without artifice as she was today in faded jeans and a blue top with a little ruffle at the hem. Her tongue darted out to lick her lower lip. Even though Hannah was right there and, despite all the reasons he shouldn't let himself be attracted to Annie, warmth flooded Seth's body. The chaste kiss on her soft cheek he couldn't forget hung between them.

"Don't you think it's a great name?" Hannah bumped his shoulder. "For Mom, I mean. If it were my song, it would be lame, but for her it's perfect."

"It *is* perfect." Like her. His fingers tingled, and he took a step back.

"I have a great idea." Hannah's grin was as open and uncomplicated as Dylan's used to be. "Most of the kids at my school listen to your show, and when I told them how you sang for us at my grandma's house, a bunch of them want to hear you sing, too."

"Hannah—" Annie shot her daughter a warning glance.

"Hear me out before you say no. I think you and Mom should sing 'Country on the Radio' together. You know, that Blake Shelton song?" She hummed a few bars and swayed in time. "Grandma's a huge Blake Shelton fan. It's real embarrassing sometimes, but she'd love it if you sang one of his songs. Since you play country music on the station, that song is perfect, don't you think? I have the music." Hannah gave him a hopeful look, mixed with the kind of face Seth remembered Dylan making a few years back. Like adults were a different species and teenagers only tolerated them because they were a source of food, money, and rides to wherever the kid wanted to go.

"Seth is already accompanying us and hosting the show. Maybe he doesn't want to do anything more." Annie's face flushed as rosy as her geraniums.

"Sure, why not? It would be fun," Seth said. "Besides, when we first talked about the fundraiser, I said I'd be happy to sing with you." And since Irish Falls was like the town in Blake's song, Hannah's idea was clever and sweet. He and Annie would bring the house down if they closed the show with it. "What do you say, Annie-Bella?"

Her breath stuttered. "Okay."

"Only family call my mom Annie-Bella." Hannah glanced between them, her expression quizzical.

"I'm sorry, I—"

"It's fine." Annie sat on the piano bench and shuffled sheet music.

Seth rubbed the back of his neck. Her nickname had slipped out, but somehow it felt as right as her house and everything else about her.

"Since this fundraiser is about helping families and bringing everyone together, why don't you invite your son to come and see the show?" Annie half turned on the bench. "Can he get time off work for the Memorial Day weekend?"

Seth's heart constricted. "I asked him about visiting a while back, but he's got plans with his girlfriend and her family."

"Oh." Her expression was thoughtful. "Well, if you want to go and see him after the weekend, I could ask Steve if he's free to cover the show for you if it's only a few days. You must want to go back to LA, too. When you came here, you didn't expect to stay long. You must need to pick up clothes and whatever."

"I had some things shipped out." Like Jake, Seth travelled light and, for everything else, there was online shopping. Although he didn't want to go to LA, he did want to see his son. Maybe Dylan's plans had changed since that one stilted phone call. And if he could talk to him face-to-face, he'd have a better chance of fixing what had gone wrong between them.

"It's too bad Dylan can't be here, but since you won't be spending time with him, you have to join our family's

Memorial Day barbecue." Along with the chirpy tone in her voice, Hannah's riot of curly red hair and big eyes were an irresistible combination. "My grandma always says the more the merrier. Holidays are huge in our family. Even Groundhog Day is an event."

"Hannah." Annie sat rigid on the piano bench, with a panicked expression.

"I appreciate the thought, but we'll see." Seth tried to smile at Hannah. He'd never been big on holidays, large or small, although he'd made an effort when Dylan was little. "If we're going to sing 'Country on the Radio,' we'd better practice it." He grabbed the guitar and strummed a few chords. Music would get his mind back where it belonged, and the strings against his fingers soothed him like they always did.

He had to fix the mess he'd made of his own family before he got involved with someone else's. He moved to the far side of the room and gazed out the French doors into Annie's backyard, where a robin drank from a stone bird bath.

"Whatever's gone wrong between you and Dylan, it'll be all right." Annie's voice was soft at his side. "I always tell Hannah that no matter how bad you think things are, you always have a chance to start over."

"You think so?" He blinked and his throat burned. He wasn't used to feeling so off balance—with his son, work, and, most of all, a woman.

"I'm sure of it." She touched his arm, gentle but fleeting.

Seth gulped. "Thanks." He'd tried to convince himself there was no place for a woman in his life, at least not now. But he already knew life didn't always happen the way you expected. Maybe he couldn't let himself think about opening up his life to Annie, but he also didn't want to think about what it would be like to leave here and leave her behind.

Chapter 12

"You look fantastic." Sitting cross-legged on the end of Annie's bed, with her elbows on a stack of blue and white ruffled pillows, Tara gave her a warm smile.

"Awesome." Holly hovered beside Annie.

Annie considered herself in the mirror on the back of the closet door. The jeans Tara had helped her pick out, on their shopping trip to the outlet mall in Lake George, hugged her hips and accentuated curves she'd forgotten she had. "Maybe this top is too low cut." She turned sideways and sucked in her stomach by instinct.

"Not with a rack like yours." Next to Tara on the bed, Rowan's voice was amused. "Most of the time I see you in a Quinn's apron, so I'd almost forgotten what you've got underneath. It's not only your voice that's going to give Irish Falls a show."

"Drop it, Rowan." Her sister had hit on one of the many things Annie was afraid of. The jade top Tara had also insisted she buy had a scoop neck edged with tiny silver sparkles and was even more formfitting than the jeans. She craned her head over her shoulder to get a back view.

Tara got up from the bed and lifted Annie's hair away from her neck. "I'll put your hair up, but if I leave a few curls to brush your shoulders, you'll look so sexy you'll knock Seth off his boots." She gave a throaty laugh.

"Assuming Annie wants to knock the guy sideways." Rowan got up, too, and swung her purse by its strap.

"Why wouldn't she?" Holly patted Annie's bare

shoulders. "You look beautiful, honey, and you'll sing like an angel on Saturday night. We'll all be there to cheer you on."

"Thank you." But having her whole family there was another kind of stress. What if she disappointed them, as well as herself?

"I'm sorry I teased you." Rowan blew Annie a kiss. "I have to go because the kids have soccer practice tonight, but you totally rock that outfit. You're going to rock the Black Duck, too." Her footsteps clattered on the uncarpeted stairs, then the front door banged behind her.

"I should head out, too. It's nearly suppertime, and my guys need to be fed." Holly hugged Annie. "You can do this. Don't doubt yourself and don't let old hurts stop you from trying new things. Go for it. Won't you always wonder 'what if,' if you don't?"

As Holly waggled her fingers in a good-bye, unexpected tears pricked at the backs of Annie's eyes. Leave it to Holly to cut through the noise and get to the heart of the issue—her heart, too. She swallowed the lump in her throat that was as much from the tenderness in Holly's voice as about the memories that still made her fearful of drawing attention to herself.

"I love Irish Falls, and I love my life here." Annie fumbled with the bags her new clothes had been packed in.

"Nobody says you don't." Tara's tone was gentle. "But Holly's right and, if you ask me, maybe you've wondered 'what if' for years. Lately, though, you get this look in your eyes like you're thinking about being somewhere else."

"Don't be ridiculous." Annie padded to the bedroom window.

The leaves on the two big maple trees that guarded the backyard like sentinels had begun to fill out, and the lilac bushes by the back porch had fragrant purple blooms.

"Even though Irish Falls is home, you can still leave it

and spread your wings. Like I did with Adam." Tara's mouth trembled.

Annie looped a comforting arm around her sister. "I spread my wings when I went to Nashville. Besides, it's not like I'm trapped here. I leave all the time. We went shopping today, didn't we?"

"Today doesn't count, and if you'd truly spread your wings, you'd have been able to finish college and work somewhere else but the bakery." There was a hint of exasperation in Tara's tone. "Apart from the time you and Hannah went to Disney World with Mom and Duncan, when did you last travel anywhere out of state for more than a day or two? Rowan and I wanted you to come to Toronto with us last year, but you wouldn't."

"Only because I didn't want to leave Hannah. She had her first summer job." Once, her daughter had been too small, and now Annie fretted about what the teen might get up to in her absence. "You also know money's tight for me. I have to save for Hannah's future." Annie's stomach hardened.

"That's why everything I found for you was on sale. You'll look like a million dollars for under a hundred bucks." Tara's smile was smug. "Those sparkly earrings I used to wear for parties will look perfect with that top, and you can borrow my black heels."

"What do you mean used to wear? You'll wear those earrings again." Annie studied her reflection again in the mirror.

"Nope. You can have them." Sadness lurked behind Tara's bright smile.

"I . . . you . . ."

"Leave it, okay?" Tara bit her lip. "It's your time to shine."

"Adam wouldn't have—"

"Adam's not here." Tara's clipped voice came from inside the closet where she rummaged for empty hangers.

"True, but—"

"I'll bring my shoes to work tomorrow." She cut Annie off again. "You need to practice walking in heels before Saturday."

"What if I fall on my butt?" Apart from Jake's funeral, Annie couldn't remember the last time she'd worn any shoes except sneakers.

"You'll get right back up and show everyone what we Quinn girls are made of." Tara's mouth curved into a lopsided smile. "And before you say anything else, it's easier for me to give you advice than take it myself, even though I might need it." She handed Annie the hangers and moved toward the bedroom door. "If you're really worried about the shoes, you could wear those old boots on the shelf in your basement. I don't know why you don't take them to Goodwill. You never wear them."

Annie's heart gave a sickening thud. She'd learn to walk in Tara's heels if it killed her. She hadn't worn those boots in almost seventeen years, and she didn't plan to ever wear them again, but she kept them as a reminder of what and who she didn't want to be. She followed her sister down the stairs. "You'll still come over on Saturday and help me get ready?"

"Of course." Tara slipped into the pair of vertiginous cobalt blue heels she'd bought earlier. "I'll even make sure Hannah doesn't wear too much makeup, seeing as she's not likely to listen to you."

"Like Nana Gerry always said, less is more." Annie made herself smile.

"Except when it comes to a guy like Seth. Then more is so much more." Tara's answering smile turned wicked. "When you get nervous about the show, remember the women in the audience won't be looking at you. With how Seth heats up the airwaves, can you imagine what he'll be like on stage?"

Annie didn't have to imagine it. She glimpsed it every time they rehearsed together, and it dug up emotions she thought she'd made peace with. A shiver coursed through her. Couldn't, shouldn't, wouldn't. She repeated the words in her head. Yet, in spite of everything, she was still drawn to him way more than she should be—in life, as well as music.

~ ~ ~

On Friday morning, Seth tucked the cardboard box under the desk in his small office at the station. Would Annie be as happy with his surprise as Tara said, or had he overstepped one of those invisible barriers she put up between them at every turn?

Summertime tunes from the lunchtime oldies show washed over him as he turned to the computer to answer e-mails. In a few hours, the Memorial Day weekend would kick off for families all across the country, but so far, Seth's phone had stayed silent. And each time he thought about Dylan heading to the Hamptons, his heart squeezed a little more.

"Tara said you wanted to talk to me." Annie's voice came from outside the half-open office door. "Did you hear from your son?"

He swiveled in his chair and gestured her to come in and sit beside him. "No, not yet."

"You have to keep trying." Her tone was encouraging, although Seth couldn't feel encouraged.

"I will." Except, Dylan was an adult, and if he didn't want to talk, Seth couldn't force him to. "We used to be close, but now I don't think he wants me in his life. He's caught up with his girlfriend—a whole new life, really."

"You're his dad. Nobody can replace you."

Apart from a guy who could help him get a job and a girlfriend whose folks had the kind of summer place Seth had grown up with. He exhaled. He should be happy Dylan had those opportunities.

"He thought I was interfering in his life, but I wanted to look out for him. When he went to college, it was his first time away from home, and I thought . . ." Whatever he'd thought and then said were wrong.

"I bet Dylan thought, too." Annie's tone was understanding. "You'll work it out. Be patient."

But patience wasn't something Seth was good at. "I was going to text him again, but . . ."

"Go ahead, but don't sound like you're pushing. Be friendly and low key. Tell him about the station and other stuff here. If he knows you have your own life, maybe he'll share more of his." She gave a self-deprecating shrug. "What do I know? I have a daughter who doesn't want to go to college and won't listen much to me, either."

"You know more than me. Until this past year, Dylan was a pretty easy kid. I thought I'd gotten through the teen years fine, but he saved all the teenage rebellion for college." He gave her a bemused smile. Annie wore an apron patterned with an American flag overtop denim shorts and a white T-shirt. She also sported a pair of sparkly red, white, and blue sneakers. "I didn't think people got dressed up for Memorial Day."

"Remember Hannah said holidays in our family are big? Dressing up is part of that. My dad started it when we were little, because he thought it helped customers get in the holiday spirit. At Christmas, I wear reindeer antlers for two weeks." She gave him a sheepish grin. "If you'd turned up here a few weeks earlier, you'd have seen me in Easter Bunny ears."

Now that was a sight he'd have enjoyed. "Did you have a cottontail, too?" He choked back a laugh. Over the past while, they'd fallen into this kind of teasing that was not only fun but had an unanticipated sexy edge.

"No." Her grin broadened. "And don't even think about it or give Brendan ideas for next year." Her face flushed before her smile slipped away. "Because of Adam, we have a special reason to mark Memorial Day." She fiddled with her apron ties and gazed out the office window, where flags and bunting were draped from each storefront.

"Yeah." How would he have coped if Dylan had wanted to join the military? At least, so far, he was thankful he hadn't had to find out. "You look tired." Her eyes were purple-shadowed and her shoulders hunched forward.

"We baked and iced three hundred cupcakes this morning to fill advance orders for the weekend. I'm used to standing all day, but that kitchen gets hot." She shrugged and winced.

He couldn't imagine that many cupcakes, and his heart filled with tenderness and something else. "You better not be scheduled to work tomorrow. You need to be well rested before you sing."

"I will be." Her tone was amused. "Tara, Rowan, and Holly have researched performance tips for singers so, as well as monitoring what I eat and how much I sleep, they've got me gargling with warm salt water and using this special throat spray Tara ordered off the Internet to coat my vocal cords." There was an appealing twinkle in her eyes. "Humoring them is easier than arguing. Besides, I'd have to use my voice to argue. Tara and Holly won't even let me serve at the counter today because I'd have to talk to people, so there's no way they're letting me anywhere near the bakery tomorrow."

"Singing at the fundraiser's important, and they're looking out for you like they should."

Annie looked out for everyone else more than she looked out for herself.

He reached under the desk and pulled out the cardboard box. "I got something to wish you luck."

"A present?" The words came out in a whisper, and she took the box from him like it held dynamite. "You shouldn't have."

"I wanted to."

She was a good friend to him. This was a friendly gift, nothing more. His stomach contracted at the lie.

Annie set the box on the desk and pulled at the brown paper and tape.

"I bet you won't guess what's inside." Not if Tara had kept the secret.

She lifted the lid and pulled out sheets of packing tissue. "It's . . . you gave me . . ." Her face crumpled, and she took one of the boots and hugged it to her chest.

"You can't get up there and sing without a decent pair of boots." His voice was gruff. "Tara told me your size so they should fit. She also helped me pick out the pair she thought you'd like."

"They're beautiful." She stroked the soft brown leather with the braided detail up one side, and a tear rolled down her cheeks. "But I can't accept them. They're too expensive. I've borrowed a pair of Tara's shoes." Her voice cracked.

"There's no way I'm sending these boots back. You were good to Jake. Consider it a thank you. Besides, Tara told me you can't walk properly in her shoes, so how are you going to get up on stage and sing?"

"I'll manage." She touched one boot with a gentle finger. "These are perfect, but I still can't . . ." She stopped and made a choked sound.

"Hey." Seth reached over and gave her a one-armed hug. "Don't cry. Tara said you'd be thrilled. We never meant to upset you."

"Tara doesn't . . ." Annie sniffed and swiped a hand across her face. "Tara doesn't know, but Hannah's dad gave me a pair of boots a long time ago. He said if I stuck with him and did what he wanted, I'd make it big in Nashville, and the boots were supposed to be for luck. They weren't. They didn't bring me anything but bad luck."

Seth flinched at the tortured expression on Annie's face and hurt in her eyes. He'd like to take out the guy who'd made her look like that—who'd destroyed her self-belief and made her question her talent. "What happened back then is the past. Singing at the fundraiser is a new start. These boots can be part of that. And I'll be right beside you, along with Hannah."

"But what if I fail? Every time I think about it, I feel like I'm going to throw up."

"You won't fail as long as you try. And if something doesn't work out, you'll pick yourself up and try again." Like he was doing with Dylan and in Irish Falls. "I'll ask the bartender at the Black Duck to put a bucket by the mike." Although he was teasing, Seth kept his voice gentle.

"Very funny." She gave him a faint smile and wrapped her arms around her stomach. "I thought I was over what happened with Hannah's dad, but maybe I'm not. He . . ." Her mouth tightened. "He was nice at first. I thought he was the best thing to ever happen to me. But then . . . he changed. By that time, I'd gotten sucked in and couldn't get out. When I got pregnant, he was so mad. He told me I had to get rid of the baby . . . otherwise . . ." She shivered. "I was young and scared, but I couldn't."

"Did he hurt you? I mean . . . physically?" Seth's body tensed, and heat flashed through him. The guy had sure hurt her emotionally, but those were the scars that couldn't be seen. He clenched his fists.

Her chin jerked.

"Did you call the police or talk to anyone at your school?"

She shook her head. "Mom wanted me to, but I didn't think anyone would believe me. I was so scared and Todd made me feel . . . worthless, stupid even." Her voice was rough and laced with pain.

The backs of Seth's eyes burned and he dug his nails into his palms. "How did you get away from him?"

"One evening we were at the restaurant where I worked weekends, and Todd was talking to some guys. I slipped out to go the bathroom and then . . . I ran. I took the first chance I had to keep me and my baby safe. Except for my purse, and what I was wearing and the boots on my feet, I left everything else behind in my dorm room. I made it to the bus station and called Mom. She bought me a ticket on the first bus heading north, and I came home. I gave up my scholarship. I was pregnant and sick and couldn't even take my finals."

His stomach rolled. He couldn't comprehend what Annie's life had been like then. It was a miracle she'd survived. "You're an inspiration." He swallowed. "Hannah's lucky to have you."

"I'm lucky to have her, too." Her breathing rasped. "She doesn't know the details, but she knows her dad didn't want her, or me, either. She knows he wasn't a good man."

"You did what you had to do keep yourself safe." Seth pushed the words out. His throat was raw, his chest heavy. "And you kept Hannah safe, too. You're a good mom, and Hannah's a great girl. That's all that matters."

At least Jake had been part of his life for a little while and he'd cared for his mom when she'd needed him. Even though he'd made some big mistakes, Jake must have cared for him, too. He'd never have left him the station if he hadn't. It was easy to judge, but he hadn't walked Jake's path. And compared to Todd, Jake had been a prince.

He unclenched his stiff fists. How could a guy treat a woman like Todd had treated Annie? He'd heard stuff like that happened, but he'd never known anyone it had happened to—or at least who'd talked about it happening. He swallowed several times. "Hannah told me her dad had never been in her life. If that's the case, and if he didn't come after you right away, he won't bother you." Seth's throat closed again.

"Maybe so, but I can't . . . some of that fear is still there, even now." The words were ripped out of her in a harsh cry. "Todd took a lot of things from me, but there's no way he'll ever take my daughter." She grabbed a tissue from the box on the desk and shredded it.

The heaviness in Seth's chest spread to his stomach. That was why Annie was as good as hiding out here. "Is what happened with Todd why you stopped singing?"

"Yeah." Her voice was low and her expression haunted. "I'd do anything to protect Hannah and singing at this fundraiser—it's public, you know?"

Seth sucked in a sharp breath, his heart breaking for her and what she'd gone through. "You haven't heard from him in what, sixteen years?"

"Almost seventeen." There was a new strength in her voice. "I never told him where I came from. Back then, I was ashamed of being from a place like Irish Falls, and I sort of let him think I was from California. He wasn't interested, so I didn't talk about my family, but there was also something about him I didn't trust. I should have listened to my instincts."

"You were still smart." Seth took Annie's cold hands. "I bet Todd moved on as soon as you left town. He didn't want a baby, and guys like him are scum. The way he hurt you, he probably hurt other women, too. If he's not dead, he should be in jail. Did you ever try to find out what happened to him?"

"Once." Her mouth twisted. "When Nana Gerry died, she left me some money. I used it to hire a private investigator, but beyond the first few years, and apart from some bars where Todd worked and a band he was part of, nothing else turned up. The PI said maybe Todd was using a different name or Smith wasn't his real name in the first place. Apparently, it's surprisingly easy for people to disappear." Her tone was bitter.

"Maybe he didn't want to be found any more than you did."

"But even so, how did I get taken in? And once I saw what was happening, why didn't I leave right away?" Annie's hands shook. "Todd was handsome and charming, though, and I thought . . . he told me he'd help me make it big and I didn't need college. I trusted him."

Seth's stomach roiled. "You can't blame yourself. You were young. He took advantage of you." His ex-wife had lots of dreams, too, and although she'd liked the idea of a baby, the reality was different. But at least Dylan knew who his mom was and Amanda had always tried to have some kind of relationship with him. "I understand if singing at the fundraiser is too much for you and—"

"No." She took one hand away from his and raised a gentle finger to his lips. "I have enough regrets. I don't want to regret not singing tomorrow night, too." She straightened her shoulders. "You may have to scrape me off the stage after it's over, but if I don't sing, I'll never be truly free of Todd or able to let go of how he made me feel." Her laugh was hollow. "Besides, these are kickass boots. It would be a shame to waste them."

"Then don't." Seth squeezed Annie's hand. "Have you talked to anyone else about this?"

"My sisters a bit, but not really." Her eyes were enormous—and haunted—in her white face. "I wanted to forget about what happened. Mom and Brendan said I should get child support, but I never wanted it. Today, though, these boots from you . . . they reminded me . . ." She shrugged, and her expression was bleak.

"I understand." His chest constricted because he understood more than he wanted. And he was falling for her—falling so hard maybe he was already a goner. But too many ugly things had happened to her and, like him, she had too many memories of things she'd left behind, as well as too many fears.

He could look out for her and help her with her music. And maybe, with some of his industry contacts, he could do some digging so that no matter if he was dead or alive, she could put Todd out of her life once and for all.

But for Annie's sake, as well as his own, he couldn't let himself fall any further, or hope for anything beyond friendship.

Chapter 13

"Breathe, Mom." Hannah flipped her hair away from her face and tapped one foot in time to the cheers for the Irish dance troupe, whose talent-show winning performance had brought the audience to its feet. "Chill and feel the energy from the crowd."

"Shouldn't that be my line?" Annie forced the words out. She could barely speak, so how could she get up on that stage in a few minutes and sing?

She scanned the Black Duck. For tonight's show, the staff had opened the folding doors between the bar and restaurant to make one big space. Red, white, and blue bunting hung from the ceiling, and each round table was decorated with a small American flag stuck in a Mason jar with lilacs and greenery. The scent of the spring flowers mingled with the aroma of hot dogs, burgers, and fries.

"You're gonna be great." Hannah squeezed her hand. "I'll love you forever for letting me do this."

"I'm your mother. You have to love me forever." But as Annie laughed, the thick blanket of fear that had enveloped her since before she'd gotten out of bed that morning eased. She could do this. She'd sung to bigger crowds than this one. Her family and friends were here, and they loved her, whether she sang a note or not. They wouldn't betray her, either. And since telling Seth about Todd, she felt lighter than she had for years, maybe ever.

"You're not too disappointed about coming third in the talent show?" She studied Hannah's face. Her daughter hadn't seemed upset, but Annie had to be sure.

"Nope." Hannah gave her a half-smile. "Sure, I'd liked to have won, but those dancers are great. And what chance did I have against Mr. Flaherty and his dog in their routine with top hats?"

Annie laughed. "You're a good sport, and I'm proud of you."

"I'm proud of you, too." Hannah's voice was serious.

Annie's eyes smarted, and the crowd clapped again as Seth came to the front of the stage, a microphone in one hand and Jake's Gibson slung over his other shoulder. "You've been a great audience tonight, and we've raised a lot of money for folks who need it."

As he thanked everyone, from the mayor to the PTA, Annie's breath got short again and she stared at her boots. New boots, new start. She repeated the words in her head in two-two time.

"We've got a special treat for you now."

She looked up and met Seth's gaze on the stage above her. His white shirt glowed in the spotlight and black jeans hugged his thighs. "Annie Quinn had the idea for this talent show, and she's worked harder than anyone to put it together. Now she and her daughter, Hannah, are going to sing for us. And what's even better is they're singing a song Annie wrote. Let's give a big Irish Falls welcome to two hometown girls singing 'My Hometown Heart.' Annie and Hannah Quinn."

Annie sucked air into her constricted lungs and reached for Seth's hand to navigate the few steps up to the stage.

"The first time I heard this song, I knew it was special. I'm sure you'll agree." Seth handed Annie the microphone and gave her a small wink. It gave her courage, and her heart stilled its frantic pace.

"Go for it, Annie-Bella," he said under the noise of the crowd.

Annie wrapped her hands around the mike and smiled at the audience, without seeing them. She coiled her toes inside her boots. This was it. It was her show and she planned on owning it.

Time slowed as the crowd settled, and she inhaled the rush of expectancy. She nodded at Seth, and the first notes of her song came out of Jake's guitar. The sound was rich and haunting, and it wrapped around her and reached every corner of the room to catch the crowd's attention and hold.

Then she opened her mouth and sang like she'd never sung before. She didn't sing for the audience, or even for Hannah, who stood off to one side, her voice rising in harmony like they'd rehearsed. She didn't sing for Seth, either, who accompanied her with such tenderness and sensitivity, like the guitar, the music, and his fingers were one. She sang for herself to conquer old fears, heal old hurts, and to prove something she needed to prove.

When the last note drifted into the half-darkness, silence hit her. Had everyone hated it? She glanced at Seth. He quirked an eyebrow and a small smile played around a corner of his mouth.

Then the applause broke over her like a wave, along with shouts and cheers. The crowd stood and stamped their feet and, above it all, a piercing whistle rang out. Brendan.

Her brother stood at the back of the room near the door wearing a black T-shirt with "Security Volunteer" on it in white letters. He gave her a thumbs-up and smiled. The tension in Annie's shoulders eased. There was no way Todd would ever have found her here. She'd worried about nothing.

Hannah grabbed her hand. "Way to go, Mom." Her daughter's face was flushed and her eyes were bright. "You rocked it."

"You did, too." Except for right at the beginning, though, Annie hadn't registered Hannah. She'd only heard her voice—her real voice, instead of the one she'd gotten used to hearing when she sang with the choir. Emotion bubbled up to choke her. Excitement, relief, and so much happiness she might have been floating several feet above the stage.

"You both rocked it. I'm so proud of you." Seth hugged them before he held up a hand to quiet the crowd. "Thanks for showing Annie and Hannah how much you liked 'My Hometown Heart.' It's a song that reaches deep inside and touches you, and I hope we get to hear it again on the radio someday."

"The radio?" Annie darted a glance at Seth as the crowd roared approval.

"Why not?" He grinned.

Hannah bounced at her side. "I want to do this again. I want to do it for the rest of my life. It's totally wild, you know?"

Annie slung an arm around Hannah's shoulders. She knew that wildness too well, but she wouldn't dim Hannah's excitement, at least not tonight. "I'm glad you had fun, honey. Seeing you happy makes me happy."

Seth started to speak again, and the crowd hushed. "We're closing this show with one last song. It's a Blake Shelton tune. Hannah chose it, and Annie and I are singing it together for everybody who listens to my morning show and as a thank you for supporting local radio. Although I haven't lived here long, I know how much Irish Falls loves country music so 'Country on the Radio' is for you."

Hannah slipped off the stage, and Annie and Seth sang together. The music swirled and forged a palpable connection between them. When they finished, there was that same hush as before, and then another crash of applause.

"You were fantastic." Tara pulled Annie off the stage and into a hug.

"We knew you could do it." Wearing a raspberry-pink PTA shirt, Rowan joined the hug. "You looked gorgeous, you sang gorgeous, and if I could do what you do, there's no way I'd spend my life baking cupcakes." She gave a quick laugh. "Or, in my case, teaching kids improper fractions."

"I like baking." But she liked singing more. Annie's heart gave a dull thud as the truth slithered through her. But she wasn't a kid any more, and she had responsibilities.

"I'm so proud of you, Annie." Her mom's face shone as she wrapped Annie in a hug in her turn. "It's been so long, I'd almost forgotten what a pair of lungs you have. Your dad is up there in heaven bursting with pride, too." Her voice was husky, and she hugged Annie closer.

"Well done." Duncan reached around her mom to pat Annie's shoulder. He was paler than usual and had dark circles under his eyes. "You're a pro."

Annie's throat got tight and she blinked away the sudden moisture behind her eyes. "I need a few minutes to freshen up." She tugged on Tara's arm. "If Hannah looks for me, let her know?"

"Sure." Tara nodded. "Are you okay?"

"Yeah." And she'd make herself believe it when she'd put the pieces of herself back together again. Even though it was only a small-town roadhouse, being up on that stage had cracked her wide open to leave her way too raw and exposed.

Tara gave her an understanding smile, followed by another hug. "I love you, Annie-Bella, and tonight is only the start. You have to keep singing. You can't stop now."

Annie gulped as she pushed her way through the crowd and nodded and smiled to acknowledge the congratulations. She reached the back door and grabbed her sweater from behind the screened area that served as a dressing room for the talent show performers. When she pulled open the door, a welcome blast of cool air washed over her, and moonlight dappled the flagstone path that wound from the Black Duck's patio toward the dark forest behind.

She walked along the path until it ended at a split-rail fence, her boots making a soft thud on the stones. She stopped, shrugged into her sweater, and rested her arms on top of a weathered wooden rail. Apart from the faint splash of water on rocks from the river far below, the night was silent and still, waiting.

The crisp pine-scented air tickled her nose. Her heartbeat slowed and the roaring in her ears faded. Animal tracks indented the mud around the fence—coyotes and white-tailed deer. Her dad had known this land like the back of his hand, and he'd made sure his kids did, too.

"Once you're a northern girl, you're always a northern girl." She couldn't remember the sound of her dad's voice, but she remembered his words and how he'd lifted her up to sit on this same fence when it was taller than she was.

Lacing her fingers together, she stared into the velvety shadows of the trees. The wind flicked the leaves with a gentle rustle. She'd proved to herself she could get up on a stage and sing again. She'd told herself all she had to do was sing once and her life would be the same as it was before, but she'd been wrong. And what was she going to do about it?

~ ~ ~

Seth shut the back door of the Black Duck behind him—the same door Annie had gone out of five minutes before. He squinted as his eyes adapted to the dark night. "Annie?" He started down a path made of stones. The grass on either side was wet, and the cool air had a peaty smell.

At the end of the path, by a fence, a figure turned. Overhanging tree branches shadowed Annie's face, but a shaft of moonlight stole through to illuminate her hair.

"Hey." Her voice was flat.

"I saw you leave and I was worried about you." He held out a paper cup. "I brought you some water. What's wrong?"

The vibrant woman he'd sung with on the stage had almost disappeared, and she looked smaller, almost frail.

Annie took the cup. "Thanks. Singing. It—" She

swallowed some water. "Although it gave me something—something important—it took something away too."

He moved to join her under the tree. "Music can do that."

"I needed a few minutes to put myself back together." She gave him a faint smile.

"I understand." The show had taken something from him, too. "I'll go. I just wanted to make sure you were okay." He took a step back, and his boot heels sunk into the damp ground.

"No, stay." She curved her hands around the cup of water and stared at her feet. "You were up there with me. You know what it's like. If you sing from your heart, you give a piece of yourself to the audience. Before tonight, I hadn't done that in a long time."

"You did yourself proud, and I don't only mean the singing." His voice got rough.

"You helped me do it. You helped Hannah, too."

The little sparkles on Annie's top peeped between her sweater buttons and winked at him below a strip of creamy skin.

His mouth went dry. "Did you see Hannah's expression when she sang?"

"No." Her laugh was embarrassed. "I can't let Hannah guess, but once I got up there, I forgot about her. The music took over. I forgot about the audience, too. You're a great accompanist."

"You're easy to accompany." And when he'd played for her, there had been a bond between them that went beyond the music. "Hannah's a natural performer. With luck and hard work, she could be the real deal someday."

"Maybe, but she's still young." Annie drained the water and crumpled the empty cup.

"How old were you when you first sang to an audience?"

"Eight, at a school Christmas concert." She gave Seth a dry smile. "But apart from that, the first time I sang to people I didn't know was at a music festival when I was almost thirteen. I bugged my mom to let me take part, and she finally gave in. My dad had just died, and I was lost. But when I sang . . ." She stopped and shivered.

"You found yourself again?" He slung an arm around her hunched shoulders.

"How did you know?" She tilted her head to look at him.

"Because that happened to me when I was around that age." He looped a loose curl of her hair around his fingers. "I saw your face tonight. You loved singing as much as Hannah did, maybe even more."

"I did, but it's complicated." She leaned against him, and Seth's nerve ends tingled.

"Aw, Annie-Bella." His voice hitched as he turned her around and took her in his arms. "It's more than the singing that's complicated. I told myself I wouldn't do this, but I can't help it." And he was tired of fighting whatever *this* was. He brushed his mouth along her jaw and then covered her lips with his.

She moaned and stumbled against him as he traced the seam of her lips and coaxed her mouth open. The paper cup brushed his side as it fell to the ground, and she wrapped her arms around his waist.

As Seth deepened the kiss, she ran her hands up his back, and his muscles corded under her touch.

"I . . ." Reluctantly, he dragged his mouth away from hers. "I want to kiss you, and touch you, and . . ." His heart thudded as he slipped one hand under her sweater. Even through her silky top, her skin was hot. "I couldn't keep my eyes off you tonight."

She stiffened. "Because I look different?"

"No." He dropped kisses along the curve of her neck, and she moaned again. "This outfit is great, but I can't keep my eyes off you in your bakery apron, either."

"But when I sang . . ." She gasped as his hand explored farther and traced the generous curve of her breast.

"I saw all of you, the real you." His breath got short, and when her hand fumbled with the buttons on his shirt front, he quivered. Her hand connected with his bare chest, and his body flooded with warmth. "Yes . . ."

"No." She pulled her hand away like she'd been burned and stepped from the shelter of his arms. "I'm sorry." Her voice was dull.

"But . . ." Seth swallowed and clenched his fists.

Her face flushed, and her chest heaved.

"I thought you wanted this too."

"Maybe I do, but I can't . . . Hannah's in there, and I . . ." Above the neck of her sweater her skin flushed dark red. "It's not you. It's me." Her voice was high, and her expression strained.

"I won't hurt you." He took a deep breath. What Todd had done to her was even worse than he'd thought. "Or Hannah, either."

"I didn't mean . . ." Annie yanked at her sweater. "I shouldn't have led you on."

"You didn't." Seth buttoned his shirt and stuffed it back into his jeans. "You were into me, and I was into you, but I won't take it any further." He scraped a hand across his face. "Not unless you tell me you want me to. It's your call."

"I wish . . ." Her voice cracked, and the moonlight threw the naked vulnerability in her eyes into sharp—and even more painful—relief.

"Me too." And that was the problem with wishes. They were meaningless. He crossed his arms over his chest so he wouldn't take her in his arms again.

"Annie?" The door of the Black Duck banged open. "There you are." Tara's voice rang out in the heavy silence. "The buffet's open, and they're going to draw raffle prizes. Mom needs us. First up is Quinn's wedding cake."

"I have to go." Annie's voice was small, and she licked her lips.

"Of course." Seth's phone dinged in the pocket of his jeans to signal an incoming text.

"Annie?" Tara's voice got louder. "We're waiting for you. Unless you want half the family out here, get your butt in gear."

"I'll be right there." She turned to Seth as the door shut behind her sister. "Thank you for tonight. Helping me with my song, accompanying me, singing with me. I . . . you . . ." An expression that might have been regret flickered in the depths of her eyes. "If things were different . . . if I was different."

"Yeah." He swallowed, then she turned away and walked back up the shadowy path. "Annie?"

"What?" The chubby moon gilded her features with silver.

"You write songs from your heart. You sing from your heart. Have you ever wondered what would happen if you lived from your heart?"

She held his gaze for a long moment. "It's not that simple."

"Isn't it? For a woman who's all about heart, I'd have thought living from your heart would be the simplest thing of all."

"Then maybe you should do it, too." Her voice was a whisper in the night before she moved to the door, pulled it open, and disappeared inside.

Seth's heart slammed in his chest. Annie was right, and why did he think he could judge her for something he wasn't doing? His phone dinged again, and he fumbled it out of his pocket and stared at the screen. As he read the text, a jolt went through his body.

Dylan had finally reached out. And for the first time in months, his son needed him.

Chapter 14

"Your show was good." His dark brown hair still bedhead rumpled, Dylan stood outside the open studio door with Dolly by his side. He avoided looking at Seth directly, like he'd done the night before when Seth picked him up five miles outside Irish Falls beside his broken-down car.

"Thanks." Seth gave his son a cautious smile. "I don't usually do it on Sunday, but since it's a long weekend, I gave the regular guy a day off." At the time, Seth hadn't had any other plans. "I appreciate you listening." He checked to make sure he'd pushed the button for the subscription service. Since he was the only one here this weekend, apart from the morning show, there wouldn't be any live programs.

"No problem." Dylan glanced at his sweats and wrinkled Drake T-shirt. "You have coffee?"

"There's a pot in the kitchen down the hall." Seth gestured. "Grab a mug from the cupboard over the sink."

Dylan padded to the galley kitchen and crockery clattered.

"Who dressed you up, Dolly?" Seth eyed the red, white, and blue bow tied to the dog's collar.

"I found it beneath that tree by the waterfall when I took her out earlier." His son ambled back into the booth and sat in the chair across from Seth's then put a *Peanuts* coffee mug on the desk. "The one with pieces of paper and charm things tied to it." He pulled a lid off a plastic box and took out a cookie.

"That's the Irish Falls wishing tree. People tie wishes to it because they think the tree makes those wishes come true."

"Weird." Dylan slurped coffee. "But it's the kind of shit Mom would like."

"Dylan." Seth stopped. His kid was an adult. The time for correcting his language was gone, along with bedtime stories, kicking around a ball together in the park, and helping with science fair projects.

"Sorry." Dylan grin was self-conscious. "All I meant is Mom's as flaky as ever."

"Have you heard from her lately?" Seth tensed. Was Dylan turning up here with no warning something to do with Amanda?

Dylan shrugged and fiddled with his silver stud earring. "She calls me once a month or so. Last I heard she was singing with a band off the strip in Vegas. She sounded good, I guess. The same as always, anyway."

Except, she wouldn't have sounded like a mom. Not like Annie. Seth bit back a sigh. "Your mom loves you."

"Sure." Dylan's voice was expressionless. "I'm bummed I missed your show last night. If my car hadn't overheated, I'd have made it in time."

"Thanks for making the effort." Seth leaned back. Apart from the earring and shaggier hair, Dylan looked the same as he always had, but there was something new in his expression—like life had knocked some of the teenage bravado out of him.

"It's not a big deal." Dylan shrugged and gulped a mouthful of coffee, but not before Seth glimpsed the flash of hurt in his son's brown eyes.

"It is to me." Seth chose his words with care. "You must have been looking forward to spending the weekend with Mackenzie and her family. The Hamptons are pretty, although the area gets busy—"

"She dumped me." A pulse worked in Dylan's jaw. "Go ahead and say it. You were right about her and everything else. Are you happy?"

"Of course not. I'm sorry." Seth picked up his empty coffee mug and set it down again without seeing it. "You really liked Mackenzie."

"I did, but it turns out she was two-timing me with a guy I thought was a friend."

Seth's heart twisted. "She doesn't know what she's missing."

"Like Mom?" There was a cynical note in his son's voice. "She sure never missed me."

And she'd missed all the big milestones in Dylan's life, too—including this one. "Your mom's a free spirit and maybe someday—"

"I'm not counting on it." The anger in Dylan's expression tore at Seth's heart. "I wasn't serious about Mackenzie, but . . ."

"You weren't expecting her to cheat on you, either." Seth moved around the broadcast desk and gave Dylan's shoulder a hesitant pat. "You'll meet the right woman someday and, when you do, you'll know it."

"You never did." Dylan's tone was bleak.

"That doesn't mean you won't." Even though Seth tasted bile, he made himself continue. "There are a lot of girls out there who know the meaning of commitment." Like Annie, except she was all woman. His heartbeat sped up, and his legs trembled. He eased back and sat on the edge of the desk.

"I lost my job, too." Dylan's voice caught and he cleared his throat. "Mackenzie's dad found someone else. My boss at the pizza place said he'd take me back, but . . . I guess I blew it. You tried to tell me to slow down, but I didn't listen."

Seth studied his son's bent head and the red flush that crept across his cheeks. "A man has to make his own mistakes and own them, too. I should have treated you like a man. I was wrong to butt in." He sucked in a breath. "I wanted to help, but I can see how you thought I was interfering."

"I should have realized you were looking out for me. And what I said to you . . . I behaved like a spoiled brat, especially when you must have been dealing with crap of your own." His Adam's apple bobbed. "Well. I thought I should come and tell you in person. I can only stay until tomorrow afternoon. I start back at the pizza place on Tuesday, but you're my dad, and we've gone through a lot together and, well, you know."

"Yeah, I do." Seth let out a huge breath. It wouldn't be all easy from now on, but thanks to Annie, he hadn't made things worse, and he and Dylan had this precious chance to make a fresh start.

"You were right about my car, too." Dylan's laugh was rueful. "It's a pile of junk. What a waste of money."

"Do you need—?"

"Nope." His son shook his head. "Apart from college, I'm not taking money from you. If I want to be an adult, I better start acting like one."

"It's good you want to be self-sufficient, but not even money for a bus ticket?" Seth grinned. "Maybe you didn't see the look the tow truck guy gave your car last night, but I did. I don't think you're going to be driving it anywhere soon, if ever."

"It's okay." Dylan grinned back. "Mackenzie's dad must have felt bad about letting me go. He gave me a whole month's pay."

"And you took it?" Seth laughed, partly with amusement but more with relief. He had his boy back, and the whole world looked brighter.

"Course I did. He should feel guilty." Dylan's mouth narrowed. "I don't mind about missing the Hamptons, and golf is kind of lame, but I thought Mackenzie really liked me."

And his son hurt like Seth hurt when Amanda walked out on the two of them, onto a tour bus and into the arms of a rock star wannabe. But unlike him, Dylan had learned his lesson before there was a kid involved or he had a wedding ring on his finger.

"You'll know better next time." His chest got tight.

Unlike him, there would be a next time.

"Yeah." Dylan's voice was gruff and he bent to scratch Dolly's ears. "She's sure cute. Are you taking her back to LA with you?"

"I want to." Seth tented his fingers on his knees. Condo rules or not, there was no way he'd leave Dolly behind. "But see, the thing is, the terms of Jake's will mean I have to run this station for six months before I can sell it." Although that didn't seem as bad as it had at first, it still wasn't what Seth would have chosen.

"Downer." Seth glimpsed Jake in the lines of his son's jaw and nose.

"Since you're sticking around today, what do you want to do? There are some trails outside town where we could go hiking, or we could head over to a lake and—"

He stopped as the outside door opened and Annie came into the station. "Oh." She hovered outside the studio. "I didn't realize you had company." She glanced between him and Dylan and her face went pink.

He gestured her to come in. "Annie, my son, Dylan." As he made the introductions, Dylan got to his feet, brushed cookie crumbs off his sweats, and took Annie's hand. Seth's heart swelled. Although he'd made mistakes in raising him, his son was becoming a good man and that was all that mattered.

"Pleased to meet you." Annie stepped back. "Your dad didn't mention . . ." She glanced at Seth again.

"It was kind of a surprise." Dylan gave an uneasy laugh.

"The best kind." Seth moved to stand beside his son.

Dylan held out the box of cookies to her. "Do you want one? These are great."

"Cookies?" Annie looked between the box and Dylan. "Maple pecan cookies?"

"I dunno." Dylan took another one. "They have some kind of nut in them."

Annie's mouth twitched, and then her laugh rang out. "I made those cookies for my family's Memorial Day weekend picnic. Since everyone's off for the holiday, I left them in the station kitchen so my daughter and her friends wouldn't find them."

"How many did you eat?" Seth looked from the half-empty box to the telltale crumbs on Dylan's face.

"I didn't count." Dylan flushed. "I'm sorry. I thought . . . I didn't think. I can buy you more cookies at a store, but I guess they wouldn't be the same."

"I didn't think, either." Seth rubbed a hand across the back of his neck. "Sherri brought cookies for everyone on Friday, and I assumed those were the leftovers."

Annie laughed again. "No worries. We already have a ton of food for the picnic. If you don't have plans for today, you two are welcome to join us." When she looked at Seth, her smile wavered.

He swallowed, still tasting the sweetness of their kiss from the night before, and the imprint of her cheek against his. "If it's okay with Dylan, it's good for me."

"Sure." His son's expression turned speculative. Then, as he glanced between Seth and Annie, he gave Seth a knowing smile.

~ ~ ~

On Monday afternoon, Annie set the last of the three cardboard boxes she'd lugged down from the attic on the coffee table in her living room. That kiss with Seth behind the Black Duck on Saturday night had been a one-time thing. She'd been caught up in the emotion of singing, nothing more, and it wouldn't happen again. Like he said, it was her call, and he'd been a perfect gentleman at her family's picnic yesterday—friendly, but not too friendly. So why had she felt peculiarly bereft?

Her stomach somersaulted as she eyed the boxes that, except for those months in Nashville, held the songs she'd written over the years. Maybe "My Hometown Heart" was a fluke. Or maybe it wasn't and she should stop being such a coward. Singing to an audience on Saturday night had been the push she needed, and she wouldn't falter now.

She straightened her shoulders and pulled the box nearest to her open. It was Memorial Day and all around town—around the country—people were remembering brave soldiers. People like Adam. She gulped at the thought of Tara's loss. The least she could do was take a look at a few songs. She pulled a sheet of music off the top of a pile and hummed a few bars before adding the lyrics.

She hit a high note and excitement fizzed through her. Todd didn't have the power to hurt her ever again. She was brave, she was powerful, and, even in her own small way, she was mighty.

Minutes or maybe hours later, the doorbell rang. Still half lost in the music, she went to the front door and tugged on it. "Hang on a second." She pulled harder, and the door swung inward, taking her with it.

"Oops." Seth snagged her arm.

Annie righted herself. "Thanks." She stuttered, almost lightheaded.

"I guess you know there's a problem with your door." His eyes twinkled. "Do you need help fixing it? I've got a toolbox in my truck."

"Brendan said he'd do it, but I don't want to bother him. Duncan's treatment starts tomorrow, and Brendan will be spending a lot of time driving him to and from the hospital."

And whenever she thought about Duncan's prostate cancer diagnosis, she got a sick feeling in the pit of her stomach.

"I'm happy to help. Hang on." He jogged to his truck parked at the curb and took out a metal box. Below his shorts, his legs were long and muscular, and she trembled. Within seconds he was back. "You should have asked me before."

"I didn't want to bother you, either. I tried to fix it myself, but I'm not very handy with stuff around the house." And she didn't like admitting there was something she couldn't handle on her own. She made herself move away from him to sit on the stairs that led to the second floor. "Did Dylan get away okay?" If she focused on his son, she'd curb those wayward thoughts.

"Yeah. He caught the bus a little while ago." He set the toolbox on the hall floor and opened it. "That car of his is toast." His hands stilled. "I owe you. One of the reasons I came by this afternoon was to thank you."

"For what?" Her thoughts froze.

"If it weren't for you, I doubt Dylan would have come here. You helped me figure out how to talk to him."

She hugged herself as desire ebbed. "Thanks to my loud Irish relatives, I know how to talk." She tried to smile.

"You're lucky to have a family that cares so much about each other." Seth picked up a screwdriver and tapped at the door hinge.

"I know." Except, sometimes all that caring made her want to run, but even if she could have, there was no place for her to run to.

Seth cleared his throat. "Being with your family at the picnic was good for Dylan. Apart from me, he hasn't had much family in his life."

"Everyone liked him." And she'd breathed a silent prayer of thanks Hannah was too young for him to notice. Her daughter had male friends, sure, but no boyfriends so far, and Annie was happy to keep it that way.

"Dylan's a good kid. Man, now. I guess." Seth gave her a half-smile. "When I look at him, I wonder where the years went."

"He looks a lot like you." She hesitated. "Did you tell him about Jake?"

"No." Seth was intent on the door, his expression inscrutable. "I'm still trying to figure things out myself."

"Hasn't he ever asked you about your family?"

Seth dumped the screwdriver back into the toolbox. "Not lately. Neither my ex nor I were big on family." He grimaced. "You need a new part for this door. I'll pick it up at the hardware store tomorrow."

"Thanks. I didn't mean to pry." She swallowed. "I've never not been big on family." Although her relatives couldn't make up for the absence of a dad in Hannah's life, they'd still filled a big gap, her brother especially.

"It's me. Amanda and I didn't know how to do family, and that still bugs me, I guess." Seth's firm lips turned up into a crooked grin, and Annie's mouth went dry.

She might not want to, but she remembered every contour of those lips and their warmth against hers—as well as how his kisses had made her feel things she'd thought she couldn't feel ever feel again.

"Is Hannah home?" He moved to sit on the stairs beside her.

"No. She's at a friend's."

"Good. I wanted to talk to you without her around."

"What about?" Her stomach fluttered.

What was the matter with her? Seth had taken her at her word. She should be relieved, but she wasn't, and she didn't know what to do about it.

"I meant what I said about hearing 'My Hometown Heart' on the radio. I have a friend who has a recording studio near

Utica. I called him this morning, and he'll give me studio space plus mixing to record your song—you and Hannah together. What do you say?" His voice had an undercurrent of excitement.

When Annie was Hannah's age, she'd have killed for an offer like that. Even now, it was tempting. "It's really generous, but . . ." Out of the corner of her eye, she glimpsed the scattered music in the living room.

"But what?" His expression held no guile. "We could also hire backup musicians at minimal cost."

She studied him. "What's the catch?"

"There isn't one. I met Pete soon after I moved to LA. We worked on a couple of songwriting projects together before he moved to the music production side. He's from Georgia, too, so he looked out for another green kid from the South." His tone was frank. "He left the West Coast a few years ago because once their kids were grown, he and his wife wanted to slow down. He does good work, and I trust him."

But could she trust Seth? She wanted to. She shifted on the hard stairs. "Even if I recorded the song, who would be interested in it? Folks here liked it when they heard it at the fundraiser, but they're my family and friends. It's not like they're going to tell me they hated it."

"The tourists liked it, too." He leaned toward her, and she caught her breath at that overwhelming masculinity. "All you need to do is sing like you did on Saturday night. When you got up on that stage, magic happened. You were a different person."

She recoiled. "You mean the real me is dull and boring?"

"Of course not." His eyes narrowed. "Is that what Hannah's dad told you?"

She shrugged like it didn't matter. "Not in so many words, but I'm a small-town girl from a place most people have never heard of. I made some stupid choices and dropped out of college because I believed someone who fed me a bunch of lines about having a future in music. Now I work in my family's bakery. End of story." Her vision blurred.

"Hey." His expression softened. "It doesn't have to be the end of your story. Whatever Todd said was wrong. There isn't anybody who hasn't made bad choices. They're only stupid if you don't learn from them and you make the same ones over again." He gave her a lopsided smile. "Lots of smart people never finished college, and a bunch of big stars come from places most people never heard of."

She drew in a breath. She'd conquered a lot of her fears, but maybe not quite all of them. "It's not only about me. Hannah . . . she's—"

"Not you." Seth's voice was firm. "You can't live Hannah's life for her. All you can do is love and guide her. She'll make her own mistakes." He clasped his hands under his chin. "It's easier to say than do, and I'm not a model dad, but anybody can see you're doing your best with her."

"Thanks." Her voice cracked.

Seth understood her in a way not even her sisters did.

"By the way . . ." His smile turned teasing. "Just to clear things up, any woman who can kiss like you sure isn't dull and boring. You rocked it on stage, but when you were kissing me, you hit it out of the park."

"I . . ." Annie's face heated.

"What happened between us on Saturday night was important."

So important she couldn't let herself think about it. "People get carried away after gigs all the time." She tried to make her tone casual.

"I don't, and I don't think you do either." Seth's breath feathered the hair at her nape. "In fact, I don't think I ever got carried away like that before."

But she had, and that was why, until now, she'd made sure it never happened again. "I'm a mom."

His soft and seductive laugh curled around her heart. "So, I'm a dad. What does parenthood have to do with anything?"

"Nothing. But . . ." She bit her bottom lip. What would it be like to live from her heart? And to explore whatever was between them? She inched closer to him on the stairs.

"Let me know what you what you want to do about the recording session." He stood and picked up his toolbox. "I'll swing by and install that new part for your door later this week."

"Wait." She scrambled to her feet. There was no reason for her not to take a chance in music—as well as life. Except, she didn't know what scared her more. Facing her fears or not taking that step and always wondering. Then, before she lost her nerve, she moved in close, stood on tiptoe in front of him, and covered his mouth with hers.

Chapter 15

Three days later, Seth closed the old photo album and slid it back into the bottom of the chest of drawers in the apartment living room. Apart from a cursory flip through it, he'd avoided the album up until now, but whether he liked it or not, Jake was part of his past, and so the pictures were too. And if whatever was between he and Annie had a chance to go anywhere—and after that kiss she'd planted on him in her front hall, he wanted it to—he owed it to her, as well as to himself, to deal with the past then put it behind him.

He stared at the picture of his mom and Jake that had fallen out of one of the plastic sleeves and onto the carpet. They sat at a rectangular table with a group of other people with scattered drinks and half-filled plates of food. They were in a restaurant or nightclub, given the dim light and high, banquette seats.

His mom had big hair and even bigger earrings, and a bearded Jake had one arm around her shoulders, his other hand resting on the curve of her pregnant belly covered by a polka-dot maternity top. Oblivious to the camera and everyone else at the table, the two of them stared into each other's eyes. Whatever had happened later, the picture proved they'd loved each other once. And they'd loved him, too.

Seth eased Dolly off his lap and went to the galley kitchen to grab a soda from the fridge. He should be happy Jake had cared about him and his mom, but instead, all he felt was sadness for what all of them had lost.

The dog ran to the door and pawed at it.

Seth set his unopened soda aside. "I took you out after Dylan called." A call that hadn't been about anything important but was still the most important call he'd had with his son in months because it was part of the two of them inching their way back to what they'd once shared.

Dolly whined and looked at him with soulful brown eyes.

"Okay, five minutes and then bed." Although the early morning starts were getting easier, he should have been asleep half an hour ago. Once he'd started looking at the album, though, he couldn't stop.

Seth grabbed Dolly's leash from a hook and stuck his feet into his sneakers.

At a light knock on the door, Dolly erupted into a chorus of barks.

He pulled open the door. "Annie. What is it? Has something happened to Hannah or your family?"

"No. They're fine." Her hair was windblown, and she was out of breath. "It's . . . you have to come outside and see. When I saw your light still on, and the station door was unlocked, I came in. Half the town is over by the wishing tree. Didn't you notice?"

"No. I've been busy . . . with stuff. See what?" Seth pulled on a sweatshirt, clipped Dolly's leash to her collar, and shut the apartment door behind them.

"The northern lights. You heard of them, city guy?" Her smile warmed him like it always did, along with that underlying sizzle of sexual attraction.

"You mean nature's light show, otherwise known as the Aurora Borealis?" He teased her back.

"Yep." She skipped down the stairs outside the station, and Seth followed her along the path to the wishing tree, with Dolly at his heels. "We rarely see them here. I've only ever seen them once before. Look." She pointed.

Seth sucked in a breath. He'd seen pictures, sure, but they couldn't compare to the reality. "Wow."

"Amazing, aren't they?" Her voice was an awed whisper.

"They sure are." Even Dolly was quiet as flashes of green, purple, and blue light lit up the sky.

Annie moved closer to his side. "When I was about ten, my mom and dad woke my sisters and Brendan and me up late one night to see the northern lights. We got bundled into our parkas and came out here."

"Did you write a song about it?"

"Not then, but when I was older."

His heart caught at the wistful expression in her eyes.

"Seeing the lights with my dad is a special memory. In a way, I wrote the song in remembrance of him."

"Will you sing it for me sometime?" He held his breath.

"Sure." There was a smile in her voice. "I think you'd have liked my dad. He was the kind of guy who believed in God, family, and country. He liked hockey in winter and fishing in summer. He was also smart about business and had a fantastic sense of humor."

"He sounds great. A lot like Brendan, actually." Heat radiated through Seth's chest. In sharing an important part of her past with him, Annie had also given him a piece of her soul.

"He was." Her smile was tender and her eyes were bright. "Brendan looks like Dad too, at least how I remember him."

"I'm honored you'll sing for me again." And humbled she finally trusted him enough to take that next step.

"I've thought about the recording session too." Her voice was soft. "I'll do it. My dad wouldn't have wanted me to give up on a dream. He always told us to reach for the stars. Even if you didn't get there, he said you had to try and maybe you'd catch the moon instead."

"Your dad would be proud of you." Seth's tongue got thick. "I'm proud of you, too." In the light breeze, the wishes and tokens tied to the wishing tree rustled like a flock of benevolent birds.

"I haven't done it yet."

"You will." He knew that about her. "Because if you don't, Tara and Rowan will kick your butt."

Her chuckle warmed the darkness. "Like you wouldn't."

"Maybe." But he wanted to kiss her more. He glanced at her bright hair and the soft curve of her cheek, and his body stirred.

"Singing at the fundraiser was the kick in the butt I needed to start putting my past behind me." Her tone was wistful. "All my songs have been in boxes, but when I looked at them this week, I realized the most important part of my life has been in a box too. I already decided I needed to change my life so I'd have something for me after Hannah left home, but I didn't think it could be my music."

Seth put a hand to his chest. Had the most important part of his life been in a box too? Had he been so focused on the past, he hadn't let himself think about the future? And had he hung onto Dylan and interfered in his life because he hadn't wanted to let him go? "Even after Hannah leaves home, she'll still be part of your life."

"Not like she is now." Annie's voice was sad. "She won't need me in the same way. When Dylan was here, I looked at him and saw Hannah in a few years. It's great that she needs her own life, but I'm not ready for it." She gave a dry laugh. "I don't think any mom is ever ready for their kid to fly the nest, but Hannah's all I've ever had. I don't want to stop her growing up, but it's time I looked beyond her, my family, and the bakery and did something more for me. I'm taking a pottery class, and I signed up for an online college course, but my music . . . I can't ignore it any longer. It's like a big ache inside. I need to see where music might take me."

Seth shifted from one foot to the other, and the technicolor display in the sky wavered. He wasn't anything like Annie. He'd done lots of stuff for himself, separate from Dylan. But maybe he'd overcompensated with his son because he'd wanted to give Dylan everything he hadn't had growing up and then hadn't known when to stop. "You're a wise woman."

"If I am, I got it from my mom. She was a great teacher. She still is. The way she's handling Duncan's illness . . ." She stopped and cleared her throat.

He touched her shoulder. "Duncan's going to be fine."

"I know, but even though Mom and the doctors are saying all the right things, it's still another reminder that life is short. And compared to those lights up there, we're a pretty small part of the universe." Her expression was pensive.

"That sounds like another song." Seth's breathing slowed. No matter what they talked about, or what they were doing, Annie calmed and centered him.

"One I haven't written."

"Yet." Even though a bunch of folks from town were nearby, he and Annie could have been in another world.

"You believe in me, don't you?" She tilted her head toward him.

"Always." He did, and it wasn't an idle assertion. Seth sucked in a quick breath. How had it happened? He hadn't known Annie long, but it felt like forever, and his connection with her defied logical explanation.

"What are you two doing over here all cozy?" At Rowan's voice behind them, Seth started.

"We aren't cozy." Annie's face went red. "What are you two doing sneaking up on people?" She glanced at Tara behind Rowan.

"Coming up to two people in the middle of a crowd isn't sneaking." Tara's voice had a teasing note. "Shouldn't you be in bed? You're not a morning person."

"Like either of you are." Annie's voice softened and she grinned at her sisters.

"Unlike you and Tara, I don't start work until eight." Rowan gestured to the dark-haired boy and girl at her side. "My kids should be in bed, but we couldn't miss this." She glanced around. "Where's Hannah?"

"As far away from me as possible with some friends from school." Annie's laugh was strained. "Your two are still young enough, but at Hannah's age, it's not cool to hang out with your mom."

Rowan flicked a speculative glance at Seth. "There are other advantages to having a kid who is older."

Annie exhaled. "Button it."

"We're going. The show is ending anyway." After Tara glanced between Seth and Annie, a slow smile spread across her face. "At least one of them is."

"Good night." Annie's voice was firm.

"Don't do anything we wouldn't do." Rowan shooed her kids in the direction of several other women with children, and her eyes twinkled.

"That gives me a lot of scope, doesn't it?" Annie made a face.

As soon as Rowan and Tara were out of earshot, the laugh Seth couldn't hold back spilled out. "Now I know why folks talk about the Quinn sisters in action."

"My sisters and I are close, but I'm still my own person."

At Annie's prim tone, Seth sobered. "Of course you are. Thanks for showing me the northern lights. Sharing them with you was good." No, it was fabulous. When he'd come to Irish Falls and ended up staying, he'd thought he wanted to be alone. But somewhere along the line, things had changed. He'd made friends, like Brendan, the guys he worked with at the station, and Annie, too. Except, she was more than a friend.

"The first time I saw the northern lights, I thought they were magic. A part of me still wants to believe that."

Her face shone in the moonlight, and a jolt of awareness shot through him. The leaves on the wishing tree made a gentle swishing sound, and he stilled.

Although the past he didn't want to think about still loomed large and, even though he'd always been a sceptic, maybe there was something in that tree after all. Although it might be awkward and uncertain for both of them, he and Annie were tiptoeing toward something—something special. And if that wasn't magic, what was?

~ ~ ~

Hannah was fine at her friend's place. Annie had no reason to doubt her daughter. Singing more of her songs for Seth would be fine, too. It would help her prepare for the recording session only two weeks away. Annie took a deep breath and gathered up the folder of music, her purse, and a still-warm loaf of soda bread wrapped in a tea towel from her kitchen counter. She only had to walk over to Seth's place and show him some of her other songs like they'd arranged.

Ten minutes—and more deep breaths later—she rapped on the apartment door she now thought of as Seth's, not Jake's.

"Hey." Seth opened the door and gestured her in. "I was about to text you. Can Hannah come over later? I'd like to do more work with her on the harmony for 'My Hometown Heart.'"

"Sure. Her last exam is this week so she's at a friend's house studying, but she'll be done in a few hours." At least that's where Hannah had said she'd be and, despite that persistent twinge of uncertainty—one that had intensified since the talent show—Annie was being too suspicious. She handed him the loaf of bread.

"Thanks." Seth's eyes gleamed, and her mouth went dry. His expression hinted at more than a simple thank you for baking.

She kicked off her shoes and moved across the small entry and into the combined living/dining room. Apart from the big-screen TV and premium dog bed, the place was as basic as it had been when Jake lived here. "Mom says you can't resist Quinn's soda bread," Annie said.

"Among other things." Seth's slow gaze slid from the top of her head to the tips of her toes before zeroing in on the folder of music she clutched to her chest.

"Want to get started?" She made her voice bright. "I walked over so I didn't bring my guitar. I thought we could use the Gibson."

"Sure." Seth went to the hall closet and opened it.

Annie couldn't help herself. She stared after him, feasting her gaze on all that hot masculinity. It was so unfair. She only had to look at a cupcake, and she put on half a pound, but although he inhaled Tara's signature butter tarts and almost everything else that came out of the bakery kitchen, there wasn't an ounce of spare flesh on him. Well-worn jeans hugged his hips, and a white T-shirt sculpted that toned chest. Below the jeans, his feet were bare, and his dark hair was damp and tousled like he'd just showered.

"What's up?" He turned around and came back to the sofa with the guitar case. He waited for her to sit and then sat beside her.

"Nothing." She straightened and kept the music folder between them.

"Is it singing new songs for me?" His mouth curved into a heart-melting smile. "You know how much I love 'My Hometown Heart.'"

She flushed and fumbled with the guitar case. "What if it's a one-off?"

"I doubt it, but so what if you're a one-hit wonder? Isn't that better than being a no-hit wonder?" His voice was amused.

"I guess so." She picked up the guitar and cradled it. "It's not only the singing." Although, whenever she thought about trusting Seth enough to share more of her music with him, she still almost broke out in a cold sweat.

"Is Hannah giving you grief?" His tone turned warm and comforting.

"Not really, but I have this feeling." She linked her fingers together. "I can't put my finger on it, but something's not right with her. I thought being in the talent show would help, and it did, but still . . ."

"Maternal intuition." Seth's smile was rueful. "Even though Dylan's mom wasn't around much while he was growing up, he could never get anything past her. Me, on the other hand." He shrugged. "I was an easier mark."

"I used to think I understood Hannah, but this spring, she's changed." A heaviness lodged in Annie's stomach. "Whenever I try to talk to her, she shuts me out. At first I thought it was only about her not wanting to go to college, but now it seems to be about everything. And since the talent show, she's withdrawn again."

"Have you talked to your mom or your sisters?"

"I can't." So why had she found it so easy to open up to him? "Mom's worried about Duncan, and Rowan's divorce is hitting her hard. As for Tara, she and Adam couldn't have kids. She'd give anything to have a child, so if she heard me complaining about mine . . . I don't want to hurt her." She fingered the guitar pick and didn't look at him.

"We both know teenagers go through phases. Look what I've been going through with Dylan." Seth pulled Annie into the crook of his arm. "From what I've seen, Hannah's a good kid."

"She is, but Duncan getting sick has upset her more than she lets on. The two of them are close. She never knew my dad, and since she never knew her dad, either, Duncan is somewhere between a grandfather and a father. If he should die . . ." Annie squeezed her eyes tight shut.

"Don't even think that." Seth's voice was his radio voice—deep, rich, and reassuring.

"I know, but sometimes I can't help it. Like I know Hannah's hurting, but I can't seem to help her."

"The recording session might be good for her." He cupped her chin. "Good for both of you. And for you, it could be the first step in a new career."

"I don't think—"

"So, don't." Seth's face was inches from hers. Tiny laugh lines fanned out around his eyes, and he smelled of clean laundry, mint toothpaste, and fresh air. "You're talented, and I won't be the only one to think so. Whatever happened in Nashville and at Belmont, you didn't fail. You gave it your best shot, and now you've got Hannah, who you wouldn't trade for any number of hit songs. If you ask me, you're right where you're supposed to be. It's all about perspective."

Warmth suffused Annie's body, and she felt lighter, almost carefree. "How did you get to be so smart, city guy?"

"The same way you did." Seth's laugh rumbled. "When life kicks you in the butt, it gives you lessons for free."

She'd always have regrets, but maybe she wouldn't trade the lessons she'd learned because without them, she wouldn't be here with this man. She had to look forward, not back. "Do you want to hear more of my tunes?" She reached for the folder and pulled sheets of her handwritten music out of it.

"I thought you'd never ask." He smiled as he set up a music stand.

She took a deep breath, stood, and launched into a song she'd written the day after the fundraiser when she'd been high on Seth's kisses and adrenaline. As she moved from one piece to the next, she let the notes carry her away from the apartment to that place beyond herself where music always took her.

When she finally stopped, the room swam back into focus and Seth still sat on the sofa unmoving. He opened his mouth, closed it again, and patted Dolly, who must have gotten up beside him while she'd been singing.

Blood rushed through her. Maybe her songs weren't as good as she thought and he was trying to find a nice way to tell her.

He leaned forward and stared at her like he'd never seen her before. "I'm guessing you didn't write those kinds of songs when you were in Nashville."

"No. Back then, I didn't know who I was, and I was embarrassed about where I came from. I'm not that girl anymore." She hugged the guitar.

"I'm glad you aren't." His eyes went wide and he gave her a big smile. "Those songs are like a breath of fresh air. Don't ever doubt yourself again. Even though I like what I heard, we've still got work to do to get ready for the recording session. This is your chance, Annie. Grab it with both hands, hold tight, and see where the ride takes you."

At his words, the last of the fear she'd carried deep inside for so many years loosened and disintegrated, to be replaced by excitement and new confidence. "Then what are we waiting for? I'll work as hard as I need to. I won't let you down."

"As if you could ever do that. I—"

Annie's phone rang and cut off whatever Seth had been about to say. "Hold that thought." She reached behind Dolly to pull the phone from her purse where she'd left it on the sofa. "Hey, Hannah." She listened, trying to make sense of words that made no sense. "You what? Where?" She went cold, and her heart raced. "I'll get there as fast as I can."

Seth took her arm, and she swayed toward him. "What

is it? Is Hannah hurt?"

"Not as far as I know." Her voice hitched, and she could barely breathe. "She's at the police station on the other side of the mountain. She and the friend she was supposed to be studying with somehow ended up with an eighteen-year-old kid driving drunk. The police found them in a ditch twelve miles outside of town."

"What about her friend and the driver?" Seth's words came out in an urgent staccato.

"I think they're okay, but I don't . . . she . . . I don't have any details." Her body shook. "Why would she—? She could have been killed. I have to go."

A set of keys jingled. "I'll drive you." Seth still had a hold of her arm.

She set the guitar aside and put a hand to her head. "What if Hannah was drinking, too? What if there was open alcohol in the car? Isn't that illegal?"

"Usually." His voice was grim. "Here." He handed her purse to her, and Dolly's cold nose nudged her arm. "Shoes?"

"By the door." She shoved her feet into them, while he found his own shoes and clipped a leash on Dolly.

"What if Hannah gets a criminal record?" Annie gulped. "She's got her whole life ahead of her."

"She's lucky. It's still ahead of her." Seth shepherded her out of the apartment and locked both the apartment and station doors behind them. "Don't panic until you know all the facts. What exactly did she say?"

"Apart from the accident, that she's at the police station and needs me to pick her up." The warm wind cut across her face as she stumbled across the station parking lot toward Seth's truck.

"All kids do dumb things at one time or another." His hand covered hers in a brief caress as he helped her into the truck, and Dolly followed. "It sounds like this one could have been a whole lot worse."

It could, but right now, Annie couldn't think about that. A black cloud of fear pressed down to smother her. She wrapped a hand around Dolly's collar and closed her eyes as the truck engine came to life.

She had so many hopes for Hannah—so many dreams. She'd kept her safe for almost seventeen years. All she'd worried about was Todd somehow finding them. She'd never imagined something like this.

She opened her eyes again as the truck hit a pothole in front of the elementary school. It seemed like yesterday Hannah had gone there every morning with her princess backpack and matching lunchbox, waving before she got on the school bus. How could everything have gone so wrong?

Chapter 16

"Are you hungry?" Seth studied Annie perched on the edge of a straight-backed chair in a small office at the police station. Her face was gray and pinched. "There's chicken noodle soup in the vending machine."

"I can't eat anything." She rubbed her arms. "Hannah?"

The teen shook her head. Slumped in a chair beside Annie, a reddish bruise ran along one side of her jaw.

"Drink something then. Tea, a soda, or more coffee?" He gestured to the sludge-like brew in a *Star Wars* mug on the table in front of her.

"No." She put a hand to her mouth.

Seth's belly knotted. Dylan had made his share of mistakes, but so far not one like this. He stared out the window behind the table. Gray clouds massed above the mountain, and wind stirred the branches of the pine trees beyond the parking lot. His truck was parked outside, and Dolly's head poked through the partially-open window.

"I screwed up." Hannah rolled the hem of her T-shirt up and down. "I'm sorry."

"I know you are, and I'm not mad. Disappointed in your behavior? Yes. Scared, too." Annie let out a long breath. "And what I still don't get is why you got into a car with a kid who'd been drinking? You told me you were going to Natalie's to study."

"I was. It just happened." Hannah squirmed on the chair. "Zach drove by and saw us on the porch. When he asked if we wanted to go for a ride, we thought it would only be in town. We didn't know he'd been drinking then."

"But as soon as you did, why didn't you tell him to stop the car so you could get out? Or call the police or me? That's the biggest reason why you have a phone." Annie's chin trembled. "If that wasn't an emergency, I don't know what was."

"I couldn't. I'd have looked stupid." Hannah grimaced.

"Better stupid than dead." Annie's voice faltered.

Hannah flushed and darted a glance at Seth. "I thought you'd be busy."

"How could you think I'd ever be too busy for you?"

"Forget it." Hannah tucked her chin into her chest.

"How can I?" Annie massaged her temples. "I'm so thankful you're okay, but you could have . . . and on Sunday afternoon."

"Would it have been better if it was Saturday night?" Hannah worried her bottom lip.

"Of course not." Annie's expression tensed. "But I thought you had more sense, and even if you didn't see alcohol in the car, didn't you smell it? Zach was so far over the legal limit, it's a wonder he even made it out of town, let alone all the way over here."

"We wanted to have some fun."

"Fun? When did driving drunk become fun for you?" Annie's voice rose.

"Zach's cute, and he's a senior. He has a football scholarship to Penn State." Hannah mumbled the words.

"According to one of the officers out there, Zach likely has a leg fracture to remind him of his stupidity and keep him off any football field for a good long while, as well as a court case in his future for underage drinking and driving under the influence. And Natalie might have broken her wrist." Annie covered her face with her hands.

Seth winced. "I'll go out to the waiting room. You two need your privacy." And he shouldn't be in the middle of someone else's family drama. Maybe he should have stayed in the waiting room to begin with, but until they found out what was going on with Hannah, he didn't want to leave Annie alone.

She lifted her head. "Maybe we do, but you can't go out there. By now, that waiting room will be full of Quinns, Quinns by marriage, and a bunch of McEvoys—that was Mom's maiden name. They all live nearby, and if you go out there, it'll be as good as a deer wandering into camp in hunting season."

Seth pressed a hand to his temple. "We haven't been here long so how—"

"A few minutes after we went into the ditch, a couple of Grandma's cousins drove by and stopped. They called the police." Hannah's voice was small. "They'd have called a few people, and then they'd have called other people . . ." She stopped and bowed her head. "Nothing is ever private for long around here. I made a fool of myself, and Mom too."

"Oh, honey." Annie gave Hannah a faint smile. "It's not so bad we can't fix it. At least the beer was in the trunk and you weren't drinking. I don't like what you did today, but I still love you."

"Despite everything, you got lucky, kiddo." It wasn't as if Seth hadn't done dumb things in high school, but the only consequences had been extra chores and a few detentions here and there.

"But everyone else . . ." Hannah's gaze darted to the door. "I don't want to face them." She slid farther down in the chair.

"Then you don't have to. At least not right now." Seth couldn't change what had happened, but maybe he could make things a bit better than they were. "There has to be a back door. While you wait for the rest of the paperwork, I'll find out."

Annie's eyes softened. "Thanks. I don't really want to face everyone myself right now."

His gaze held hers for a long moment and something shifted near his heart. "Sit tight. I'll be back soon. I spotted another office at the end of the hall so I can avoid the waiting room." But even if he had to walk through fifty waiting rooms filled with Annie's family, it didn't matter. Family or not, anybody who said anything bad about her or Hannah would have to deal with him.

"Okay." Her voice was low. "Thanks for being here for us."

"Thank you from me too." Several tears rolled down Hannah's bruised face.

"No problem." Adrenaline surged through Seth's body. Not only had Todd treated Annie like dirt, but he hadn't wanted a baby who'd become this precious girl.

He moved to the office door on unsteady legs. He wanted to help Annie and protect her, but this was a whole lot more than that. *Love*. The word zinged through him and left him breathless. He couldn't be falling in love with her, could he?

He pushed open the door and stepped into the institutional beige hallway then pressed a hand to his chest. He thought he'd loved Amanda, but he hadn't, not really, and she hadn't loved him, either. The two of them had been kids caught up in a rush of sex, music, and dreams of a glittering future.

Grown-up love was different. It was quieter, steadier, and there in good times and bad. His skin tingled, and his heart raced. When he'd thought about finding out where things might go with Annie, he'd never considered it could take him somewhere this serious. Somewhere that felt a whole lot like a real family, home, and commitment—everything he'd never thought he'd have.

~ ~ ~

Annie hesitated outside Hannah's closed bedroom door. In the silent house, the late-afternoon sun made a checkerboard pattern on the sloping pine floor of the upstairs hall. Five days after the accident, her daughter still only spoke to her when she had to and, when she wasn't at school, had spent most of her time holed up in her bedroom under the eaves.

Taking a deep breath, Annie tapped on the door.

"What?" Her daughter's voice was wary.

"I want to talk to you." Annie's chest had a fluttery feeling and her muscles constricted.

"What about?"

"I'm not talking to you through a closed door." Her mom had told her parenting a teenage girl was tough, but until now, she hadn't realized how tough.

The door swung inward, and her daughter's face appeared on the other side. The bruises from the accident had faded to a yellowish-purple, but Annie worried more about the emotional wounds.

"Thank you." Annie moved into the room. Instead of its usual state of untidiness, it was almost painfully neat. Only the rumpled teal comforter and pair of mismatched socks in the middle of the floor disturbed the pristine order.

"Whatever." Hannah went to the window, turned her back on Annie, and stared into the backyard.

Annie wrung her hands. "Your room looks . . . different . . . good."

The teen gave an exaggerated shrug.

"I've said I'm not mad at you for what happened, but we have to talk about it." More importantly, they had to talk about Hannah's throwaway comment at the police station about Annie being too busy for her. The angry words had lodged in Annie's heart like a poisoned arrow and, each time she relived them, the poison seeped deeper and hardened into her soul.

"Why?" Hannah half turned from the window and, mixed with her sulky expression, was defensiveness and maybe even fear. "Wasn't it enough you took away my phone and grounded me so I missed the class pool party?"

"I need to make sure you understand what you did was serious and how much you scared me." Annie still woke up at night imagining what might have happened. "We also can't keep on not talking to each other like this." She was the adult, so she had to take the lead in trying to fix what had gone wrong between them.

"Don't you have a rehearsal with Seth or something?" Hannah stared at her bare feet. Beneath the hem of her ripped jeans, her toenails sported bright red polish.

"Not today." And there it was. The elephant in the room, or maybe the whole house. Big, gray, lumbering, and almost as destructive as a real elephant would have been to their little world. "Do you have a problem with me rehearsing with Seth?"

"Why would I?" Hannah's words were too quick and her tone too sharp.

"I don't know." Annie wanted to run back down the stairs and maybe out of the house, but she had to face this, whatever it was. "Why don't you try telling me?"

Hannah stared at her for several endless seconds. "Music was always my thing, not yours, but now . . . it's not Seth. Not exactly, anyway." Hannah's voice got low. "I like him and all, but . . ." She fiddled with an edge of her T-shirt.

"But what?" Even if Annie might not want to hear the answer, she had to ask the question. She sat on the edge of Hannah's bed and patted the comforter beside her.

"I never thought music was so important to you, but with 'My Hometown Heart,' and singing at the fundraiser . . . it . . . everything." Hannah sat on the opposite side of the bed, as far from Annie as possible.

"Music was always important to me, but I forgot how much." Annie's throat closed, and the backs of her eyes burned.

"Because of my dad?" Hannah's shoulders were hunched.

Annie gave a jerky nod.

"I know you said he didn't want me, but what really happened?" Her daughter's voice hitched.

"No, he didn't." Annie pressed her lips together. "He . . . didn't want you to even be born, so I ran away. A few years later, I tried to find out what happened to him, but I couldn't." And she'd lived most of the past seventeen years with a fear that lurked in the background of her life. "I gave up my music because I somehow thought it would help keep me safe, keep you safe, too."

"But why? I don't understand." Hannah's expression was both hurt and puzzled.

"I know it doesn't make sense, does it? But I was young, mixed up, and scared. I wasn't thinking clearly, and then that mixed-up thinking became a habit." Her chest burned.

"Did you love my dad?" Hannah's voice was halting.

"I thought I did, at least at first. When I met him, he was fun to be with. We both liked music, and we wrote songs together. I thought he could help me. But when I got pregnant with you, he changed." Sweat pooled between her breasts. "It was like he wanted to control my life, and I couldn't. . . he got so angry. I was afraid of him."

Hannah slid across the bed toward her. "I'm sorry." Her voice thickened with tears.

Annie looped her hand with her daughter's. "He also started drinking more, so when you got in that car with Zach, it brought stuff back for me. I can't lose you, and I thought . . ." She took her daughter's hand and squeezed.

"I . . . you won't lose me." Hannah squeezed back. "I'll never do anything like that again."

Some of the pressure in Annie's chest eased. "Because I met your dad, I didn't do a lot of things in my life maybe I could have. I wanted you, don't think I didn't, but that's why I want you to go to college and do all the stuff I never had a chance to."

"I'm not you." Hannah's voice was earnest. "And I'm not him, either."

"No, you're your own person, and I'm glad of it." Annie tried to smile. "And maybe I was wrong. Why would a guy like him ever have tracked me down? He was from Florida, he never mentioned any family, and I don't think he'd ever been farther north than Kentucky. But, being with your dad changed me and since then I've never wanted to stand out."

"But now you do?" Hannah's tone was careful. "With the singing and songwriting?"

"I don't know." Annie owed it to her daughter to be honest. "It's confusing." The understatement of the month, if not the year. "Probably nothing will come of this recording session."

"But if it does?" Hannah's expression was more adult than child.

"Like Nana Gerry used to say, I'll cross that bridge when I come to it." Her heart skittered. "But whatever happens, I want you to be part of it. Do you believe me?"

"I guess." Hannah still searched her face. "The thing with Zach snowballed. It was exciting. I mean, why would a guy like him pay attention to Natalie and me? He hangs around with cheerleaders. And you were so excited about the song and working with Seth, I kind of felt . . . I don't know . . . left out maybe?"

"Oh, honey." Annie's heart compressed. "I never knew. I thought you were excited about the song and singing at the fundraiser too."

"I was, but then when it took off, maybe I also got a bit jealous. And when Seth turned up at the police station with you, he was great and all, but it was still kind of weird." She fiddled with a strand of hair.

"I understand." It had been kind of weird for Annie, too. For the first time in her life, someone apart from her family and Jake had looked out for her. Seth hadn't taken over, but he'd been the kind of support she hadn't known she'd needed.

"Do you think you could, I don't know, like maybe try again to find my dad?" Hannah's voice was hesitant. "I don't want to meet him or anything, but so we know what happened to him? If he's still out there somewhere? I don't want to go through my life thinking I might run into him."

"Of course I can." Annie had avoided the whole Todd issue for so many years it had become a habit—one she had to break.

"If you give me more information, I could look on the Internet. You can find out stuff about almost anyone there." Hannah looked at their joined hands then looped her free arm around Annie's rigid shoulders.

"We can look together." No matter what they found, she could face it with Hannah by her side. "About Seth and the recording session, will you still sing with me? It wouldn't be the same without you."

"Try to keep me away." Her daughter's voice lightened. "Who else are you going to find to sing backup vocals?"

"I don't want anybody but you." Annie's heart pinched. When it came to backup vocals, she didn't, but when it came to her life, things weren't so simple.

"About Zach, I made a big mistake. I should have known better."

"You learned your lesson, so we won't say anything more about it." And in time, maybe Annie's fear would fade like Hannah's bruises.

"Natalie's folks are so pissed they're sending her to visit family in South Dakota for three whole weeks as soon as school lets out." Hannah made a face. "As if a broken wrist isn't bad enough, she's going to be staring at wheat fields for days. Her mom says it will give her time to think about what she did. I'm glad we don't have any relatives for you to ship me off to."

No. All Annie's relatives were clustered in this little area, and that created a whole other set of problems, including parenting advice on her doorstep. Almost every female member of her family within a twenty-mile radius had popped into the bakery this week to talk about Hannah. They'd asked about Seth too, darting furtive glances at the ceiling, as if he could somehow hear them through the floor. South Dakota wheat fields were surprisingly appealing right now.

Hannah scooted closer to Annie. "I still don't know what I want to do about college, but maybe . . ." She let out a long breath. "I'll talk to the guidance counsellor before school ends. I can see why it might be a good idea to keep some options open."

"That's great." Annie's eyes watered.

"I love you, Mom." Hannah's voice cracked.

"I love you, too, sweetheart."

"About my dad . . ." Hannah nestled against Annie like she'd done as a small child. "Nothing he did can ever hurt you again. It can't hurt me, either."

Annie shivered. Despite her daughter's confident words, if only she could be so sure.

Chapter 17

All Annie had to do was sing. It was about the music, not her. Not about her and Seth, either. It had been a lot of years, but apart from some drool-worthy equipment, recording studios hadn't changed much, at least not in the ways that mattered. They all held a little bit of magic and echoes of the hopes and dreams of the musicians who'd passed through them over the years.

From the main road, the place looked like an ordinary upstate New York clapboard farmhouse nestled into a stand of trees on several acres of land. But behind the house another building, custom designed and soundproofed, held a comfortable studio with state-of-the art equipment and acoustics.

"Are you okay?" She glanced at Hannah, who sat in a purple beanbag chair in the middle of the reception area. Although her daughter's cuts and bruises had healed, that was only on the outside. Despite their talk, Hannah still had some bruises on the inside and maybe always would.

"Why wouldn't I be?" Hannah picked at a hangnail on her thumb.

Annie set Jake's guitar case on a low table and took out the Gibson. "I thought you were more excited about doing the recording, that's all. If there's anything . . . I mean . . ."

"It's not that. You've included me every step of the way, and I *am* excited but . . ." She stared at the turquoise boots Annie, Tara, and Rowan had all chipped in to buy for her sixteenth birthday. "What if I mess this up for you?"

"Why would you? And even if you, me, or anyone else makes a mistake, we can try again. It's not like this is a live performance. Besides, you did great at the fundraiser."

"It's not the same." Hannah got to her feet and looked out one of the floor-to-ceiling windows at the stunning view of the southern Adirondacks. "I know everybody in Irish Falls, but it's different here. How could someone like me belong in a place like this? You can almost smell the money, you know? And those guys in there? They're so professional."

"Oh, honey, of course you belong here." Except, if she was right, her daughter felt like Annie had all those years ago in Nashville—a small-town girl way out of her depth and comfort zone. "I know it's scary, but we're doing this together. You'll be fine. As for the backup musicians, it's their job. They're here to help us." Although Annie had been in a recording studio before, she was as nervous as Hannah, maybe more.

The outside door swung open, and an older guy with shaggy gray-blond hair Seth had introduced earlier as his friend, Pete Johannsen, came into the reception area, then Seth with a picnic cooler, and Tara.

"Surprise." Tara grinned. "I'm here for moral support and snack delivery." She gestured to the cooler Seth set on a desk. "How's my favorite young woman?" She slung an arm around Hannah, and the teen gave her an awkward hug in return.

"I can't believe it." Annie's heart squeezed. "You drove all the way over here, but you never said a word."

"I swore Seth to secrecy." Tara's smile broadened, and she took drinks and food containers out of the cooler. "I didn't drive here by myself. I came with Rowan and her kids. They'll pick me up later after they go on some scenic train ride." She handed Annie a bottle of water. "This is a big deal for you and Hannah. Of course I'd be here. Rowan wanted to come, but you know how active her two are. She was worried they might break something."

Annie curled her fingers around the ice-cold water. Her family might be nosy and interfering, but they always had her back. "Rowan . . . she and the kids need time together, too." Because, although joint custody was fair, it was also hard.

"Yeah, they do." Tara's tone was strained. "So, tell me everything." She glanced around. "I've never been in a recording studio before."

"What do you want to know?" Pete grinned at Tara. He had the same mellow Southern accent as Seth, and, although he must be in his late fifties, hair flopped over his forehead to give him a sexy Nordic rock star look.

"Has anybody famous recorded a song here?" Her sister gave him a shy smile.

Pete's blue eyes crinkled at the corners. "Sure, but most of them like to keep a low profile."

"Wow." Hannah sidled up beside Annie and let out a soft breath.

"Lots of big names have been through the same studio where you and your mom are going to be singing." Pete's smile widened.

"That is so awesome." Hannah's voice came out in an excited squeak.

"Why don't you help the backup guys finish getting set up in there and give your aunt a tour?" Pete inclined his head toward Tara. "We'll join you in a minute. My wife's sorry she's not here to meet you all. She's babysitting our grandkids today. Being closer to our daughter and her family is one of the reasons we moved here."

"Family first." Tara's voice caught and then her heels tapped on the polished floor as she followed Hannah in the direction of the studio.

Annie turned to Seth. "We're booked for a few hours,

right?"

He nodded. "Longer if we need it."

"Seth and I worked together a lot over the years. He knows music, so if he says you're good, you must be." Pete studied Annie, and her face heated under his scrutiny. "We go way back. See?" He gestured to a picture in the middle of a wall of framed photos behind the reception desk.

Annie moved closer to look. A much younger Seth stared out at her from the faded color snapshot. He wore jeans, a graphic T-shirt, and a backward baseball cap over his dark hair and had a guitar slung low. A girl with long brown hair, in a black T-shirt and short denim shorts, stood in front of a microphone backed by two other guys, one behind a drum kit, the other holding a bass guitar. Pete, younger and blonder, stood off to the side with a clipboard.

She glanced at Seth. "You must have still been a teenager."

"I'd just turned eighteen. That picture was taken soon after I got to LA," Seth said. "Back then, I was in a band and Pete helped us record a demo. We were bad country meets bad rock and roll and, except for Amanda, we had bad hair, and bad clothes, but Pete took us in hand and helped us figure out who we were and got us some gigs."

"Amanda?" Annie glanced between the two men and then back at the girl in the picture.

"My ex-wife. Dylan's mom." Seth's voice was expressionless.

"Oh." Annie studied the picture again. The girl was a knock-out, but there was a hardness to her, like she knew how pretty she was and didn't hesitate to use it.

"She had a decent voice, and she was savvy when it came to production and promotion." Pete's tone was dry. "Ruthless too. You didn't get in her way when she wanted something." He glanced at Seth with a fatherly expression.

"But without real talent and a bad attitude . . ." He stopped and shrugged.

Seth rubbed a hand against his chest. "We were kids with a dream." He stared at the photo, his gaze unfocused. "Although that dream didn't take me where I thought it would, it still helped me get started in the music business."

Hannah's boots clattered, and Annie looked up. "Mom, it's amazing. The musicians are really nice, and you won't believe it when I tell you who they've played with." Her daughter's eyes sparkled.

"You ready, Annie?" Seth's blue-gray gaze met hers.

"As ready as I'll ever be." She pushed her shoulders back, even as her heart raced and her mouth went dry.

She'd been wrong. Today wasn't only about the music. It was about her and Seth, too. By bringing her here, he'd given her a glimpse of his past and how he'd come to be the man she knew. The man she was falling into something special with, day by day, and song by song.

~ ~ ~

After the last echo of Annie's voice faded, Seth turned to Pete, who sat beside him in the cramped control room. "What do you think?"

"You sure can pick them. Ever thought about a new career in talent scouting?" His friend chuckled, but his blue eyes narrowed in concentration. "She's got the voice, but you said she wrote that song, too? 'My Hometown Heart?'"

"Annie wrote all the songs she sang today." Although she and Hannah were only recording "My Hometown Heart," Seth had asked them to sing a few others as well to warm up and so the backup musicians could get a sense of their voices.

"You've struck gold, buddy." Pete leaned back. "Those songs of hers are magic."

Seth looked through the glass at Annie and Hannah.

Annie sat on a low stool and cradled Jake's guitar. When she looked up to speak to the keyboard player, a tall guy with cropped brown hair and glasses, her expression was animated.

"Do you think Rick would be interested in hearing her? Remember when we worked together on that jazz project, he said he was always looking for new talent for the label?" Unlike some people in the music business, Rick was solid and loyal, not someone who only hung around because they thought Seth could help them in their career and disappeared when his life crashed and burned.

Pete chuckled. "Does the guy like making money? Sure, he'd want to hear her." Pete swiveled in his chair until his back was to Annie, Hannah, and the band. "Annie can sing, sure, but it's her songwriting I bet he'd be more interested in. Have you asked her to work with you?"

Seth shook his head. "No." He'd only just started writing songs for himself again. His muse was still too fragile to share it with anyone. "Annie's pretty set on keeping her life the way it is. It took a lot of convincing to get her to record this one song." He turned his chair around too so he didn't have to see the keyboard player flirting with Annie—and fight a sudden, irrational urge to charge out of the control room and throttle a kid who couldn't have been more than twenty-three. "She also wants to protect Hannah. You know what this business is like."

"I do, but Hannah seems like a girl who'll get what she wants." Pete's smile was amused. "She's got talent, youth, and looks on her side, so if she works hard and sticks to it, who knows what might happen? But I doubt Rick would be interested in her, at least not yet. However, the guy is connected with a lot of people who'd kill to record a song like Annie's."

"True, but I have to take it slow." Seth rubbed a hand through his hair, a sinking feeling in his stomach. "Annie's a single parent, and Hannah's dad was out of the picture before she was born. Annie went to Nashville when she only a year or so older than Hannah and met him there. He was a musician and, from the sounds of it, a real dick. Thanks to him, when I met Annie, she was afraid to sing or draw attention to herself in any way. She's come a long way since April."

"Not only in her music." Pete spoke around a mouthful of one of Tara's butter tarts. "Why didn't you tell me you're having a thing with her?" He gave Seth a slow sideways smile.

"It's . . . nothing's official." Seth heartbeat hammered in his ears and he stared at his boots.

Pete snorted. "You've fallen for more than Annie's music. You were about to pitch a fit the way that keyboard guy looked at her. If you ask me, it's about time."

"I didn't ask you." Seth's tone was harsher than he'd intended. He swung his chair back around.

On the other side of the window, Annie strummed the guitar with a faraway look on her face, and the keyboard player had gone back to where he was supposed to be behind Hannah.

"Sorry, I haven't . . . we haven't . . ."

"No, but you're fixing to, and soon." Pete swiveled and tilted his head to one side. "What's Amanda up to these days?"

"The usual." Seth's stomach knotted.

"Too bad." Pete shrugged. "But it's nothing to do with you."

It wasn't, so after all these years, why was Seth still so wary of getting involved with any other woman? And why was he so scared to think about, let alone say, the word love?

"Why did you marry Amanda anyway? That was one break-up I saw coming a mile away." Pete grabbed another butter tart.

"She got pregnant. I wanted to do the right thing." Except, it had turned out to be the wrong thing—not only for him, but Dylan too. "It is what it is." And as much as he'd beat himself up for his choices, it didn't change the outcome and he didn't want to imagine what his life would be like without his son.

"My wife and I will have to take a trip to Irish Falls one of these days." Pete waved a half-eaten tart in Seth's direction. "These are great. And if there are any other singers like Annie tucked away in that valley, the two of us could start some kind of new business venture."

"My lumpy bed is yours any time you want it." Pete was a cross between the big brother and the dad Seth had never had. "You'd still work with me after . . .?"

"Why not?" Pete licked his sticky fingers. "None of what happened in LA was your fault. Anybody who knows you would never think you'd be involved in any wrongdoing. And once things settle . . . people there have short memories, you'll be fine. You'll go back, won't you?"

"I guess so." Although the prospect was less appealing than it used to be. "For now, though, the radio station gig is working out." He glanced at Annie, who had her back to him, chatting to the keyboard player again, her red-gold hair cascading down her back. "If you visit, you can guest on my morning show."

"Don't count on it." Pete grinned. "I never liked the limelight. I thought I'd miss LA, but I don't. People here are real, you know?" His expression sobered. "I'm heading for retirement, but you should still be in the fast lane. Next you'll tell me you've got a dog and you're playing in a darts league in some country bar."

"One out of two." And it sure felt good. "The dog is called Dolly." Seth grinned back. "Irish Falls has grown on me."

"The place or the woman?"

"None of your business." Seth gave Pete a flat stare. "I don't kiss and tell."

"Bless your heart." Pete elbowed him, then his deep laugh rolled out. "Living in the boonies sure has changed you."

"For the better." Seth made a face. "There are more cows than clubs around here, too."

"A few of those cows in that field are mine. I've started a hobby farm." Pete looked away, and his teasing expression slipped. "Life's short and it's precious. My wife had a breast cancer scare before we moved here. She's fine, but it put a lot of things into perspective for me. I want to grow old with my family around me, and I spent too much time sitting in freeway traffic. What I've got here is real living."

Whereas, despite his songwriting success, the clients, and the flashy parties, Seth had been drifting in LA. He'd packed a lot into his life, but, apart from the time he spent with Dylan, how much of it had been real living?

"How's my godson?" Pete's voice warmed.

"Dylan's great." And since his Memorial Day weekend visit, his son messaged and called more than he had, and although the two of them didn't share what they once did, maybe they were building something better.

"In spite of Amanda, you got lucky, and you raised a good kid." Pete's voice was gruff. "In the end, what you leave behind is all that matters."

"Thanks." Seth's throat tightened.

There was a tap on the control room door, then it opened and Annie stuck her head through. "So, how were we? Hannah's convinced we're the next hot country-pop duo, so when she comes back from the restroom, please break it to her gently." Her smile was droll. "You two have been in here long enough to listen to that recording ten times over."

"You were great." Pete stood. "I want to work on a few

more things and smooth out a couple of edges, but why don't you take five while I talk to the guys out there?"

Annie stepped away to let Pete through the doorway, and Seth gestured her to the chair his friend had vacated. "He's right. You *were* great. I hope hearing somebody else say it, apart from me, means you'll believe it."

"Maybe." Annie grinned. Tendrils of hair curled around her face, and her eyes sparkled. "But now I've done it, I have to admit singing here today felt good. You were right."

Seth grinned back. "I can't wait to play this recording of 'My Hometown Heart' on my show. Trust me, that song is magic."

"I don't believe in magic anymore." Annie's smile disappeared. "Maybe I never will again, at least not until I find out what happened to Todd. Hannah and I looked on the Internet, but we couldn't find anything."

He let out a breath. "Let me help you."

"You'd do that for me?"

"Sure. Don't you trust me?"

She looked down. "As much as I can trust anyone. "If you haven't noticed, I have a problem with trust."

He touched her clenched hands, a brief caress. "You're not the only one."

She gave him a jerky nod. "I guess folks in Irish Falls want to hear my song again."

"They sure do."

Annie had no idea—and now wasn't the time to tell her—but playing the song on his show would only be the start.

"There's something about it that touches people."

Like something about her touched him. His heart seemed to freeze, and then it pounded as his gaze locked with hers. "Annie . . . I . . ." He stopped and licked his lips.

"What?" She rolled her chair closer to his.

What they'd been skirting around for weeks hung

between them. It was what they both wanted and couldn't resist any longer. "Hannah . . ."

"Asked me if she could go home with Tara, Rowan and the kids. After we finish here, they want to go to a mall. Tara said Hannah could spend the night at her place." Annie blew out several short breaths.

Not only was it what they both wanted, but they were old enough to go into it without expectations, regrets, or disappointment. "So we'll be on our own for the ride back?" Seth's stomach rolled.

"If it's okay with you." She stumbled over the words and avoided his gaze.

It was more than okay, but maybe he needed to put the brakes on. Maybe she wasn't thinking what he was. "We could have an early dinner here first. Hannah says you like Tex Mex. Pete told me about a place that's really good. We could celebrate recording your song." Seth tried to work moisture into his mouth. If dinner was all it was, he was okay with that. Whatever happened between them after dinner would be her call.

"That sounds . . . fun." Annie touched his forearm, and heat tingled along Seth's nerve ends.

"Great." He cleared his throat, and Annie pulled her hand away as Pete came back into the booth.

"Are you ready to run through your song again, Annie? Hannah and the guys are all set." Pete glanced between the two of them and, when his gaze landed on Seth, his smile was way too perceptive.

"Absolutely," Annie said. And when she smiled at Seth, her smile was soft and full of sweet promise.

Chapter 18

Annie eased the kitchen door closed on Dolly, then turned back to Seth. Either he was bigger, or her house had all of a sudden shrunk. Or maybe it was neither of those things and she was simply more aware of him than ever before. "Are you sure Dolly will be okay in there?"

"She'll be fine." In the muted light, his eyes were dark blue with flecks of silver. "I bet she's happier than those cats of yours."

Annie didn't need the reminder. Hazel and Olivia were used to having the run of the house, but because of Dolly, the kitchen was now off limits. Figuring out logistics for kids and pets when you had a man stay over was only one of the complications of dating at her age.

Although she and Seth weren't actually dating, were they? She also hadn't invited him to stay overnight, so she could still change her mind. She sucked in her stomach. She'd been a lot thinner the last time she'd gotten naked with a man, and that was a much more important complication.

"Would you like a drink? I can open a bottle of wine or I have juice, soda or hot cocoa. Although it's June, it can still get chilly at night." Annie rubbed her hands down the front of her jeans. She was babbling. And why had she suggested cocoa? It wasn't the kind of drink you offered a guy if you were thinking about seducing him.

He shook his head. "I'm not thirsty."

"Was Dolly okay today with Brendan and Holly?" Annie twirled a piece of hair between her fingers. The stairs to the second floor loomed in front of her—stairs that led to her bedroom halfway along the upstairs hall.

"Brendan said Dolly sat by their front door most of the day like she was listening for my truck. When I picked her up, she almost turned somersaults, she was so excited." Seth's fingers covered hers and then tunneled into her hair.

"Dolly likes you." Her breathing sped up as he massaged the tight muscles at the back of her neck, his fingers warm and touch sensual.

Seth's laugh was low. "I hope you like me, too."

"Of course." She shivered as his fingers traced behind her ear and then along her jaw. Liking him wasn't in doubt. But what if she let herself like him too much?

His hand slipped down her back. "I sure like you."

Liking each other was good. It meant they were friends. Annie gulped as his hand slid around her waist and up toward her breasts.

"Hannah and my sisters got back okay." She trembled as Seth stroked her sides through her top. "Tara said she'll take Hannah out for breakfast tomorrow morning. The Black Duck does a special Sunday breakfast and—"

"Does that mean you want me to stick around until tomorrow morning?" His tone was amused, and then his breath hitched as his hand slipped sideways to cover the slope of her breast.

Her skin burned, and she held her breath. This was what she wanted, wasn't it? She'd given him all the right signals at the studio, over dinner, and on the drive back to Irish Falls. But it had been so long. Like doing that recording. What if she'd forgotten what she'd once known how to do? She arched closer to him then stilled.

His hand fell away from her breast. "Do you want me to stop?" He took a step back, and her body cooled. "It's okay if you changed your mind."

"No, I meant . . . I want this." And it wasn't only to banish Todd's ghost forever, a man who'd exerted too much power over her even long after he was no longer in her life. It was part of becoming the woman she wanted to be—one who didn't live her life in fear and who listened to—and lived from—her heart. She took his hand and led him up the stairs. "Have you changed your mind?"

"No." His voice was hoarse. At the top of the stairs, he looked left and right along the narrow hall. "Which way?"

She nodded left. Golden light from the lamp on the bedside table she'd turned on earlier shone through her half-open bedroom door.

Seth swung her into his arms for the few steps to the door and pushed it all the way open before closing it behind them.

Her bed was covered with its familiar floral comforter and stacked with plump pillows. Her pine dresser and matching dressing table sat along opposite walls, with a rocking chair in the corner by the window. Several dark blue rag rugs were scattered across the plank floor. Although the room looked the same as always, it felt different. She was different.

She tucked her face into the crook of Seth's chin. He must have stopped at his apartment to shower in the short time between dropping her off at home and going to pick up Dolly, because he wore a fresh blue shirt and different jeans. He also smelled of something crisp and citrusy. She kissed the side of his neck, and he shuddered. He set her on the edge of the bed and smoothed her hair away from her face.

"The first thing I noticed about you was your hair." He wound a tendril around his fingers.

"Even though I was wearing a hairnet because I was at work?" Annie traced the strong contours of his face. He must have shaved, too, because his skin was smooth beneath her fingers, with no beard stubble.

"There were a few little curls sticking out from under the net. I'd never seen anyone with hair like yours." He dropped a gentle kiss on the curve of her cheek. "I wanted to pull the net off to see if the rest of your hair was as pretty as those curls. Then when you came back from the kitchen with Jake's key, I saw it was."

Something shifted near Annie's heart, and her knees went weak. "When Tara's around, nobody looks at me, but you did." And then, as now, the expression on his face all those weeks ago had sent the same heat through her.

"How could I not?" Seth eased her back onto the ruffled pillows at the head of the bed and gave her a slow smile before he lay beside her.

"When you're one of three sisters close in age, sometimes it feels like that's all you are. You also get labelled. Tara's the pretty one, Rowan's the smart one, and I'm the musical one. I'm the quiet one too so, even before I went to Nashville, I got used to blending into the background."

"I've never compared you with your sisters, and I won't." Seth's voice got rough and, as he leaned on one elbow to look into her face, his gaze was tender. "You're your own woman all the way through."

"I won't compare you with anyone else, either. I did to begin with, but only because on the surface you reminded me of Todd." Her breath caught. "But now, you don't and you haven't for ages. I . . ." She stopped and bit her lip.

"You what?" Seth's voice was soft, and there was no judgment in his tone.

"It was easier when I thought you were like Todd because it meant . . . I wouldn't . . ." Her face got warm. "I didn't want to be attracted to you, but I couldn't stop it."

He reached for her hand and laced her fingers with his. "I couldn't stop it, either. I don't want to hurt you, and I hope you trust me at least a little bit."

Her throat clogged. She did. She wouldn't sleep with him otherwise. "A part of me trusted you right from the start. A lot of people would have taken Dolly to a shelter, but you didn't. A lot of people who were new in town wouldn't have pitched in like you did when the river flooded and some folks lost everything."

"I didn't do much." He squeezed her hand. "Talking on the radio isn't a big deal."

"At a time like that, it was." She squeezed back. "Besides, even though you might not have wanted folks to know, you were heaving sandbags, too."

His cheeks reddened. "How?"

"I have family everywhere, remember?" She gave him a small smile. "And no matter how you feel about Jake and what he did to you, you've still respected his station and his show, but you've made it your own."

"Thank you." His gaze never left hers, and his eyes glowed in the lamplight.

"But most of all, you helped me believe in myself again." Annie pressed her free hand to her chest. "Without you, I'd never have been able to sing at the fundraiser or do that recording today."

"Sure you would." Seth's voice was a whisper between them. "All I did was give you a little nudge." He took his hand away from hers to play with the lacing tie on her navy top. "You drove me crazy during the recording, you know that?"

"How?" She traced the contours of his back through his shirt.

"You know exactly how." He shuddered as she slid her hand beneath his shirt to caress the warm skin of his back. "It's a wonder that keyboard guy could play." His chuckle was low and sexy. "From the way you held the mike, to how you moved in those jeans, and then this shirt." He traced the curve of her breasts, harder this time.

"It isn't low cut." She shivered and leaned into his touch.

"It doesn't have to be." In several deft moves, he undid the ribbon tie and eased the top up and over her head. "You could wear a flour sack and turn me on, so it doesn't take much, but this . . ." He sucked in a breath. "And until now, I didn't know what you had on underneath." His heated gaze landed on the aqua push-up bra she'd bought to wear for courage at the recording. "You're beautiful."

Along with his words, that heat warmed her and gave her confidence. It had been a long time since she'd felt beautiful, let alone had a man tell her so. "I'm glad you like it."

"Like it?" His laugh was wicked, and he dipped a finger into the deep valley between her breasts. "And all these little freckles . . ." The tip of his finger lingered on each one in a sensual caress. "They're beautiful, too."

"I'm a redhead. Freckles come with the territory." Her heart swelled as she fumbled with the buttons on his shirt.

"What a territory." He grinned and, when she undid the last button, he shrugged out of the shirt and dropped it onto the rug beside the bed.

"You have a tattoo." She reached out to trace the stylized music note on his right shoulder.

"I got it when I was in that band." His breathing was labored.

She pushed away the memory of how Todd had wanted her to get tattoos like his. Except, she'd always resisted. It was the one thing she'd stood up for herself about. She fingered his belt buckle.

Seth's eyes darkened. "I want to be with you, Annie. I've wanted it for weeks."

"Me too." She unbuckled his belt and undid the top button of his jeans.

He let out a strangled groan. "I don't sleep around."

"Me neither." And if she thought about how long it had been for her, she'd lose her nerve.

He pulled a condom out of one of the pockets of his jeans and then reached for her again.

She licked her lips. She could show him her body and let him in, at least as much as she could ever let him or any other man in. She wasn't the Annie Quinn who worked in her family's bakery, sat in the back row of the choir, or one of the Quinn sisters, either. Instead, she was the woman who'd recorded in a real studio a song she'd written. And Pete, as well as the studio musicians, guys who knew the business and had worked with some big names, had admired and respected her work.

She was finally the woman she'd always wanted to be.

~ ~ ~

Seth's heart thumped as he cradled Annie in his arms. Everything about her body was soft and delicate, but there was a strong woman inside that petite but curvy frame.

She murmured something unintelligible, and he stilled.

"What is it?" His whole body shook. They'd only just made love, but he already wanted her again.

"I . . ." Her lips wobbled and her eyes glistened. She let out another inarticulate cry, rolled onto her side, and curled her knees up toward her chest.

Shit. She was crying. He gulped. He hadn't hurt her, had he? "I'm sorry. I'll make it better for you next time. I couldn't hold back."

As she'd moved with him and murmured sweet words, he'd lost himself, body and soul.

"You couldn't make it any better for me." Her voice was raw.

He stroked her back. "Then what?"

Her shoulders tensed. "I thought I could . . . I did . . . but now . . ."

"Hey, you were great." He eased her into the curve of his body and pulled the rumpled sheet over them.

"That was a big deal for me."

"It was a big deal for me, too." Sex with her was different than it had been with anyone else, ever. Better, more comfortable, and somehow entirely right. Even this homey bedroom that wasn't fancy, but was the kind he'd like to come home to at the end of a long day, fit him in a way nothing else ever had.

"Except, I thought I could sleep with you and I'd be the same." Her voice was lifeless. "But I'm not."

"What do you mean?" His heart contracted and he held her tighter.

"Apart from that extra ten pounds you were polite enough not to mention . . ." Her hollow laugh ripped at his guts. "This . . . being with you changed me."

"It changed me too. And I didn't notice any extra weight. You're gorgeous, all of you, inside and out. I wouldn't change anything about you."

Because he loved her. *Love*. Unfamiliar emotion surged through him. It *was* love he felt for her, and, for the first time, it wasn't scary. He wanted to give her the sun, the moon and all the stars, but it was too soon to tell her that. He'd start by making sure her ex was out of the picture once and for all. Even before they'd talked about Todd earlier, he'd already done some digging. But now he'd look harder because he knew what he risked losing.

"Your ex-wife . . ." Annie's voice was small and muffled by the sheet. "Did you love her?"

"I thought I did." He rolled onto his back and stared at the smooth white ceiling. Now he knew what love was, how could he have thought he'd ever loved Amanda? "But she didn't love me, and as soon as a guy came along she saw as a better meal ticket, that was it." For the first time, saying those words didn't bring the usual pain. "As for Dylan, Amanda didn't want to be a mom." And no matter how much he'd wanted to make things work, if only for Dylan's sake,

Amanda hadn't.

"I'm sorry." Annie rolled back to face him and linked her fingers with his.

"It was a long time ago. I was a different man." Almost to his surprise, it was true. He traced the outline of her heart-shaped face. Besides, Amanda hadn't only given him Dylan but, because of her, he recognized what he'd found with Annie.

"It was my lucky day when you walked into the bakery." There was new strength and vibrancy in her voice, as if she'd cast off something that had been weighing her down.

"Mine too." His voice was hoarse, and he was hyper-aware of every part of his body—and hers. "I don't want to waste time looking back. Not when there's a whole lot to look forward to." He was sure of it, and he'd help her so she'd be sure, too.

The last little bit of doubt and uncertainty in her eyes was replaced by a look both teasing and provocative. "You said you'd make it better for me next time. I should hold you to that promise, don't you think?"

Seth groaned as her fingers drifted beneath the quilt. "Good idea." He pushed the words out. Annie was soft, warm, and pliant in his arms. And his last thought, before he slipped into blissful oblivion again, was no matter what it took, he was in this for the long haul.

Chapter 19

"I'm ready." Annie licked her lips and tried to focus on the interview, and not that it was Seth interviewing her. Yet, as he sat across from her in the radio station's small broadcast booth, all she could think of was how he'd rocked her world, not only last Saturday night, but Sunday morning as well.

"Me too." Hannah bounced on the chair next to hers. "This is so exciting." Ordinarily, Hannah wouldn't have been out of bed at seven forty-five on a Friday morning during summer vacation, but she was as bright-eyed as Annie had ever seen her.

As Seth adjusted his headset and began talking, Annie dug her nails into her palms. Even when he talked about something like the town council meeting, her stomach flip flopped. And when he gestured with his hands, she remembered exactly how those skilled hands had caressed her body.

"I have two guests with me in the studio today," he said. "Annie Quinn and her daughter, Hannah, are here to talk about the song they recorded last week. I know many of you loved 'My Hometown Heart' when they sang it at the flood relief fundraiser, and those of you who didn't hear it then are in for something special. Annie, you wrote 'My Hometown Heart.' Can you tell us what it means to you?"

This was it, the first question. Somehow, she got her mouth open, leaned toward the microphone, and words came out. "I wrote 'My Hometown Heart' about Irish Falls. It's about what this town, and the people who live here, mean to me. It's about family and friendship and how, even though seasons change and years go by, what really matters in life stays the same."

Seth nodded, and the warmth and encouragement in his smile helped her go on.

"It's about how in good times and bad, everyone here sticks together, and the power of hope, and maybe even wishes, help to get us through."

Annie steadied her breathing as Seth turned to Hannah and asked her what it had been like to make a recording. He was so relaxed it was like they weren't on air at all. She could have been talking to him in her kitchen.

"Do you remember the first time you sang in public, Annie?"

"Miss Leslie, my third-grade teacher, asked me to sing 'Away in a Manger' at the school Christmas concert. I was so scared, I pulled my elf hat over my face to hide, and then I couldn't get the hat off when it was time to sing. She had to come on stage and help me."

Seth laughed, and Annie put a hand to her mouth. That story hadn't been what she'd intended to say. She'd planned to talk about singing in that concert with the school choir because it wasn't personal, but she'd forgotten about everybody listening.

As the first notes of "My Hometown Heart" swirled around the studio, Seth took his headset off and gestured to her and Hannah to do the same. "Both of you were great. And your story about the Christmas concert was so funny, Annie. You didn't mention you were going to talk about that."

"It popped out." Annie laced her fingers together. "I'm sorry. Did I mess up?"

"No. Not at all." His eyes glinted with fun, as well as an intimacy that hadn't been there before they'd made love. "Might Miss Leslie have been listening?"

"Probably, except she's been Mrs. Moffatt for years." Annie curled her hands around her stomach and eased back into the chair. And a bunch of the kids she'd been at school with were likely listening, including several who'd been elves with her.

"Mrs. Moffatt taught me third grade too." Hannah grinned at Seth.

"If she heard the show, and if she wasn't a fan before, you've got a fan for life." Seth's expression sobered. "It was fine today, but when you're interviewed again, be careful what you say. There are people who'll pounce on the smallest thing and try to use it against you."

Annie's palms went damp. This interview was a one-off. She'd already learned to not trust people in this business. "I forgot." But she wouldn't again. She reached for Hannah's hand.

Her daughter's eyes were closed and she swayed in time to the music.

"You were super, sweetie. A real pro."

Hannah's eyes flipped open and she grinned. "If it wasn't vacation, I'd have been real popular at school today."

"You can give your friends the web link. I'll archive this interview." Seth put a finger to his lips to indicate they were going back on air and slid his headset back on. Then he asked a few more questions and thanked them for joining him. "I'll be playing 'My Hometown Heart' a lot on my show, but you can also get an autographed CD at Quinn's Bakery on Malone Street in the heart of beautiful downtown Irish Falls. Drop by Quinn's for all your tasty treats for the July Fourth weekend and pick up a musical treat, too."

"What?" Annie mouthed the word at him, but Seth shook his head. She covered her face with her hands. Why was Brendan selling CDs in the bakery? Or was it Tara? She gritted her teeth.

"To take us into the news and weather, here's Whitney Houston with one of Annie's favorite tunes, 'One Moment in

Time.' It's a special request for Annie and Hannah with lots of love from proud mom and grandma, Maureen McNeill."

As the song she'd listened to so many times as a teenager swirled around her, Annie glanced out the studio window. Brendan crossed the reception area with a tray holding two mugs, a bottle of apple juice, and a plate of butter tarts while Sherri, the receptionist, talked into her phone headset behind a desk. Her brother meant well. Her mom did, too. The song request was sweet, but on top of the interview, it was too much. A wave of heat flashed over her, and she motioned to Hannah to stay where she was, shook her head at Seth, wrenched her headset off, and eased out the studio door.

"Great interview." Brendan met her outside the door as she closed it behind her. "I bet the phone line is lighting up with requests for 'My Hometown Heart.'" He glanced toward Sherri, who continued to talk into her headset but grinned and gave them a thumbs-up. "Mrs. Moffatt already called the bakery. Holly said she was tickled to get a mention on the radio."

"Thank you, but . . ." Annie brought her voice down an octave. "What were you thinking? I never agreed to autographed CDs." She put her hands on her hips and stared her brother down.

"I—we—thought you'd be happy." Brendan cleared his throat and set the tray on top of a filing cabinet.

"We?" Annie picked up a butter tart. After the stress of the last quarter hour, she'd earned every one of its sweet and gooey calories.

"Me, Holly, Tara, Rowan, Mom, and Duncan." Brendan hesitated and glanced at the studio window. "Seth too because he helped us get the CDs." A faint flush crept up his cheeks. "Mom said she'd tell you beforehand, but from the look on your face, I guess she didn't. She wrote that bit about 'tasty treats' herself and asked Seth to say it. He gave her the advertising spot for free."

Annie let out a breath. "I . . ."

Brendan took both her hands. "Don't blame Seth or any of us. We're all so proud of you. When you sang at the fundraiser, it was like a light got switched on inside you. You finally believed in yourself like we always have. None of us want to hurt you. We just want to see the real Annie. She's been gone for a lot of years, but now she's back."

Her throat got tight and she swallowed. "I'm sorry." She gave her brother a sheepish smile.

"We wanted to show you how much we love you in the only way we knew how." Brendan squeezed her hands and then released them. "As for Seth, we're all happy for the two of you."

"What? You . . ." Her face burned. "How?"

"Next time he stays the night, you might want to tell him to walk or park his truck somewhere else instead of in front of your house." Brendan's eyes twinkled. "Between the late-night and early morning dog walkers in this town, you didn't have a hope of keeping that sleepover a secret."

Annie sat on the edge of the desk before her unsteady legs gave out on her. "He . . . I." A laugh bubbled out. "Busted."

Brendan bent to give her a hug. "Good for you, and not only about the singing. You've got your life back."

"Almost." And Seth would help her with that last little bit. "Love you, Bren."

"Love you, too." She wrapped her arms around her brother's neck. He smelled of fresh-baked bread and a warm summer morning. "Now go sign that stack of CDs Seth has got in a box in his office. Mom took a bunch of pre-orders in case he ran out."

After the station door had shut behind Brendan, Annie moved to the window overlooking the falls, Sherri's excited voice still on the phone behind her. The wishing tree was in full leaf. The last time she'd wished on it was before she'd left for Nashville and college—her one and only step out into the big world. But first Seth, and now Brendan, had made her think about hopes, dreams, and maybe even wishes again.

Seth's voice reached her through the overhead speakers. "The response to Annie and Hannah Quinn's recording of 'My Hometown Heart' has already been huge. By popular request, I'm going to play it again for you. Hannah's still here with me, so if you have any more questions for our own teen music star in waiting, ask away."

As her voice singing "My Hometown Heart" replaced Seth's liquid Georgia drawl, Annie's vision blurred and the wishing tree blurred right along with it. Even though she hadn't meant to, she'd fallen in love with him. Her pulse raced and she took a large, savoring breath. She'd opened her heart and her life to him in a way she'd only ever done through her songs, and although she might not have wanted to admit it, she'd never have done that if this wasn't love. She'd never have slept with him, either.

But even though Seth hadn't talked about leaving Irish Falls lately, he wasn't the kind of guy to make a life here, at least a forever one. And how could she make a life anywhere else? She stared at the wishing tree again then turned away from the window. Even if she'd started to let herself believe in wishes—and maybe even dreams coming true—she still couldn't wish for what she wanted most.

~ ~ ~

"You won't be disappointed." Three days later, Seth held his cell phone against his ear with one hand and gripped Dolly's leash with the other. "Annie's got a great voice, but it's her songwriting that will really blow you away."

He'd almost forgotten how much he missed the buzz of talking to a producer like Rick, who knew his stuff. This call was speculative, so there was no sense in telling Annie yet and getting her hopes up about something that might never happen. But he wanted to do something good for her that would make her eyes sparkle like they had when she'd made the recording.

"If you don't believe me, talk to Pete or his studio musicians." Seth moved onto the bridge so Dolly could follow a scent. "All I'm asking is you take a few minutes to listen to Annie's song and tell me what you think."

"You always knew how to wear me down, Taggart." There was a flicker of amusement in Rick's tone as his voice boomed in Seth's ear. "Because it's you, I'll listen, but no promises, you hear me?"

"I hear you." Seth sagged against the rail of the bridge. "And thanks." He'd done it. He still had the old magic. And that magic was in the songs he'd written over the past few weeks, too. He'd get back in the game when he was ready, but, for now, he was comfortable where he was.

"You bet you should thank me." Rick laughed. "My time is money."

Even as his chest got heavy, Seth made himself laugh back. Over the past few months, he'd learned that time was worth so much more than could be measured in dollars and cents. Its real value was in how, and with who, you spent it.

He ended the call and rubbed a hand through his hair. He wanted to get his songwriting career back on track, and maybe setting something up to help Annie could not only be the break she needed but also the one he needed to restore his credibility. So why was he obsessing over the big questions in life? He scanned the overcast sky and drew in a breath. If he'd been back in Georgia, he'd have said the clouds were settling to stay awhile and rain was coming. But along with everything else, the weather was so different here—not like Georgia or LA, either.

"Seth?" Annie's voice rose above the rush of river water beneath the bridge.

He turned as she clattered up behind him. "I thought you were at work this afternoon."

"I was, but Holly is covering for me." Her lips tilted into the gentle smile that never failed to make Seth smile, too. "I went to the post office for the mail. Hannah talked to her guidance counselor about colleges before school ended. The counselor contacted colleges and asked them to send Hannah information." She waved a big brown envelope at him. "This must be some of it. After talking to you, and then the counselor, I think Hannah might have turned a corner with the whole college idea."

"That's great." Seth slid his hand into Annie's as Dolly nosed the ground at his side.

"It is. I'm so proud of her. And now Duncan's doing better, life's good. I'm happy." She veered off the sidewalk onto a gravel path and tugged Seth's hand. "Do you have a few minutes?"

"For you? Always." He was happy, too. He'd almost forgotten what happiness felt like. Or maybe it was contentment. Whatever it was, and along with that still-so-surprising love, it had soaked into him like a soft summer rain and healed the scars of a too-long winter.

He followed her along a grassy path behind Malone Street until she stopped by the falls. Water tumbled over the jagged rocks and soaked the moss and ferns growing out of each little crevice. Above his head, a string of bells someone had hung from a low branch of the wishing tree tinkled in the breeze. "What's up?"

"I've been thinking more about my music." She moved closer and laid her head on his shoulder. "Recording the song was great, and the interview on your show was better than I expected, but it was enough, you know? And since I donated some of the money from selling those CDs to the flood relief fund, I feel better about it all."

"I . . ." He swallowed as the trust in her expression pierced his heart.

"I might even do a show at a fair, but if so, it will be on my terms." Her eyes shone. "I'm making the decisions about any music career that will be right for me. I'm taking small, steady steps and it feels good to do that and not be scared. You've helped me, but you've never taken over. I appreciate that."

Except, he'd called Rick about her song and he hadn't told her. Seth's stomach heaved. "Annie, I need to talk to you." If he didn't, this might not end well.

"Later." She gave him a teasing grin and put a finger to his lips. "The rain has started, and you're not wearing a jacket. Haven't you learned about Adirondack weather by now?"

"I guess not." His mouth had a sour taste.

"Maybe you need a shower to warm up so you don't catch cold." Her teasing tone had a sensual undercurrent, and the humid summer air became charged with unmistakable meaning. "Because of the weather, we're not busy this afternoon, so I don't have to get back to the bakery right away." She lowered her voice and touched his arm. "And your apartment's really close." As the wind pushed the rain in a horizontal sheet, she slipped the envelope under her rain jacket and then tugged on his hand.

He broke into a run beside her, and Dolly loped between them. He'd wanted to help Annie, but would she see it that way? Or, once she knew the truth, would she think it was only about him trying to resurrect his career and regain respect from people who'd doubted him?

Chapter 20

Annie studied the cake she'd set on the trestle table in the party room at the Black Duck. She'd designed and decorated it in the shape of a guitar and written happy birthday in black icing across the bottom.

"You're worrying too much. Seth will love it." At her side, Tara squeezed her elbow.

"Maybe a surprise party isn't such a good idea."

Seth had never mentioned his birthday, but Annie remembered it from the day he arrived in town and she'd asked to see identification.

"Dylan is all for it, isn't he?" Tara's tone reassured her. "Besides, since Seth has that birthday slot on his show, it's only right folks have a chance to celebrate his birthday, too, and this is the closest Saturday to it."

"What if he doesn't like surprises?" Whether a surprise, or planned months in advance, her family loved parties, but Seth hadn't grown up in a family like hers.

"He likes you, doesn't he? He'll be thrilled you went to all this effort for him. The way he looks at you, and how you look at him, the two of you are head over boot heels for each other." Tara's eyes twinkled.

"Is it that obvious?" Annie smoothed her top, the one she'd worn to the recording session that Seth liked. Although she hadn't come right out and told her sisters she'd slept with him, and even if there hadn't been rumors swirling around town, they'd have guessed for sure. It was that sister bond. Nothing stayed secret for long.

"It's sweet." Tara set a stack of birthday napkins beside the cake. "Rowan and I are happy for you."

"Even Rowan?"

"Sure. Even though she's still mad about what happened with her ex, it doesn't mean she can't be glad for you. She wouldn't have gone to pick up Dylan from the bus stop otherwise, now would she?" Tara's smile was warm. "Everything is perfect and everyone, including Dylan, is waiting to yell surprise when Brendan brings Seth in."

"You're right." Annie tried to smile back. She wasn't used to being in a relationship, even though she and Seth hadn't talked about what was between them in those terms. Her life had changed so much in the past few months, she was still catching up. It was natural bits of the old, insecure Annie were still there, along with the new, more confident one.

"Seth will love it when you sing happy birthday to him, too." Tara swung her arm with Annie's as they walked toward the party room door. "That man is crazy about you."

Or is he only crazy about my music? Annie pushed that thought away. She and Seth made music together, but that wasn't all they did. They went to the gym together, and he was teaching her to play tennis at the outdoor courts near the school. They'd bought tickets to a community theater show at the end of August, and he'd even picked up Hannah from that kayaking course last week when Annie was late coming back from a doctor's appointment with her mom and Duncan. But even though he was a real part of her life, she still wasn't sure if she was a real part of his. He'd never even told her what had happened with his business, and she'd never felt comfortable asking him.

She moved toward Rowan and Dylan, who stood in the middle of a crowd of people near the door. As she stopped beside them, it swung inward and everyone yelled "Surprise!" like they'd planned.

"What the—" Seth darted a glance at Brendan, and his eyebrows drew together.

"It's a surprise party for your birthday." Brendan nodded toward Annie. "Every morning you celebrate somebody's birthday on the show and play the number one song on the day they were born, so Annie . . . we all thought . . ." Brendan faltered.

"Oh." Seth scanned the crowd before his gaze settled on Annie. "I've never . . . a surprise party. It's great . . . I . . . wow." Even though his smile was still strained, his eyes shone. "Dylan?" Seth's gaze swung to his son. "What are you doing here?"

"I'm part of the surprise. Annie set it up. She messaged me and asked if I wanted to come. I got a great deal on bus fare." Dylan's face went red. "I was owed a few days off work anyway, and I wanted to be here . . . with you."

"That's . . . thanks, son." Seth's voice was gruff.

Dylan's dark eyes gleamed, and the glance that passed between him and Seth told Annie everything she needed to know. They wouldn't hug each other, at least not in public. But although they might still need to talk some stuff out, the worst of the breach between them was well on the way to being healed.

She clapped her hands. "Let's get this party started. We've got enough food to feed half the town, and Tara's organized games for the kids." She took a deep breath and focused on Seth, who still stood in front of her with a dazed expression. "Happy birthday. All of us." She gestured with a sweep of her hand. "We're glad you're a part of Irish Falls, and we wanted to make sure you knew that."

"Thanks, everyone." Seth's expression relaxed, and he grinned at Dylan. "How long were you on that bus? You must be starving."

"Rowan brought snacks when she picked me up, but I

can always eat." He grinned back.

"Go on. We have lots of time to catch up." Seth touched his son's shoulder, and Dylan nudged him back before joining the line of people snaking toward the buffet.

Annie stayed back. "Seth, this party was my idea. I didn't mean to upset you or—"

"No, it's me." His smile was wistful. "My birthday has never been a big deal, at least not after my mom passed. I'd almost forgotten about it, so when I walked in here . . . I . . . nobody has ever done anything like this for me before." His breath caught. "And to have Dylan here . . ." His mouth worked. "Thank you."

"You're welcome." Annie's heart swelled with both relief and love. "People here care about you, and we wanted to show you that." And someday soon, she'd also be able to tell him she loved him. All she needed was the right moment.

His blue-gray eyes softened. "I care about you too, and I—"

"Stop monopolizing the man, Annie." Her mom elbowed her way between them. "All the food will be gone, and you'll still be standing here jawing away." She eyed Seth. "I made my maple-glazed ribs and those always go fast. You have to try a bit of everything, though. It's the first rule of a Quinn party."

"Yes, ma'am." Seth laughed and gave Annie a knowing look.

Annie laughed, too. Subtlety had never been one of her mom's strong points. And as her mom took Seth's arm and marched him to the head of the line for the buffet, he glanced over his shoulder at her. His smile had that special warmth for her alone, but there was something else in it as well— uncertainty, maybe, but also a heaviness.

Despite the warm July day, she shivered. Nana Gerry would have said a goose walked over her grave, but that was ridiculous. Those old sayings meant nothing. Seth was fine with the party. Things were great between the two of them, as well as between him and Dylan, and she was less worried about Hannah than she'd been for months. There was no reason for that little prickle of unease.

Two hours later most of the food was gone, she'd sung "Happy Birthday," accompanied by Hannah on the Black Duck's out-of-tune upright piano, and Seth had cut his cake and now only crumbs remained.

Annie bent to pick up a stray paper napkin from under the cake table as "My Hometown Heart" rang out through the speaker system once again. Although she'd heard that song too many times to count today, it still filled her with pride. Each note was a tangible reminder of how far she'd come in conquering her fears.

"Great party, Annie." Dylan beamed as she met him beside the punch bowl. "Your family made me really welcome."

"Thanks. We're all happy you could make it." She liked Dylan for himself, but she liked him even more because he was a part of Seth. She found another napkin to wipe up some spilled punch.

"Here, let me." Dylan took it from her. "I work in a restaurant, so I'm used to this." His smiled slipped. "Dad always made me clean up at home and help cook, too. He said he had to make sure I knew how to live on my own someday. My mom wasn't around much, so it was all up to him."

"That must have been hard." For Seth, as well as Dylan. At least she'd had her family to help out with Hannah when she needed them.

"My mom's pretty and all, but she's not like a mom. Not like you." Dylan mopped up the last of the spill without looking at her.

"I'm sure your mom loves you, and she must be very

proud of you." Despite what Seth had said about Amanda not wanting to be a mom, Dylan was a fine young man. How could any mother not love and be proud of him? "Your dad's real proud of you, too."

Dylan crumpled up the napkin. "Dad and I had some stuff going on and I said some stuff I shouldn't have. It got weird there for a while."

"I think it's all right now." Annie lowered her voice. "Your dad talks about you all the time, even about things you did when you were little."

Dylan made a face. "No way."

"He wants to be part of your life." And Seth had made a big effort to make things better with his son.

A flush spread across Dylan's cheeks, and he shoved his hands into the front pockets of his khaki shorts. "Since Dad met you, he's been different."

She'd sure been different since she'd met him. "Your dad has become a good friend to me." She shifted from one foot to the other. "Are you okay with that?"

"Why wouldn't I be?" Dylan's smile was awkward. "I don't want Dad to be on his own forever. Besides, you're good for him."

Annie smiled back as heat suffused her body. "Your dad raised you right."

"Maybe you could tell him that?" Dylan's smile broadened. "I don't think he's got the message his job is pretty much done."

"Although kids might like to think so, a parent's job is never done. Even when Hannah's forty, I bet I'll still be telling her to eat her vegetables and wear a hat when it's cold outside." She raised her eyebrows. "And she'll still be telling me to back off like she does now."

"She's lucky." Dylan's expression sobered. "Even though Dad gets on my case, I always know he cares."

"He sure does."

"But sometimes, it would be kind of good to have a mom to talk about stuff with, too." Dylan studied his sneakers.

"If you want . . . I . . . can . . . you can talk to me . . . as a friend." Annie cleared her throat. "I'd never tell you what to do, but I could listen if you needed it."

"I'd like that. And when I said you were like a mom, I didn't mean you were like old or anything. And you're real pretty, too." The tips of his ears went red. "My dad likes you a lot. I can tell."

"What are you two looking all serious about over here in the corner?" Seth laid a hand on the small of Annie's back.

"Nothing much." Dylan shrugged, and Annie was struck by how much he looked like Seth, as well as pictures she'd seen of a young Jake.

"Dylan is helping me clean up." She gave him a half-smile. "He told me he works in a restaurant, and I was about to ask him about college. I don't know anything about animation, except what I see in movies."

Dylan shot her a grateful glance. "It's so cool. I have my computer with me. I could show you a few of my projects. Dad, too. If you're interested, I mean."

"Of course we are. That sounds great." Seth's voice was warm, and his hand curved around Annie's waist to pull her into the curve of his body. "Maybe we could take a trip to New York City to see you before school starts again—bring Hannah, too."

Almost like they were a family. Annie sucked in a breath.

Dylan looked between them and smiled. "I'd like that. You could eat at the restaurant where I work, my treat. I have a friend with a sister Hannah's age. She could probably take her shopping."

"Shopping?" Hannah appeared at Annie's side. "Where?"

"Seth thought we could go to the city to see Dylan sometime. How would you feel about that?" Annie's smile wavered. A trip anywhere would be a big deal for them, but that kind of trip was off-the-charts big. It smacked of commitment, a future, and linking all their lives together in new and perhaps scary ways.

"Sure, I guess." Hannah's gaze ping-ponged from Annie to Seth and then over to Dylan. "It would be different . . . but good." She slipped her hand into Annie's and squeezed. "I promised Auntie Tara and Grandma I'd help clean up." She glanced back at Dylan. "Do you want to help us?"

"Sure." Dylan gave her the kind of smile a big brother would give a kid sister, and the knot in Annie's chest loosened.

Everything was working out. Any doubts were a legacy of the woman she used to be, not the one she'd become. She shoved away that pesky twinge of discomfort and smiled at Seth. Maybe, just maybe, dreams, and even wishes, really could come true.

~ ~ ~

"The girls sure looked pretty at Seth's party." Maureen took off her rings and put them on the holder then glanced in the dressing table mirror at Duncan reflected behind her. He sat on his side of their bed and took his right sock off first, then the left, the way he always did. Although that precision had once irritated her, over the past few weeks, it had brought curious comfort because it was one of the few things that was familiar and unchanged.

"Not as pretty as their mother." Duncan tossed his socks into the laundry hamper. "None of them can cook as well as you, either. Those maple-glazed ribs were flawless, and your potato salad and sweet rolls . . . you know the way to this man's heart." He rubbed his stomach then shrugged out of his shirt and it followed the socks into the hamper.

"You're full of blarney." Maureen's face warmed as she patted cream onto it.

Duncan was a man of few words, but today he'd been

more gregarious than usual and more attentive to her.

"Even Rowan looked like she was having a good time. Did you see her talking to that nice man from the town office? As for Tara, when she served the birthday cake, the new bank manager couldn't take his eyes off her. I hear he's single."

One of Duncan's rare laughs rolled out. "I was more interested in Annie and Seth." He settled back on the bed in his black boxers.

Maureen swiveled to face him. No matter how much cream she slathered onto her face, it still sagged almost as much as the rest of her did. Even in his late sixties, though, Duncan had the body of a much younger man. Her throat clenched. Although both their doctors had given them the all clear, he still slept in Rowan's old room. He'd never say so outright, but it must have something to do with her.

"Annie and Seth seem close, don't they?"

"They do, but who knows?" Duncan exhaled. "And don't you go interfering. All our kids have to live their own lives."

"But maybe . . . Annie's still young enough, if things worked out with her and Seth, there might even be another grandbaby."

"Reenie . . ." Duncan let out another sigh, heavier this time.

"I know, I know, and I won't say a word to her, but a mother can always hope." It also didn't hurt to give a little nudge in the right direction. Only this week, she'd gone to the wishing tree and tied a wedding bell charm to her wish that Annie and Seth would find lasting happiness together. She tightened the belt on her robe and moved to her side of the bed.

"No matter what happens between them, Seth's sure brought Annie out of her shell. He's a good darts player too. I plan to ask him to join the team next winter." Duncan picked up his tablet from the night table and tapped the screen. "I've been thinking we need a new lawn mower. The hardware store has a sale on."

Maureen reached out and eased the tablet away. Instead of bringing them closer together, the prostate cancer had driven another wedge between them, but that had to stop, starting now. Unless she took action, she'd spend the rest of her married life like this, she and Duncan together but apart, only talking about their kids, food, and mowing the lawn, instead of what mattered.

"You don't want a new mower?" His expression was puzzled. "Keeping the lawn nice is so important to you. I thought—"

"You're more important to me than any lawn." Maureen's heart raced as she shifted over on the bed to sit beside him. She had to stay calm and focus. She also had to think positively. "Remember how we used to talk about what we'd do when I retired? All those plans we had?"

"That was before . . . everything." His voice was a dull monotone.

"We're still alive, aren't we?" She inhaled his familiar smell. "Remember how we wanted to go to Ireland and Scotland? They're still there, too."

"Long flights wouldn't be good for your hip." He grunted and bunched a pillow behind him.

"You need to let me decide that, but even if we can't travel so far yet, we can do other things." Maureen made herself say the words she'd avoided for weeks. "Like you can sleep in the same bed as me for a start."

"I flail around. I could hurt you or wake you up. You need your sleep." He looked so earnest she almost believed him, but not quite. It was in how he wouldn't meet her gaze and fingered the edge of the sheet.

"I'll have plenty of sleep when I'm in the cemetery in

the family plot." The backs of her eyes stung and she sniffed. "And I don't want to spend what are supposed to be our golden years like this." There, she'd said it, and she couldn't take the words back, even if she wanted to, but she didn't. "I miss you, and I miss us. What happened to our date night?"

"So, we'll go on dates again. I'll take you wherever you want to go." Duncan patted her hand.

"Dates would be a good start." She'd never been comfortable talking about sex, but if she couldn't talk to her husband, who could she talk to? "Now your hospital appointments are over for a while, we could even go away for a few days. There's an inn near Lake Placid that sounds real romantic. I saw a feature about it on the local news. They have four-poster beds, whirlpool tubs, and you can even have a champagne breakfast on your private balcony."

"Don't you think we're a bit old for all that? Besides, champagne is for weddings. Why would we want to drink it at breakfast?" Duncan's gaze locked on the striped comforter as if it was a particularly absorbing puzzle.

"I need you to love me, Duncan. You're my husband, not my roommate." She put her hand on his bare thigh, and he flinched. "I know I don't look exactly like I did when we met, but I hope you . . . I . . ." She dropped her head into her hands and scrubbed at her face. Despite all his nice words, except for her cooking, he didn't want her anymore.

"Oh, Reenie." Duncan let out a breath. "You're still a good-looking woman, the best in my eyes. It's not your fault, it's me."

"You? How could it be you?" She raised her head to stare at him.

A faint flush covered his cheeks beneath the white beard stubble. "A man like me wants to take charge in the bedroom. He wants to make it good for his woman and . . ." He stopped and the flush deepened.

"It's never not been good. How can you think that?"

Maureen bit her lip. The trouble was obvious. Why hadn't she guessed?

"I'm not the man I used to be, not with my you know what and the doctors messing about." He twisted his wedding ring. "What if we . . . and I can't?" The words were a tormented groan.

"We won't know unless we try, will we?" She leaned against his familiar chest. "And if you can't right now, it doesn't matter to me. We can be more creative. It could even be fun." She tightened her fists. Somehow, she had to reach him. "If we need to, we can talk to a doctor, too. One who isn't in Irish Falls. I want to help you."

"You do?" He stilled as she traced the curve of his shoulder.

"I meant what I promised in church." Maureen maneuvered herself onto his lap. "For better, for worse, in sickness and health. We've had a lot of the for worse and in sickness lately, but in the whole time we've been married, there's always been loving. I want you, Duncan Bruce McNeill, in every part of my life, including the bedroom. Won't you let me show you?"

"My Reenie." His voice thickened as he pulled her close. "You're one heck of a woman, my woman, always."

"Duncan?" The laugh she tried to stifle rang out like she was a girl again. "My hip, I can't, at least not this way."

He eased her onto her back and looked into her eyes. She caught her breath at the gentleness, tenderness, and steadfast love in his blue gaze. "Being creative sounds good to me." He slipped her robe off one shoulder. "Maybe we could see about that trip to Scotland and Ireland after all. We could take it in stages. Iceland's somewhere in the middle. Do you remember that program on Vikings we watched?"

"No." She trembled as his lips found the sensitive part of her neck. "It doesn't matter where we go, as long as we go together." And that one step, one touch at a time, they'd find their way back to who they used to be.

"I'm still not keen on that champagne breakfast business, but we need a second honeymoon, don't you think?" His breath was warm against her cheek, his voice soft and throaty. "Our first one was pretty good."

"It was wonderful." She touched the curve of his face, dear, familiar, and constant.

"So were you." He caught her hand and kissed her palm. "You still are."

The pleasure only Duncan could bring her spiraled in the pit of Maureen's stomach. "I love you. I'll always love you."

His eyes turned dark blue. "Like I'll always love you. Thanks for not giving up on me or us."

"As if I could." She quivered as his hand dropped to her hip.

"I don't want to hurt you." He raised himself above her on his forearms.

"You won't." She took his hand and showed him where she wanted him to touch her.

He groaned like he had when they'd first started along this path and hadn't known where it would lead.

Together with desire, peace and contentment wrapped around Maureen like a warm embrace. Although her kids scoffed at it, there was something in that wishing tree after all. It had brought Duncan to her almost eleven years ago. And now it had brought him back. She turned into his body in a gesture achingly familiar, yet new. Maybe, if she kept the faith, the tree would make everything right for her family too.

Chapter 21

Annie assessed the bakery display. The red, white, and blue fourth of July decorations had been packed away for another year, and the glass cases overflowed with summer-themed cupcakes, fruit tarts, and picnic cookies. "Summer vacation, then back to school, Halloween, Thanksgiving, and Christmas." She glanced at Tara behind the counter. "Our lives are marked by baking. Does that ever bother you?"

"No." Tara raised an eyebrow. "It's reassuring. In at least one part of my life, I always know exactly what's coming up."

"I guess so." Although that predictable cycle used to be comforting, now it irritated Annie more than it should. She bit back a sigh. After all, she'd wanted an ordinary life, and it had suited her fine for almost seventeen years.

"Hannah seems to like Seth and Dylan." Tara moved two cupcakes decorated with fish farther apart.

"She does." Annie bit back another sigh. She'd worried her daughter might see Seth as competition but, apart from an initial blip, that hadn't been the case. "She says I need to have my own life."

"That's good, isn't it?" Tara's tone was careful. "Especially since you and Seth have spent so much time together lately."

"It should be but . . ." Annie shrugged. The little niggle that something wasn't quite right was still there and had only intensified since Seth's birthday party the weekend before.

"But what? From what I saw at the party, Dylan likes you, too. If you and Seth get married, you'd be a blended family. It's bound to be easier if both your kids are on board with everything from the start."

"Marriage? Who said anything about marriage?" Annie's throat went dry.

"It's a logical assumption, isn't it? You wouldn't be sleeping with the man unless you were serious about him."

She was, but was he serious about her? "Yes, but marriage is a big step."

"Ever since he yanked you out of that rut you were in, you've glowed."

"I yanked myself out of that rut, too." But Seth had helped kick-start the process.

"You sure did." Tara grinned.

"Besides, Seth's already been married once. He might not want to do it again. And I've been a single mom for all these years. I'm not in a rush for a wedding ring." Except, she'd let herself consider it, her thoughts skittering like water bugs on the surface of a pond. What would it mean to share her life with Seth and have him and Dylan as part of her family? And what would it be like to have someone to look out for her like she wanted to look out for him?

"It's good when you find the right man and make a commitment to each other. I want you to have what I did with Adam."

The poignancy in Tara's voice tugged at Annie's heart and she reached for her sister and squeezed her shoulder. "It's still early days for Seth and me."

"Don't leave it too late." Tara's eyes glistened. "If you want, you could even have another baby."

After the death of her husband, the absence of a child was her sister's other big heartache. Annie gave her an encouraging smile. "Hannah is enough for me, but your time will come, honey."

"It already did. I can't think about anyone else yet, but

even if I wanted to, how many single men near our age are around here anyway?"

Apart from tourists passing through, no more permanent single men than Annie could count on the fingers of two hands, and one of them was Seth. "The new bank manager seemed interested."

"Please. Although I might be able to overlook his *Star Trek* obsession, he wears white socks with brown sandals. That should be illegal." Tara laughed as the bell over the bakery door jingled.

Seth held the door open for Mrs. Byrne, an older woman who went to Annie's church, and then followed her to the counter.

"Hey, you." Annie's stomach flipped. She'd never felt about anyone the way she felt about him, and every day was better because she'd see him. If this wasn't love, she didn't know what it was. She moved to the coffee pot. She didn't have to ask what he wanted. He always ordered a coffee after work and sometimes added the muffin of the day or a butter tart.

"Wait. I need to talk to you."

"Sure. I finish in an hour." She glanced at Tara, who was talking to Mrs. Byrne about gluten-free Black Forest cake. "We still have a few apple muffins left, and I saved a butter tart for you."

He held out a hand across the counter to stop her pouring coffee. "If Tara can manage on her own, I need to talk to you sooner." Seth's mouth was tight. "It's important."

"Hannah?" Annie pressed a hand to her chest. Her daughter was babysitting Rowan's kids, and she'd been in here with them half an hour ago on their way to the park. She hadn't heard any sirens, but that didn't mean anything.

"As far as I know, Hannah's fine. Wouldn't someone have called you if there was a problem?"

"Yes." She relaxed her grip on her apron. Rowan's two weren't old enough to stay by themselves, but they were old enough to call for help in an emergency. "I guess I can take a break. If it gets busy, Tara can call me. What is it? Dylan?"

"He's fine, too. Let's talk upstairs at my place." Seth's voice was strained.

She fumbled with her hairnet and took both it and her apron off. The hair on the back of her neck stiffened. "Then what's wrong?"

"Nothing, I hope." Seth's smile didn't reach his eyes.

"Cover for me, okay?" She jerked her chin in Tara's direction, and her sister nodded back.

Seth held the bakery door open for her, and she went through it into the afternoon sunshine. Irish Falls looked its best in mid-July. Colorful flowers were still summer fresh and tumbled out of window boxes along Malone Street. At the Italian restaurant on the corner, sun umbrellas fluttered on the busy outdoor patio.

They went around the building and up the back stairs, Seth's footsteps thudding behind her. Then they went into the station and left the brightness of the day behind.

She trusted him, at least as much as she could trust any man. She wouldn't have slept with him, or shared her music with him, otherwise. Except, how much did she really know about Seth's life before he came here?

As she followed him down the hall to the apartment, that tendril of doubt curled up from her stomach to lodge in her windpipe. In pulling her out of a rut, had Seth pulled her into quicksand instead?

~ ~ ~

"Take a seat." Seth gestured Annie to Jake's shabby sofa. He guessed he should replace it, but for reasons he didn't want to consider too closely, he'd never let himself get too settled in this apartment or Irish Falls. "Do you want a soda?"

"No thanks. I'm not thirsty." Annie's expression was wary and, as he sat beside her, guilt punched his chest.

"I planned to talk to you when we met on the bridge. But then it started to rain and you . . . we . . ." He hadn't been able to resist her. "I didn't mean to hide anything from you, but then there was my party, and Dylan was here."

He was making excuses. He hadn't wanted to change anything about what they had together, but then Pete called late last night, followed by Rick this morning, and he couldn't wait any longer.

"So, talk." Her voice was cool, and she sat ramrod straight, like a soldier preparing for battle.

"I hope you know how much I care about you, and I'd never do anything to hurt you." His mouth went tinder dry, and his body got cold. "All I wanted was to help you and make you happy."

"I care about you, too. And you already make me happy." She took several quick breaths, and her chest heaved beneath her scoop-necked purple T-shirt.

He took her hand, and there was an empty feeling in the pit of his stomach. "See, the thing is, I sent your song, 'My Hometown Heart,' to this Nashville music producer I know. I asked him to tell me what he thought about it."

"You did what?" She yanked her hand away, and her face went white. "And without a word to me? How could you go behind my back?" Her eyes blazed blue fire, and she wrapped her arms around herself.

"I didn't want you to be disappointed if Rick wasn't interested, but if he liked your song, I thought it could be your big chance. I wanted to make that happen for you." Seth bunched his clammy hands into fists.

"It could be your big chance too, couldn't it? I heard what happened with your music publishing company and how you're not writing songs anymore. Everybody knows, it's all over the Internet, but we didn't want to upset you by saying anything." She jumped to her feet and backed away from him. "My song is *my* song. You had no right to share it with this Rick, or anybody else, without telling me first."

Guilt and shame jabbed Seth's chest. "Maybe I was wrong, but if I told you and Rick said your song was nothing special, I knew you'd be hurt. He's the kind of guy who doesn't mince words. He tells it like it is." He got to his feet and reached for her, but she stumbled backward toward the table. "You'd only started singing in public again. You believed in yourself. I didn't want you to stop. And I *am* writing my own songs. Being here, you . . . you're the reason I can write again." His stomach heaved. How could he make her understand he'd meant well? And why had he let stupid pride stop him from telling her what had happened in LA?

"I trusted you enough to share my songs with you. I even let myself . . ." She sucked in a breath and two red patches bloomed on her pale cheeks.

"Hang on, it's good news. Rick called me. He loves 'My Hometown Heart.' He talked to Pete too, and Pete told him what a class act you are." As Seth stared into her furious face, the knot in his belly got even tighter. "Rick wants to come here to meet you and hear you sing."

"When?" Her voice was icy, and she held up a hand as if to ward him off.

"Three days from now, if that timing works for you." He cringed, and the tingling in his hands spread throughout his body. "Annie, I'm sorry. I didn't think you'd be so upset. I thought you'd be happy."

"Well, I'm not." She gripped the back of one of the dinette chairs. "Let me get this straight." Her voice was low, but he heard every word with awful clarity. "You sent the recording of my song to this Rick guy, without telling me. Then you talked to him about me, and he talked to Pete, and all the while I knew nothing about any of it? Even though it's my song, my life, and maybe even my career?" She pressed a fist to her mouth.

When she put what he'd done like that, it sounded even worse. Seth's chest hurt. "Yes, that's what I did, but you have to understand, I didn't want you to get your hopes up and be disappointed."

"I'm not a child, and I understand all right." She choked out the words. "You betrayed me." She moved toward the window. "Just like Todd."

"No, I . . . how, what do you mean?"

"Todd and I sang together, too, like you and I do. And at first, he liked my songs, same as you. Then he said he'd help make them better." Her eyes got shiny. "And he took a bunch of my songs, ones we'd worked on together, and shared them with a music publisher. Then Todd made a deal for one of the songs and he didn't even name me as a songwriter."

"He had no business—"

"No, he didn't, but you had no business, either. I'm not the naïve girl I was all those years ago. I'm not pregnant, either." She stiffened. "When I confronted Todd about what he did, he said my songs wouldn't have gone anywhere without his input. According to him, I had no talent, but later, when another artist recorded my song, they made it onto the charts. And then he . . ." Her chest heaved and she made a low, guttural sound. "You already know the rest."

Seth clenched and unclenched his hands as the world spun and then seemed to slow down. "Todd was wrong. You do have talent. A man like Rick wouldn't come all the way here if you didn't."

"Even if that's true, all those times we were together, did you never think of telling me you loved my song so much you wanted to share it with him? Did you never think of asking me what I thought about that?" Her face went slack, and she pressed a hand to her temple.

"I did, but I thought you'd say no." His throat got thick.

"Maybe I would have, but you didn't even give me a choice. I should have had that choice, but, like Todd, you went behind my back. You and Pete both."

"Pete didn't do anything." The blame for this mess sat squarely on Seth's shoulders. "Rick worked with him on a couple of albums, and since Pete helped you make the recording, Rick gave him a call." If only Seth could go back and do things differently, he would, but he couldn't, so he had to finish this the best he could. "Pete and his studio musicians thought you and Hannah were great."

"Hannah?" Annie flinched. "You didn't only betray me. You betrayed my daughter, too."

"Of course I didn't." He took a deep breath and held his hands behind his back. "Whether you like it or not, Hannah's going to try to make it in the music business. You can't control that."

"Says the guy who already tried to control my career." Annie gulped. "Only last week I told you how good it felt to make my own decisions and not be scared." Her voice cracked. "I even thanked you for not taking over with my music, but all the time you . . . was it some kind of twisted joke?"

"No, never." His voice rasped.

"Well, you can call Rick and tell him he doesn't need to come here." She crossed her arms over her chest and gave him a fixed stare.

"I could, but think about it. Rick might be able to help you have a real music career. He could help you have a second chance." Sweat trickled down Seth's back under his shirt between his shoulder blades. "Don't miss this opportunity because you're mad at me. Sing for him, Annie. Not because I set it up. Sing for you."

"And if I do, then what?" Her voice rose, and she rubbed

a hand across her forehead.

"Maybe he'll want to work with you and maybe he won't, but at least you'll know. You've spent a lot of years denying who you are and what you want." Seth stared at Annie and willed her to believe him. "I made a mistake, and I'm sorrier than you can ever know, but I only had your best interests at heart. Since I opened that door, it's up to you whether you walk through it or not."

"And you?" Annie's eyes narrowed. "Unlike Todd, you didn't pass off my song as yours, but there must be a cut for you somewhere in this. Am I your second chance in the music business, too? And what about Hannah? Were you planning to get her a record deal behind my back?"

"Of course not. I'd never go behind your back with Hannah." He took a deep breath. He owed her the truth, even if she didn't want to hear it. "If I'd heard your songs when I still had my music publishing company, I'd have wanted to collaborate with you, but I don't have that company anymore. And I should have told you what happened in LA. I wanted to, but my business partner—I was embarrassed and humiliated by what happened with him. I felt like a failure. I shouldn't have felt like that with you or anyone here and I'm sorry about that, too."

"I don't care what happened in LA or how you feel." The bitterness in her voice stabbed his heart. "But if my song was a hit and people knew you'd discovered me, that wouldn't hurt you, would it? How do I know you don't want to start another company? You're a city guy. You belong in LA, not Irish Falls." Her voice was grim.

"I . . ." He'd thought he wanted LA, but lately he hadn't been sure. All he knew was he wanted her and what they had together.

"I trusted you." She paused for a heartbeat. "I trusted you so much I fell in love with you. I didn't plan to, but I did. I've wanted to tell you for weeks, but I could never find the right time. More fool me."

Blood thundered in Seth's ears. "I love you, too. And because I love you, I wanted to help you. That's why I contacted Rick about your song."

"Why should I believe you?" Her laugh was cynical. "You love my music. But me? I don't think so. If you really loved me, you'd have paid attention to what I wanted and understood who I am, all of me."

"Please . . ." He took a step toward her, and she whirled toward the door.

"No." Her voice was brittle. "It's over. The music and everything. I thought I knew you, but I don't. And maybe you don't know who you are, either." She straightened her shoulders and stuck her chin up. "You're Jake's son, but have you told anybody except me? Have you told me, or anybody else, what you're planning to do with the station once the six months Jake set out in his will are up? Or are you even planning to stay the full six months? Maybe I'll wake up one morning and you'll be gone."

"No. I wouldn't do that." Except, he didn't know what his future plans were. He'd reconciled with Dylan, but as for the rest of his life—as for Annie—he'd only thought about the day to day. And he'd let her down. His lips went numb, and he couldn't breathe.

"You also never talk much about the past or your ex-wife."

"Because that's the past." He forced the words out.

"It seems to me your past has a lot to do with your present." Her voice went flat, and her shoulders slumped. "People here like your show, and they like you. Everybody came to that birthday party because you're an important part of this town." Her chin trembled. "You let me down, but if you ever let Hannah or the people of Irish Falls down, that would be even worse."

"Annie, I'm sorry." The backs of his eyes burned, and

his legs went weak.

"I'm sorry, too." She looked at him for a long moment, her expression bleak. "Text me Rick's number and leave the music we were working on in the bakery. I don't want to hear from you again." She inhaled, and it was as if she suddenly became taller and more confident. "You were right, though. You did open a door, and it's up to me whether I walk through it or any other one."

She turned and then was gone. The apartment door shut behind her with a soft click. It would have hurt less and been less final if she'd slammed it.

Seth looked around the soulless apartment like he'd never seen it before. He couldn't change what he'd done. More important was what he had to do now.

Chapter 22

"Do you want me to talk to Seth, man to man?" Duncan hovered over Annie as she huddled in a corner of her living room sofa.

"No." Annie tried to smile, but more tears leaked out of her eyes and rolled down her cheeks. "It's not because you're my stepfather, either. Even if my own dad were still alive, I wouldn't want him talking to Seth. I'm an adult. I have to handle this myself."

"I'm never making that man a butter tart again as long as I live." From her place on the rug near Annie's feet, Tara passed her a new box of tissues.

"He can live without baking, but I appreciate the thought." Annie took a handful of tissues and blew her nose.

"I can sneak over behind the station in the middle of the night and let the air out of his tires." Rowan grinned at Annie from the footstool beside the sofa. "A friend did that to her ex. Maybe it's childish, but she said it sure felt good."

"You wouldn't." Annie let out a wheezy breath, a futile attempt at a laugh. No matter what, her family was always there when she needed them.

"No, but I can have the satisfaction of thinking about it." Rowan's smile broadened. "One small action for my sister in solidarity for mistreated women everywhere."

After Seth had ripped out her heart and stomped all over it, Annie had wanted to go home without seeing anybody, her family, especially, but she'd left her purse and keys in the bakery. And when she'd gone back downstairs, her mom and Duncan were there, and Duncan insisted on driving her home. Then Tara had texted Rowan, and the two of them had left work early to be here for her. But despite all the family support, Annie felt even worse than she had earlier in Seth's apartment.

"I should be at work. I didn't finish my shift." Except, all she wanted to do was crawl into bed and never come out again. But that would mean she'd have to change the sheets that still smelled of her and Seth together, see the guitar pick he'd forgotten on the bedside table, and the spare T-shirt he'd left in her top dresser drawer.

"Your mom called Holly, and she was happy to come back in and help out for the rest of the day." Duncan patted Annie's shoulder. "As for your mother, although she's as upset as anyone about this ruckus with Seth, she's hankered to get behind that bakery counter again. She hasn't taken to retirement easy."

An understatement, but it was good Duncan had finally recognized at least one part of her mom's unhappiness. Maybe more than one, given the kiss he'd planted on her mom's mouth before shepherding Annie out of the bakery to the car like she was a dazed accident survivor.

She looked at Duncan and her sisters. "There's also Hannah. She's supposed to bring Rowan's kids here for supper, but she can't see me like this." She scrubbed at her face.

"If it's okay with you and Rowan, I'll pick up Hannah and the other two and take them home with me instead." Duncan's voice was that of a man glad to have something practical to do that would take him away from the emotions surging through Annie's living room. "We can watch a movie and order pizza, and I'll bring them back after we eat." He patted Annie's shoulder a final time before he dug in his pocket for his car keys.

"Thanks." Annie sagged against the sofa as Rowan nodded agreement. With a few more hours to pull herself together, she'd be fine. Or, if not fine, more in control than now.

"You haven't eaten anything since this morning, honey." Tara's eyes were worried. "I'll fix whatever you want."

"I'm not hungry." Annie clutched her stomach as the front door swung shut behind Duncan. Right now, she couldn't imagine eating ever again.

"At least have another cup of tea." Tara picked up Annie's mug from the coffee table. "Or I can open some wine."

"Getting drunk won't solve anything." Annie rocked forward and back. Her body shook, and she fumbled with the blanket on the end of the sofa and wrapped herself in it. "What am I going to do?"

"You're going to call that Rick guy and, after you thank him, you tell him it would be great to meet him three days from now." Rowan's words were clipped. "And once he gets here, you're going to open your mouth and sing like the kickass woman we know you are. Tara will help you get fixed up pretty, and you're going to do yourself, your family, and Irish Falls proud."

"Rowan's right." Tara flushed rosy pink. "Don't be mad, but I texted Pete. He gave me his card when you did the recording because he wants me to make butter tarts and a cake for a surprise anniversary party he's organizing for his wife in October. He said he'd come here to help if you wanted because he knows Rick." Tara looked at the carpet and didn't meet Annie's gaze. "Since Seth's out of the picture, I thought you should keep your options open."

"Tara got your music back from Seth, too." Amusement tinged Rowan's voice. "She knew better than to let me at him."

"I may not say it often enough, but I love you guys." Annie's throat clogged.

"We love you too." Tara and Rowan joined her in a

huddle like they had when they were little—the Quinn sisters who shared an unbreakable bond.

Rowan plumped a cushion and eased it behind Annie's back. "And you love Seth, don't you?"

"I thought so, but after what he did, I . . ." Annie covered her face with her hands. Why had she blurted out that she loved him? Once she'd said the words, he'd said them back but it was as if he was compelled to. If she'd kept her mouth shut, she'd at least have some pride left.

Tara added a second cushion. "One thing at a time. Whether you love him or not can wait a few days. What matters now is you sing for that Rick and show him what you can do. Rowan and I will handle everything else, and Mom and Brendan and Holly will take care of the bakery. I bet Hannah can help out if we need her to.

Annie's head jerked up. "Hannah. She sang with me on the recording. I have to tell her what happened. She likes Seth and—"

"You're her mom. She'll be on your side, always." Rowan's voice hitched.

"Especially if she thinks there might be a record deal out of it for her." Tara grinned. "Hannah loves you more than anything. In her whole life, this thing with Seth won't be anything more than a blip."

Annie's chest clenched. For her, Seth wasn't a blip. He'd been life changing. Before he rolled into town, she hadn't let herself think much about the past. She'd convinced herself she was happy the way she was. But by letting him into her life, he'd changed both it and her and, in forcing her to look back, she'd also looked forward and thought about the possibility of having a different future.

She straightened and her gaze drifted to the piano. The new song she'd been working on with Seth was still on the music rack, the pencil he'd tucked behind his ear beside it. Even though that future no longer included him, she still wasn't going to be held hostage by her past. Unlike with Todd, she knew her own mind. She didn't like what Seth had done, but she still had a choice. And she wouldn't let herself down, or Hannah, either.

~ ~ ~

Seth hadn't seen Annie in almost twenty-four hours. Even on that long-ago day when Amanda was in labor with Dylan, time hadn't passed this slowly. He cradled the mug of cold coffee on his desk at the station as the morning farm report washed over him. He had to fix what he'd done, and he would. But that meant seeing Annie, and since the town had closed ranks around her, that wouldn't be easy.

"You look even worse than you did before the show." Brendan came into the office without knocking and sat in the chair by Seth's desk.

"Apart from telling me I look like crap, what do you want?"

"To talk to you." Brendan studied him.

Seth's heart gave a dull thud. "About Annie?"

"Yep." Brendan's brow furrowed. "Without her in the bakery, the day doesn't feel right."

Seth's day didn't feel right, either. Annie's life had melded with his so slowly he hadn't realized what a big part of it she was—until, all of a sudden, she wasn't. "She'll be back at work tomorrow, won't she?" He reached to pat Dolly.

The dog blinked then lay down with her back to him. What? He'd even offended his dog?

"No. She's taking some time off. Then Tara decided to join her." The edge to Brendan's voice made the hairs on the back of Seth's neck quiver. "Mom's in her element now she's back in the bakery full-time. Holly's working extra hours, and Hannah's helping, too."

"That's good, I guess." Seth winced. How had his life gone so far downhill so fast? Although he hadn't known everything Todd had done to Annie, if he'd stopped to think, he'd have realized that talking to Rick without telling her first was the worst thing he could have done and quickest way to destroy her trust.

"Not that you asked for my opinion, but you messed up big time." Brendan frowned. "Never go behind any woman's back, but especially not one like Annie."

"You think I don't know that now?" Seth rubbed his temples. "I thought I was doing something good for her. I saw she had a problem, and I wanted to solve it. I wanted to help her."

"See, that's how guys think." Although Brendan still eyed him like he was the lowest form of pond scum, a faint smile tugged at the corners of his mouth. "Women are way different. You should know, seeing you were married once."

"My marriage wasn't . . ." No matter how much he liked him, he couldn't talk about the disaster that had been his marriage with Brendan because he was Annie's brother. His tongue got thick. He loved Annie, but instead of doing it right, he'd spit out those precious words like they were meaningless. "I'm not married to Annie."

"No." Brendan raised an eyebrow. "But you're in some kind of relationship with her, aren't you?"

He had been, even though neither of them had ever used that word. "Yes." The tightness in his chest lifted. "At least I was." And he wanted to be again.

"So, you have to think like a woman thinks." Brendan's grin broadened. "Annie would be pissed if she knew I was here, but somebody has to talk sense into you. "What you saw as helping, she saw as you sticking your nose in her business. You didn't give her a say. You decided you knew what was best for her like she was a little kid or some helpless female."

"She's the least helpless female I know." Seth groaned and dropped his head into his heads. Even if he hadn't done pretty much what Todd had, it would still have been bad. He'd treated Annie how his grandparents had treated him when he was a kid, like he didn't have ideas and thoughts of his own. And he'd done the same thing to Dylan this past year. "I know I was wrong, but Annie won't listen to me. I told her I was sorry."

"Women don't only want words. They want actions. What kind of marriage did you have anyway?"

"Not a good one." Seth stared at Dolly stretched out on the floor. "If I did it again, I'd want to do it differently."

"Then start now." Brendan's tone was crisp. "If you don't, I'm not letting you anywhere near my sister." Although he gave Seth a fixed stare, his eyes twinkled.

"Actions, huh?" Despite himself, a smile tugged at Seth's mouth. He bent to rub Dolly's ears, and she thumped her tail against his foot.

Unlike women, dogs didn't hold grudges.

"Then I need your help."

Dolly gazed up at him.

"You too, mutt."

~ ~ ~

Rick Meyer didn't look anything like how Annie had imagined a big-shot Nashville producer would. His sandy hair was thin on top, he had a slight build, and he wore square glasses. Behind the glasses, his pale blue eyes were sharp but kind. In fact, he looked a lot like the partner in the accounting firm at the top of Malone Street who came to Quinn's each year at tax time to check the books Tara handed over.

Rick said something to Pete then raised a hand to wave Annie over to where the two of them sat at a table in front of the Black Duck's stage.

"You can do this." Rowan whispered in Annie's ear.

"We believe in you." Tara smoothed a stray curl of hair away from Annie's face.

Annie's shoes echoed as they hit the scuffed wooden floor. She was moving on with her life. She'd finally taken her old boots to a thrift store in a town twenty miles away and put the ones Seth had given her in the darkest corner of her basement. They were nice boots and she had to be practical. She'd wear them again when Seth was another part of her past—a stepping stone on the way to the woman she still wanted to be.

"Annie?" Rick got to his feet, moved around the table, and held out a hand. His handshake was warm and firm. "Seth and Pete have told me a lot about you." His smile was warm, too. "I like your song, so I decided to take a little trip north to come meet you in person." His voice had a blurry drawl, like someone who'd spent a lot of time in the south but wasn't Southern by birth. "I'm looking forward to hearing you sing."

"Thank you." Annie glanced at Pete, who nodded encouragement.

"I want to keep this real informal and relaxed." Rick scanned the Black Duck. Between them, Tara and Rowan had somehow convinced the owner to close for a couple of hours this afternoon, and Annie didn't want to think about what that might have cost Quinn's. A free bread delivery at least, maybe more.

"Sounds good." Annie pressed her lips together. She wouldn't fidget, and she wouldn't let her mouth run ahead of her brain. And most of all, she wouldn't let herself think about Seth.

Rick pushed his glasses up his nose. He wore sand chinos and a blue button-down shirt like one Duncan had, although he had to be more than ten years younger, early fifties at most. "Seth told me you can accompany yourself?"

Annie nodded because she didn't trust herself to speak.

"He asked me to give you something." Pete stood, reached under a table, and pulled out a guitar case. "He thought you might want to use this guitar today."

Jake's Gibson. Annie sucked in a breath.

Pete set the case on the table and opened it.

"Nice." Rick moved over to look. "My daddy had an old Gibson. I still play it on occasion. He passed a few years back, and I find playing it brings him closer."

Annie's eyes smarted, and she swallowed the lump in her throat. Seth knew her so well he'd know Jake was in her thoughts today. Playing Jake's guitar would be like having part of him with her.

She stood beside Pete by the open guitar case. Above the usual roadhouse scent of stale beer and fried food, there was an aroma of Jake, too—woody, citrus, and a crisp masculinity. She blinked then reached for the guitar and tucked it into the curve of her body.

"I made a passel of mistakes in my life, but you're the daughter I wished for. The daughter of my heart, Annie girl."

She started at the sound of Jake's melodious voice.

"Annie?" Pete's puzzled expression dragged her out of her reverie.

"Nothing." Her tight shoulders relaxed as warmth, mixed with a rock-solid calm, flooded her body. "I'm ready whenever you are."

"Okay, show me what you've got." Rick moved back around the table and sat in the chair again. He tilted his head back and smiled at her.

Although the words were ordinary, a part of her had waited her whole life to hear them. She went onto the small stage. In the hazy sunlight that filtered through the Black Duck's narrow windows, the stage was scarred by the hundreds of feet and all the equipment that had been dragged across it over the years. Tara and Rowan had set up a small table for her with a glass of water and a restaurant chair. She glanced toward the side of the stage and gave her sisters, with Hannah between them, a small smile.

Annie played a few chords and tuned the guitar. Fanciful or not, Jake was here with her. Maybe her dad and Nana Gerry were too. So, she sang for them, Hannah, and, most of all, for herself. "My Hometown Heart" first then Dolly Parton's "Coat of Many Colors" for Jake, and some of the other songs she'd written. The songs that came from her heart and, as the music flowed between her voice and the guitar, she couldn't tell where one began and the other ended.

Annie might only have played to an audience of two (five, if she counted her sisters and Hannah), but it was the audience she couldn't see who drew the music and performance out of her, so she was a different Annie than the one who'd made Hannah's breakfast that morning and cried into her pillow over Seth last night.

When she finished the short set, her legs trembled, and her palms were damp. Pete stood and clapped, and then her sisters and Hannah clustered around her.

"You were great, Mom." Hannah buried her face in Annie's shoulder. "If I could sing like you, I . . ." She gulped.

"Someday you'll sing even better, honey." Annie stroked her daughter's hair.

"Way to go, Annie." Rowan's voice was gruff, and her practical, usually unemotional sister's eyes were suspiciously bright.

"I'm so proud of you," Tara whispered in Annie's ear.

And Annie was proud of herself. She patted Jake's guitar and set it aside before moving away from her family. Rick got to his feet beside Pete, and his gaze snagged hers and held. Then he clapped three times, and the sound echoed in the almost-empty room.

"Nice job." Pete pulled her into a hug as she reached the table. "Can I get you water or a soda?"

"Water please." Annie sat in the chair Pete held out for her. Her legs were still rubbery, and her heart pounded as if she'd run a race.

"So." Rick eyed her across the table. "You sure can sing." He flipped the cover of his tablet closed and set it atop a green folder. "You have stage presence. You're pretty, but not in a threatening way. You've got that girl next door look a lot of men go for, but their wives and girlfriends would see you as a friend and not competition."

"But?" There was a "but" in there somewhere. The hesitation in Rick's voice was clear. She took the glass of water from Pete and waited until he sat down again.

"Seth's still got it." Rick folded his hands.

"Pardon?" Annie sipped water and crossed and uncrossed her legs.

"He could always spot talent. I used to tell him he should be a music talent scout on the side." Rick's expression was quizzical. "He told me you were good, and you are. But the question is, how bad do you want it?"

"I . . . what do you mean?" Annie wrapped her hands around the glass, and the coldness from the ice water seeped into her skin.

"How much do you want a career in music?" Rick leaned back and put his hands behind his head. "In this business, you have to push yourself forward everywhere. You also have to be on the road a lot and away from your family. Eventually, if you worked hard and got some breaks, I might be able to get you a spot to open for some big names, but you'd spend a lot of time sitting around backstage or on a tour bus. That's okay if you're twenty years old and hungry, but you seem like a real homebody."

"I am." Her eyes smarted. She wouldn't cry, at least not in public. Rick was only being honest, and honesty was good.

"There's nothing wrong with roots." Rick leaned forward, his expression intent. "No offense to the great Dolly Parton, but the only song you sang that didn't yank on my heartstrings was hers. You were singing somebody else's words, and your voice was lifeless."

"Oh." Annie looked at her hands. She'd done her best, and it had to be enough.

"I could fix that some, or a good vocal coach could. At least fix it so it isn't as noticeable, but it still comes down to how much do you want it?" Rick's gaze drilled into her.

"I don't know." Annie linked her fingers together so he wouldn't see her hands shake. What was wrong with her? All she'd ever wanted was a career in music, and now she might have a chance, why was she hesitating?

"I grew up in Nebraska." Rick's voice got a remembering tone. "I was a farm boy who spent summers working the fields and winters strumming an old guitar with a high school band. I was good at math and got a scholarship to college. My folks wanted me to be an accountant and settle in the nearest big town to our farm, but when I finished my degree, the pull of music was too strong. I got the message pretty quick I wasn't good enough to make it as a performer, but I was lucky and found my niche on the business side. I still had to want it, though, and work pretty much twenty-four-seven for a lot of years to get where I am."

Annie's insides clenched. Maybe she didn't want it as much as she thought. "Music was always my dream from when I was a little girl, but then I had my daughter, Hannah, over there." Annie inclined her head toward her daughter and sisters. "I had to put music aside, and now . . . I . . ."

She what? She was tired, emotionally spent, and she wanted to go home and not think about music, Seth, or the rest of her life—at least for the next forty-eight hours.

"Your daughter sang 'My Hometown Heart' with you on that recording." Rick glanced in Hannah's direction.

"Yes, she did." Pete broke in before Annie could get her mouth open. "Hannah's only sixteen, but you should hear her sing. Her voice is different than Annie's, but I think she's got something special."

So, this was how it would go. Rick would hear Hannah sing and, before Annie knew it, Hannah would be on the road to Nashville—maybe on a road to getting her heart broken, too. Annie sat up straighter. That wasn't how it would go because she had a say. "My daughter wants a career in music, but sixteen is too young. Hear her sing if you want, but I won't let you turn her head with false promises."

"I agree." Rick chuckled. "There are already too many teenage girls running around thinking they're the next Taylor Swift. If Hannah has real talent, it will keep for a few years. That time will also give her a chance to focus on school and get her head screwed on solid."

"Really?" Annie let out a shaky laugh.

Rick nodded and looked even more like the accountant he might have been. "My wife and I have a daughter about Hannah's age. Gracie wants to be a pediatrician. She doesn't have any musical talent or interest in the business, but even if she did, there's no way I'd let her anywhere near a studio right now."

"Thank you." Annie's head spun and relief washed over her. "I appreciate your time, but I need to think about—"

"Hang on. I'm not finished yet." Rick smiled, and the protective dad morphed back into the successful producer. "There's more than one way to have a career in music."

Annie stilled. "What do you mean?"

"Apart from that cover of Dolly's, Pete said you wrote the rest of the songs you sang today."

"Yes, although Seth helped me with some of them." Despite what Annie thought of Seth right now, he'd helped her make her songs better. "He worked with me on 'My Hometown Heart' too, so Hannah could sing backup vocals."

"Seth's a natural musician and a great guy. It's a shame he . . ." Rick stopped and something flickered in his expression Annie couldn't read. "Anyway, now I've met you, it's those songs of yours that interest me more than trying to make you into a solo act."

Annie bit her bottom lip. Todd had taken her songs, but he'd said they weren't worth anything without him. He'd mixed them up, swirled them around and changed pretty much everything about them before he'd gotten that deal.

"You're a good singer." Rick's eyes got that sharp look again. "But, from what I've heard, you have the potential to be a great songwriter—the kind a lot of folks would line up to work with. You have an innate sense of how to put words to music, and what you write about is real. That's something neither Seth nor I, nor anybody else can teach you, or package with a few harmonies. You have it or you don't, and you sure do."

Annie put a hand to her mouth and glanced at Pete then back to Rick. "You believe in me?" Her voice shook.

"I do, but more to the point, you believe in yourself. Who you are and what you want shows in every one of those songs of yours. It's also in how you want to keep your daughter away from guys like me." Rick slid a business card across the table. "Take the time you need to think about what I've said. Then call me so we can talk more." He laughed. "I want to help you get your songs heard, and with the royalties you deserve."

"I . . . thank you." Annie's voice caught.

"As for Hannah, tell her to call me in a few years." He raised an eyebrow. "No promises, but if the next Taylor is out there, I want to sign her first." He slid his tablet into a slim black briefcase. "Oh, I almost forgot. When I talked to Seth, he said you were looking for some guy. Todd something or other? He said he'd been bad news for you."

Annie's heart stuttered. "Todd Smith."

Rick pulled a piece of paper out of the green folder and pushed it across the table to her. "My assistant dug up the details and put them together for you. Todd worked as a DJ at a club some friends and I used to own. I remember him because he thought he was a songwriter. More like he was arrogant, disrespectful, and a walking cliché." He made a dismissive sound. "He was fired when my manager caught him taking money from the till. A few weeks later he got himself killed in a fight in a Miami bar. The cops came calling because our place was the last one he'd worked at. They wanted to know if he had any enemies. Who wasn't the guy's enemy?"

"I . . ." Annie fingered the paper as adrenaline flashed through her. "Thank you." She couldn't be happy about what had happened to Todd. He'd had a bad end to a bad life, but he was still Hannah's father, and she'd cared for him once. But knowing he could never bother her or anyone else ever again laid that last bit of fear to rest forever, and now her life stretched in front of her, wide open and full of possibilities.

Rick's troubled expression cleared. "You're welcome." He paused. "I want to work with you, Annie, but if and how that happens is totally your call."

Chapter 23

Seth brushed a film of soil from Jake's simple granite headstone. Whatever inner force had compelled him to come out to the cemetery had fallen silent now he was here. And like everywhere else, he couldn't stop thinking about Annie. He hadn't seen her in three days. Not at the bakery or the gym, and although he'd driven by her house a few times like a teenage boy with a crush, the curtains were always closed. In desperation, he'd even wished on the wishing tree late at night when nobody else was around.

"How can I fix things with Annie if I can't find her?" He nudged several lumps of dirt away from the base of the stone with the toe of his boot. What was he doing talking to himself? And why was this dirt churned up? The ground had been smooth the last time he'd been here soon after the headstone went in.

"Are you going to plant flowers? It's a bit late in the season this year. You'd be better off with a spray of artificial flowers for now and planting next spring."

Seth started and turned to face Annie's mom. Dressed in navy capris and a white T-shirt, she wore gardening gloves and had a small wicker basket over one arm. "Do you think Jake would have liked flowers?" His grandmother had planted a pink rosebush at his mom's grave, and Seth still sent flowers from him and Dylan to the cemetery every Mother's Day.

"Probably not, but he'd have appreciated the thought." Maureen chuckled. "He'd have liked you coming to see him even more, though."

Seth shoved his hands in the front pockets of his jeans. "I left Dolly in the truck. I should—"

"You left a window open so that dog will be fine for a few more minutes. What you should do is talk to me about what went wrong between you and my Annie." Maureen's gaze was shrewd, and she gestured to a wooden bench beneath a nearby tree. "We won't disturb Jake from there."

"Disturb him?" Seth would have laughed, but there was no humor in Maureen's tone.

She moved to sit on the bench and patted the space beside her. "You see all the soil turned up? That means the spirit is restless. Usually it's because there's unfinished business they left behind."

Since he was still a polite Southern boy, Seth tried to keep his expression neutral. The ground was churned up because of an animal, or the cemetery groundskeeper had done some work. "I don't think—"

"It seems to me you've done too much thinking and not enough feeling." Maureen patted the bench again, and Seth sat. "That man over there is fretting about you the same as I fret over Annie."

Seth stared at Maureen. "But Jake's . . . dead."

She raised her eyebrows. "That doesn't make one bit of difference. He's still watching over you, probably even more than he did when he was right here on earth."

Seth pressed his lips together. Apart from the words coming out of her mouth, Maureen looked as normal as she always did.

"You think I've lost it, don't you?" She chuckled again. "And you're trying to figure out a nice way to bundle me into your truck, keep me quiet on the drive back to town, and march me into the nearest doctor's office."

Seth gave her a bemused smile. "I've never heard you talk about restless spirits before." Although maybe he shouldn't be surprised. In a town with a wishing tree, what were a few spirits who roamed about now and then?

"People in this valley still hold to a lot of old beliefs. Maybe there's something to them, or maybe there's not, but Jake sure had unfinished business. You, for a start. What kind of man doesn't acknowledge his own son?"

Seth winced. "How did you know he was my father?"

"I suspected it the first time I saw you. You're the spitting image of Jake when he was younger. Besides, if you were really his nephew, why would he have kept it a secret all those years?" Maureen's voice was gentle. "Except for Annie, I haven't said anything to anybody, not even Duncan. Your business is your business, but folks wouldn't judge either of you. Both of you already lost too much."

Seth gripped the arm of the bench. "I . . . thanks." There was a cold, empty feeling in his chest.

"So, you and Annie." Maureen's voice became brisk. "What are your intentions toward her?"

Seth's face heated. "I want to talk to her for a start, but she told me she didn't want to hear from me. And Brendan said she was taking time off work, but I haven't seen her anywhere in town."

"She and her sisters went to a spa resort in Lake Placid for a few days. Hannah and Rowan's two are staying with Duncan and me." Maureen's expression was kind. "I doubt a few beauty treatments will heal what ails Annie, but she needed to get away."

"From me?" His heart contracted. He'd respect Annie's need for space, but that didn't mean he'd give up at the first hurdle.

"Among other things." Maureen exhaled. "You didn't hear it from me, but she'll be home tomorrow night around seven. Do you want me to keep a hold of Hannah a little longer?"

"I'd appreciate that, ma'am." A piece of the snarled knot in Seth's chest slackened.

"Annie loves you, and if what I see in your face when you look at her is right, you love her too." Maureen gazed into the distance. "That's all that matters."

"I do love her, but you make it sound so simple." And his feelings for Annie were messy and complicated.

Maureen waved a hand at the tidy graves that rambled up the peaceful hillside. "As long as the love is there, it *is* simple. When I broke my hip, there were a few days when I thought I'd soon be lying over there beside my first husband in the Quinn family plot. Thank the Lord I'm not, but realizing I could have been focuses the mind something powerful."

Seth's heartbeat sped up. "I don't want to lose Annie, but I don't know if she'll give me another chance."

"You won't know unless you keep trying." Maureen's smile gave Seth hope. "She's a lot like her dad was. When something hurts her, it goes deep, but she's real forgiving. Besides, if what's between the two of you is a true love, it won't go anywhere. That kind only gets stronger over time."

And he'd keep trying for as long as it took. "Thanks."

Maureen nodded and leaned closer. "Jake would have been proud of you. Even though he couldn't talk about it, I don't doubt he loved you." She clasped her hands to her chest. "I keep asking myself why he didn't acknowledge you. It hurts me, so I can imagine how much it hurts you. The only thing I can come up with is he wanted to give you what he thought would be a better life. He made a mistake, but who are we to judge? Neither of us knows what his life was like back then." She shrugged. "The best you can do is focus on what he gave you, not what he didn't."

Seth took a deep breath. The hurt and disappointment were still there, and maybe always would be but he couldn't let Jake's abandonment consume the rest of his life. As hard as it might be, he had to forgive, let go, and move on. "Since I wasn't here for Jake's funeral, I'd like to honor him and celebrate his life. I never got to do that, and, for myself, as much as him, I need to acknowledge him publicly as my father."

Maureen's smile warmed Seth all the way through. "You tell me what you want, and we'll all help you make it happen."

"Thank you." Seth smiled back. "As for Annie—"

Maureen's laugh was wry. "She needs you in her life as much as you need her."

He sure hoped so, because he needed Annie in every possible way. He needed her gentle touch and the way she understood him. He needed to hear her voice and make music with her again, not because it was about Nashville or LA or a record deal, but because it was something they both enjoyed.

And he needed her beside him every night in a bed they'd picked out together. In a house with her cats and his dog, where Dylan could come for vacations and Hannah would play loud music, bang doors, and leave dirty laundry on the floor like teenagers did.

But what he needed most of all was a place he could call home with her, where they could build a future together.

~ ~ ~

Tara's Jeep rolled to a stop in front of Annie's house. From her spot in the backseat, Annie unbuckled her seatbelt and grabbed the overnight bag at her feet. The spa trip had done her good. If she didn't feel happy, she at least felt lighter and more content—although that might have been due to the long talk she'd had with Hannah after singing for Rick. Since Todd was now firmly in the past, she and Hannah could look to a new future—one that would include music, but where college came first.

She leaned forward and looked between Tara and Rowan. "I should get going and—"

"Wait." Rowan twisted around from the front passenger seat. "You never told us what you're going to do about Rick." Her voice was careful.

Annie paused with her hand on the door handle. She'd talked about everything else with her sisters over the past few days—including Todd and Seth—but her music was the one topic she'd avoided, even though it had never been far from her mind. Through the open window, she breathed in the warm evening air, heavy with the fragrance of roses and other summer flowers. "I don't want to try to be a solo act, at least not in the way Rick talked about it."

"Okay." From the driver's seat, Tara exchanged a quick look with Rowan.

"I used to want to sing solo, or I thought I did, but talking to Rick made me realize I don't. Although I love to sing, I wouldn't love everything that goes along with trying to make it professionally in a place like Nashville." Warmth flooded her body. Although she might sometimes regret the path not taken, there was an unexpected release of tension, too.

"Good for you." Rowan's smile was bittersweet. "You're lucky you know what you want."

"I do." And for maybe the first time in her life, it was true. "I have Hannah to guide through to adulthood for a start, but it's more than her. I have roots here I cherish, and I don't want to pull those up. You two, Mom and Duncan, and Brendan and his family. Both the people and the place make Irish Falls my home." She took a deep breath and fiddled with the zipper on her bag. "Besides, since I've only figured out who I am and what I want, I don't want to be styled into somebody else to perform or sing songs that aren't mine. I'm not even sure I want to make another recording."

"But you have such a beautiful voice, honey. You

can't lock it away again." Tara looked back, her expression worried.

"I never said I want to lock it away. If I didn't sing, I'd miss it." Like she missed Seth. Her chest tightened. "I don't want to sing on a stage in front of thousands of people. Even if I made it in Nashville, and from what Rick said, that would be a long shot, I don't want to be a celebrity."

"Then what?" Tara tilted her head to one side.

"I'll be at the bakery early tomorrow morning as usual, and I'll keep writing my songs. I still need to think some things through, but I'll call Rick when I'm ready." And when her songwriting wasn't so wrapped up with Seth and the music they'd made together. She rubbed her chest. "First, I got caught up in the idea of making it in the music business. Then I got caught up in avoiding anything to do with the business altogether. But now? I'm older, a lot wiser, and any deal I make will be for something that's good for me and Hannah, too." She swallowed the lump in her throat. "I won't let anybody take advantage of me ever again."

"We're proud of you, Annie-Bella." Tara's voice was husky.

"I'm proud of me, too. It took a lot of years, but I'm finally okay with who and where I am." Annie smiled at her sisters. Although it would take time, someday Seth wouldn't be anything more than a bittersweet memory. "Now you two go home. We have to get up early for work tomorrow morning." She opened the door and hopped out.

Rowan grinned. "Mom must have gotten Hannah and my two to cut your grass and tidy up. I hope my place was part of whatever deal she made with them."

"It looks like they even painted the porch railing. Duncan and Brendan must have helped, too." Tara did a double take. "Do you want me to come in and wait with you until Mom brings Hannah back? Rowan can take the Jeep, and I'll walk home from here."

"No. I'll be fine. They should be here any minute." Annie stepped back onto the grass at the edge of the road. "Thanks for the trip, not bugging me about stuff, and being my sisters."

"You're welcome." Rowan's eyes glistened.

Tara sniffed. "Seth, he—"

"I'll get over him . . . this . . . everything." And maybe one day she'd even be grateful for what Seth had done. If not for him, she might not have taken that final step to seize control of her life like she'd needed to.

"But Seth works right upstairs." Tara's voice was soft.

"That doesn't mean I can't work downstairs. I won't have to see him much." Annie would make sure of it like she'd make sure she put the pieces of her heart together so well that nobody, not even Tara and Rowan, would ever guess how it had shattered into tiny pieces.

"I guess." Tara's tone was unconvinced. "Call us if you need anything." She gave a little wave before the Jeep moved away, and Annie went up the path to her house. The railing had indeed been painted, and the porch floor had also been swept and washed. Two new pots of white geraniums sat on either side of her front door, the brass doorknob shone, and the rusted mailbox she'd planned to tackle for months gleamed with fresh black paint.

Along with Hannah, the rest of the family must have worked together on this project to do something special for her. She smiled as she slid her key into the front door lock. As soon as the door swung open, Hazel and Olivia greeted her with loud meows and wound themselves around her legs.

She dropped her bag in the hall and bent to pat them, but no sooner had she touched Hazel's favorite spot between her ears than the tabby shot through the half-open door with Olivia in pursuit, a blur of white and gray fur.

Annie lunged after them and skidded to a halt at the top of the porch steps. Both cats sat on the railing, their tails twitching in tandem as they eyed Dolly. Olivia hissed, a fluffy miniature bundle of outrage. The dog stood in the middle of the sidewalk wagging her tail, and Brendan held her leash.

"Hey." Annie went down the steps to greet her brother. "I just got home. What are you two doing here?" She reached up and returned Brendan's hug. "Where's Holly?"

"At home." Brendan released her and his hazel eyes twinkled. "Dolly and I waited for you down the street. We have a surprise."

"Didn't I already get it? The yard and porch look great thanks to you, Hannah, and whoever else helped." She moved back toward the house and shepherded the hissing cats inside.

"It wasn't me, or Hannah, either." Brendan followed her up the porch steps. "Except for me unlocking your tool shed, nobody else in the family had anything to do with this."

"Then who?" She shut the door behind the cats and studied the new white paint on the porch railing.

"Look on Dolly's collar." Brendan gestured to the green ribbon looped around the fancy pink collar Seth had bought the dog. A small pink organza pouch dangled from the ribbon, almost hidden by the fur under Dolly's chin.

Annie knelt on the porch, and her fingers tingled as she fumbled with the parcel.

Dolly turned her head and nosed Annie's hand.

"What have you got?" As Annie took the bag from the dog's collar, something inside crackled.

"We're only the delivery team. You have to open it and find out." There was a smile in Brendan's voice.

Annie's stomach fluttered. She'd told Seth never to contact her again, so had he sent Brendan and Dolly because he knew she wouldn't turn them away? And if so, why? Her legs wobbled as she got to her feet.

"See you at work in the morning?" Brendan grinned.

"Of course." Annie drew in a breath and let it out again. Had she misjudged Seth?

"Great, I've missed your coffee." Brendan patted her stiff shoulder. "I missed you too, Annie-Bella."

The lump in Annie's throat swelled and all she could do was nod. After her brother and Dolly went back down the front walk, she went into the house and sat on the stairs, still clutching the little pouch in one hand. She tugged on the loop that held it closed and pulled out a small piece of paper folded in four quarters with her name on it in black letters.

As she unfolded the paper, a miniature silver key charm on a fine chain slid into her palm. She fingered it as she read the note.

"'I know you don't want to talk to me, but I hope you'll listen to my show on Monday morning at seven forty-five.'"

Annie got goose bumps as she read Seth's decisive script.

"'Rick's given you a key to your future, but you have the key to my heart.'" Seth's name was scrawled below, followed by a postscript in smaller writing. "'I did the work around your house because I wanted to help you, not because I think you can't do it yourself.'"

She blinked away the sudden hot rush of tears. Outside the house, a car door slammed. Hannah's voice rang out, and footsteps pounded on the front walk. Annie rubbed a hand across her eyes and slid Seth's note, the organza bag, and the key necklace into a pocket of her hoodie.

He wasn't the kind of man to make a statement in front of the whole town, was he? Maybe he didn't mean what she thought he did. She squeezed her hands at her sides. Or maybe he did.

Her stomach quivered with hope, excitement, and that rock-solid sense of self-belief that was new. No matter what did or didn't happen between her and Seth, she'd be okay— she and Hannah both.

Chapter 24

"Where is your head this morning?" Tara grabbed the canister from Annie. "I need ginger, not cocoa powder. Regular gingerbread cookies, remember? You said you'd give me a hand."

"I did. Sorry." Annie blew out several short breaths and glanced at the wall clock in the bakery kitchen. Only two more minutes until seven forty-five.

"Maybe it's too soon for you to be back at work." Holly looked up from the pan of scones she was about to slide into an oven. "Brendan will be finished with that phone call in the office soon. We can manage without you if you want to take a break, or even go home."

"I'm fine." She gave them her best fake smile and fumbled in a drawer for a clean set of measuring spoons.

"No, you're not." Tara's eyes narrowed, and she took the spoons from Annie's shaky fingers. "Holly's right. You should go home."

Annie touched the key charm that dangled from the chain around her neck beneath her apron and snuck another glance at the clock. Although she'd fallen in love with Seth, she'd been afraid to fully trust him. And, worst of all, she'd judged him against Todd and thrown what had happened with his company in his face like a taunt. "I have to stay here. At least for the next few minutes."

"Then you can unpack the shipment of cake boxes that came in while we were away." Tara gave her an exasperated look. "You shouldn't be anywhere near food preparation right now."

"Did you hear what Seth said? How can there be a traffic jam across the bridge this morning?" Holly gestured to the radio then shut the oven door and set the timer. "It's not even eight, and the weather's perfect."

"I heard more people are looping through town because of that construction by—"

"Would you two be quiet?" Annie cut Tara off and clenched her hands in her apron. "It doesn't matter why or even if there's a traffic jam. It's not like either of you will be driving across the bridge this morning."

"But . . ." Tara snapped her mouth closed, and both she and Holly stared at Annie in astonishment.

"I'm sorry." Her voice came out in a whisper. It was seven forty-six. Maybe the bakery clock was fast. Annie jumped as the back door opened, and Rowan came through it.

"Can I get a coffee and cinnamon bun to go? I need caffeine and sugar before facing those summer school kids and—"

"Shush," Annie, Tara, and Holly said together.

Annie reached for the radio and turned up the volume.

"For all your farm equipment needs, head to the John Deere dealership where Keith and his friendly team will be pleased to help you." Seth's voice faded out and was followed by an advertising spot for the local cheese factory.

"What's going on?" Rowan moved farther into the kitchen and picked up the coffee pot.

"Nothing." The hands on the clock inched toward seven forty-seven. Maybe it was a trick. Annie didn't think she was that gullible, but she'd already proven she wasn't a good judge of character so—

"This next tune is special." Seth was back, and his silky voice enveloped Annie like it always did, a comforting shield against life's storms. "When I first came to Irish Falls, I thought I'd forgotten how to write songs. I thought I'd forgotten a lot of things and, until a few months ago, I didn't believe life had anything more to offer me or I could trust anyone again. It turns out I was wrong."

In the background, a dog barked, and Seth made a shushing noise. "I owe a lot to this town. And I owe even more to someone here who helped me turn my life around and shared her life and heart with me."

Three pairs of eyes swiveled to look at Annie.

"If she still wants it, this woman has my heart, too." Seth's voice got quiet, and Annie held her breath. "I love you, Annie Quinn. I was afraid to feel it, and, for a long time, I was afraid to say it. Then when I did say it, I messed up. I shared your song with a guy I trusted could help you with your career because, at the time, I thought that's all I could give you. It turns out I was wrong. I can give you all of me if you want it." His breath stuttered, and he cleared his throat.

Annie's legs went weak, and she gripped the edge of the counter to keep herself upright.

"Ooh." Her sisters and Holly clustered around her.

"Since most folks have heard how I did wrong by you, it's only right they also hear how I really feel about you. This song is called 'Key to My Heart and Soul,' and I wrote it for you, Annie."

Annie sucked in a breath, and her pulse raced as the first haunting chords from Jake's Gibson echoed in the silent kitchen. Then Seth's voice reached into her heart and soul, and she licked her lips as all the love she had for him rolled over her in a wave.

Seth really loved her. She should be embarrassed he'd announced it on the radio, but she wasn't. Not only had he been honest with her, he'd been honest with her family and community, too. She tugged on her apron strings, but Tara already had the ties undone.

"Go." In the silence after the song ended, Rowan's voice was gruff, and she pulled the apron and hairnet off of Annie and gave her a gentle push toward the door.

Annie pressed a hand to heart. "I . . . he said . . ."

"He loves you." Tara's gaze was tender.

"He sure does." Holly patted her eyes with the end of a tea towel. "That was the most romantic thing I've ever heard."

It was the most romantic thing Annie had ever heard too, and Seth had done it for her. She looked around the kitchen. "I should . . ." She swallowed hard.

"You should go up to the station is what you should do. What *I* should do is put this gingerbread dough in the fridge and start a batch of butter tarts." Tara gave Annie a tremulous smile. "That man can have as many as he wants. I won't charge him, either."

Annie's laugh mixed with a sob as she hugged her sisters and Holly. She hadn't believed she and Seth could work. She'd thought he was another man who wanted her music, but not her love. But she'd been wrong and upstairs, waiting for her, was the second chance she'd never thought she'd have.

~ ~ ~

Seth gulped a mouthful of tepid coffee. Had Annie read his note, or had she tossed the whole thing in the trash unopened? And if she had read it, had she listened to his show, or had she made Tara and Holly change the bakery radio to another station? As the words of a song he barely heard echoed through his headset, he checked the time on the computer.

Annie was downstairs. He'd have put money on it. Although he hadn't seen her, the building felt different when she was in it. Happier, for a start, but it also had a sense of comfort, ease, and that the world was a better place simply because she was nearby.

He'd wanted to do the right thing, but what if once again

it turned out to be the wrong thing and he'd made a fool of himself in earshot of the whole town?

He glanced at Dolly who sat in her dog bed in a corner of the studio.

"What do you think, Dolly? Did you like the song I sang for Annie?" After he'd set the Gibson down, Seth had gone straight into the next three songs on the playlist, and then it would be the pre-recorded thought of the day from the Baptist minister.

The dog scampered to the studio door.

Seth's head jerked up. Annie stood in reception in a green T-shirt and black shorts. Oblivious to Sherri, who sat at her desk with her mouth half-open, Annie's gaze met his and held.

The outside door swung open, and Brendan came through it. He said something to Annie, and she gave him a tentative smile. Then he gestured to Seth.

Seth made himself get out of his chair and, on legs like jelly, he opened the studio door. He glanced between Annie and her brother.

"I'm taking over for you for the next half hour." Brendan's tone said he wouldn't take no for an answer.

"I can't walk out partway through the show." Except, his fingers tingled, his heart raced, and he wanted to forget all about the show.

"Sure you can." Brendan grinned. "It's small-town radio and, after what you did, folks will want to know there's going to be a happy ending."

Would there be? Seth eased Dolly aside and took a step toward Annie, who still stared at him, her expression uncertain.

"I want one." Her mouth trembled, and her eyes were soft. "That happy ending, I mean."

"Me too." Seth took a deep breath as Brendan slipped into the studio behind him. "Annie . . . I . . ." His throat constricted and, for the first time in as long as he could remember, he felt complete, whole. "Come here." He looped his arm through hers and led her down the hall to his apartment, closing the door on Dolly, Sherri and everyone else.

In the small entryway, he turned to her and took both her hands in his. "I'm sorry, and I hope you know how much I mean it."

"I sure do." She squeezed his hands and together they moved into the living room. "I'm sorry, too. You aren't Todd, you aren't anything like him, but I judged you as if you were, and I said horrible things about your company in LA and your songwriting." She stopped and stared at their entwined hands.

"I deserved it. I should have told you about everything a long time ago. My business partner cheated me. Not the way Todd cheated you but still . . ." He scrubbed a hand across his face. "I want to clear my name. I'm taking the guy to court but . . . there might still be people who think the worst of me."

"They don't matter." Her steady gaze met his filled with love and everything he'd ever hoped for and needed. "I believe in you and everyone here does too." She swallowed. "Rick, he . . ."

"He told me what happened to Todd." Seth reached out to pull her close. "It's over. We don't have to talk about him again. But I want you to know it's you I care about, not the music. Although I like making music with you, if all you want is to keep it as a hobby, that's fine. I had no right to try and take over."

"I . . ." Her face worked. "You . . ." She stumbled back and sat on the sofa, bringing him with her. "When you said you loved me, right on air . . . I . . ." Tears trickled down her cheeks, and Seth took one hand away from hers to brush them away.

"I meant it more than I've ever meant anything in my life." He tried to smile. "Apart from how I love my son, I didn't know anything else about what love was until I met you, and then when you said you'd fallen in love with me, although I said it back, I was confused. I guess I didn't think I was lovable. If my own father couldn't stick around for me and my grandparents didn't really want me, what hope did I have? And then, Amanda left me as soon as another guy she thought had better prospects came along. But you loved me for me, not because you were supposed to or for what I might be able to do for your career."

"Always." Annie nestled into his shoulder and tucked her head under his chin.

"Dylan told me what you said to him. That you'd be happy to talk to him like a friend. He needs that. He needs you in his life, too."

"Like Hannah needs you." Annie's voice was low. "Not as a dad, but as a friend and mentor. Another man in her life apart from Duncan and Brendan she can count on."

"Until you walked out the door, I didn't know love could feel like this." He leaned against her.

"Like what?" Her expression was puzzled.

"Like coming home." When he pulled her into his chest, her body fit to his like it belonged there. "And now I want to figure out where we go from here."

"Me too." Her eyes filled with warmth and love.

"It'll take time because this is new for me." His face got hot. "I haven't had good role models for relationships. Not like you with your folks and now your mom and Duncan. I need your help to get things right."

"Like I need your help. I'm the one who was stuck in old, comfortable patterns." She gave him a chagrined smile. "I wanted to do something with my music, but I was scared. Apart from the thing with Todd, that's why I got so mad at you for sharing my song with Rick." She traced the curve of his shoulder, and his body trembled. "We can help each other."

"Of course we can." He caught her hand in his. "This is a new start for both of us."

"All of us, Hannah and Dylan too." Her voice hitched. "Like a . . ."

"Like a family." And it would be the kind of family he'd longed for all his life but never had.

"I love you, Seth. I didn't plan on it. I tried to avoid it because I was scared of love, let alone getting involved with someone in the music business. But you're so much a part of my life, I can't imagine you not being in it. You're not a city guy. You're *my* guy."

"That's good because I plan to stick around." He kissed the top of her head and smelled cinnamon, floral shampoo, and a sweetness that was all her, the woman he loved with his whole heart and soul. "We have a lot of stuff to work out, but I want to work on it together—forever."

"Me too." Her voice was raw.

"For you and us, I've got all the time in the world." Seth pulled her closer.

"Umm . . ." Annie pushed against his chest and giggled. "You have to get back to the show."

"I guess I do. Who knows what your brother is doing out there." He captured her mouth in a kiss so sweet it made him ache, then drew back slightly and studied the tiny freckles dotted across the bridge of her nose. "What do you want me to tell my listeners about that happy ending they're hoping for?"

"Tell them we're working on it." Annie's mouth curved into the smile he loved best. "And that you have the key to my heart and soul, too."

Epilogue

October, three months later

"I ran this bakery fine when you were still in diapers. I can manage for a week while you and Seth are in Nashville." Annie's mom put her hands on her hips and gave Annie the look she remembered from childhood—loving but with a hint of steel.

"Besides, what are Brendan, Holly, and I? Chopped liver?" Tara swatted Annie's arm. "Hannah will pitch in after school and on Saturdays, if we need her to, and our new apprentice starts tomorrow." Tara glanced at Holly and Brendan huddled over an order list on the far side of the bakery kitchen. "You have more important things to think about nowadays than the muffin of the day."

Annie smiled at her sister. "The success of this bakery will always be important to me, but I still can't believe all the rest of it." She and Tara moved out to the store with a tray of Halloween-themed cupcakes.

"What part can't you believe?" Tara's tone was amused. "That, thanks to Rick, people are falling over themselves to record your songs? Or you're able to have a career in music while still living in Irish Falls and working part-time here? Or Seth looks at you like you're a yummy butter tart he wants to eat right up?"

"All of the above!" Annie laughed and slid a cupcake with orange frosting into the display case.

The bell over the door jingled and Seth came in.

Annie's heart skipped a beat like it always did when she saw him. There was something about a man in jeans, boots, and a white T-shirt beneath an untucked shirt. Or maybe it was only him. Whatever it was, the past three months had been happier than she could have ever imagined.

"Ready?" He nodded at Tara as his boots hit the floor in that syncopated rhythm Annie would never tire of.

She reached into the fridge behind the counter for the plastic container she'd packed earlier and then grabbed forks, paper plates, and napkins and dropped them into a Quinn's bag.

"Have fun." Tara waved, and Annie waved back as the door jingled again and shut behind her and Seth.

"So, what's your surprise?" Seth glanced at the lively street decorated with pumpkins, fall wreaths, hay bales and a smiling trio of inflatable ghosts, and then at the sun that shone as warm as it had in August.

"Follow me." Annie took his hand in hers as they walked around the bakery toward Irish Falls. She gestured him to the picnic table by the wishing tree. "Take a seat."

Seth did as she asked and eyed the bag she set on the table.

"Today's a special day." She sat beside him and bumped his shoulder.

He quirked an eyebrow. "Every day with you is special for me."

She smiled and tried to focus. "Today is extra special because it's exactly six months ago you came to Irish Falls." She opened the bag and took out the plastic container. "That day, you overheard me say my Nanaimo Bar Cheesecake was better than sex. I was so embarrassed I haven't made that cheesecake since, but this morning I did because it was the best way I could think of to show you how much I love you and what you've brought to my life." She popped the lid on the box and set out two plates, forks, and napkins.

Seth's eyes darkened. "Last night in our bed wasn't enough?"

"This isn't only about sex." Annie's face heated.

"Says the woman who thinks her cheesecake is better than sex." Seth took a mouthful of cake, chewed it, and swallowed. "Good, but never better than sex, at least not with you." He set down the fork and reached for her hand. Along with the teasing glint in his eyes, there was something more serious, and Annie caught her breath.

"I remember everything about you from the first day I walked into Quinn's until now." His voice got husky. "And I also remembered today was a special day. You already know I'm not going to sell the station, and now I've cleared my name and got my reputation back, if things work out how I plan, I can do my songwriting and some music talent scouting with Pete and Rick while being based here. I don't want to go back to LA to stay so we have to keep figuring out a way of life that works for both of us."

"And Hannah and Dylan." Annie twined her fingers with his.

Although there'd been a few bumps along the way, Seth's son and her daughter were at the heart of the new family they were building. Hannah had a big brother to look out for her, and Dylan had a little sister he cherished.

"That's why I talked to both of them before I talked to you." Seth took his hand away from hers and dug in the front pocket of his jeans. "Even your cats have stopped hissing at Dolly. If that's not a sign, I don't know what is."

He cradled a small blue velvet box in the palm of his hand, and Annie's heart got stuck in her throat. "I found this in Jake's safety deposit box at the bank a while ago. There was a note with it in my mom's writing." He moved closer to her on the narrow picnic bench and flipped open the box to reveal a ruby and diamond ring in the shape of a flower. "Jake gave this ring to my mom before I was born. I remember Mom wearing it sometimes, but I didn't know it was from him. When Mom died, my grandmother must have given the ring back to him."

Annie sucked in a breath as emotion surged through her.

Seth took her left hand in his. "Despite everything, Jake loved my mom, like I love you, and I'd be honored if you'd wear this ring and marry me. It's not a traditional engagement ring, and if you don't like it, I'll get you something else, but I still want you to have it."

"Of course I'll marry you, and I don't want any ring but this one. I love it." Annie's vision blurred, and the ring blurred along with it. She swallowed and sniffed. "And I love you more than any ring."

"I love you too, Annie-Bella, and Jake loved both of us." Seth handed her a napkin, and she patted her eyes. "Somewhere, I'm sure he knows about us and is glad. From a few papers I found at the bank, he had an even rougher life before he came here than I thought. Maybe it was better he didn't try to get custody of me back then. He probably wouldn't have been able to be a dad and who knows what might have happened to me."

Annie glanced at the wishing tree. Its branches were partly leafless now, but the little papers and trinkets tied to them whispered in the light breeze—a promise of another spring and new wishes to come. "Although Jake never told me what he wished for on this tree, I think it must have had something to do with you."

"And you." Seth slipped the ring on her fourth finger. "Look at that, it's a perfect fit."

"Like it was meant to be." Annie held out her hand, and the ring sparkled in the sun. "I once told you I didn't believe in wishes. I gave up wishing on this tree because none of my wishes ever came true. It turns out I wished for the wrong things." She looked at Seth and the love in his eyes for her.

"A wish is only a wish, but you helped me figure out what I really wanted and how to make it a reality."

Seth's chuckle was low and sexy. "Always, Annie-Bella." He pulled her close for a hug.

Above them, the branches of the wishing tree sighed. Annie glanced up and, for a moment, it was as if the faint outlines of Jake, Nana Gerry, and her dad flickered between the tree and the sky. "I love him," she whispered, "and he loves me, and we'll take good care of each other and our family."

"And your family to come." The faint words echoed on the wind.

"Did you say something?" Seth looked up, a question in his eyes.

"No." It must have been a trick of her mind. She was as fanciful as the older women who came to Quinn's to drink tea and chat around the small tables Tara had added and who clung to old Irish superstitions, even though most of them had never set foot on Irish soil. "We'd better head back. The wind is picking up and there's a cloud coming over the mountain. Fall is finally here. We can finish the cheesecake at home."

"No offense to your cheesecake, but I'd rather do something else at home." In a heartbeat, Seth's smile went from sweet to sensual.

Annie laughed. "You would, would you?" She got to her feet and packed up the little picnic.

"You bet." He stood beside her.

She gave him a teasing grin and looked at the tree one last time. "Thank you," she mouthed.

Although she'd temporarily lost her faith in wishes and the wishing tree, with Seth, her greatest wish of all—the one she couldn't let herself make—had come true.

Jen Gilroy:

Jen Gilroy worked in higher education and international marketing and business development before trading the corporate 9-5 to write contemporary romance and women's fiction with heart, home, and hope.

After many years living and working in England, she returned to where her roots run deep and lives in a small town in Eastern Ontario, Canada with her husband, teen daughter and a floppy-eared hound. When she's not writing, Jen enjoys reading, travel, singing, and ballet. She's also known for her love of ice cream, shoes, and vintage finds.

Jen's first book, *The Cottage at Firefly Lake* (and first book in her *Firefly Lake* series), was a finalist for Romance Writers of America's (RWA) Golden Heart® award in 2015. It was also shortlisted for the Romantic Novelists' Association (RNA) Joan Hessayon Award 2017.

She's a member of RWA, RNA, and the Women's Fiction Writers Association (WFWA).

Website: www.jengilroy.com
Blog: http://www.jengilroy.com/category/blog/
Facebook: www.facebook.com/JenGilroyAuthor
Twitter: www.twitter.com/JenGilroy1
Newsletter: https://www.jengilroy.com/subscribe-to-jens-newsletter/